## ALSO BY VICKI LEWIS THOMPSON

*Werewolf in Alaska*
*Werewolf in Denver*
*Werewolf in Seattle*
*Werewolf in Greenwich Village*
(A Penguin Special)
*Werewolf in the North Woods*
*A Werewolf in Manhattan*
*Chick with a Charm*
*Blonde with a Wand*
*Over Hexed*
*Wild & Hexy*
*Casual Hex*

# CRAZY
## *for the*
# COWBOY

## *A Sexy Texans Novel*

## Vicki Lewis Thompson

A SIGNET ECLIPSE BOOK

SIGNET ECLIPSE
Published by the Penguin Group
Penguin Group (USA) LLC, 375 Hudson Street,
New York, New York 10014

USA | Canada | UK | Ireland | Australia | New Zealand | India | South Africa | China
penguin.com
A Penguin Random House Company

First published by Signet Eclipse, an imprint of New American Library,
a division of Penguin Group (USA) LLC

First Printing, May 2015

ISBN 978-0-451-47139-0

Printed in the United States of America
10  9  8  7  6  5  4  3  2  1

# ACKNOWLEDGMENTS

I'm grateful for my editor Claire Zion's continued belief in me, and for the guidance of my agent, Jenny Bent. And as always, I wouldn't function nearly as well without my amazing assistant, Audrey Sharpe.

# CHAPTER 1

"Somebody should take a paintbrush to Sadie's left nipple." Vince Durant studied the six-by-ten mural on the far wall of Sadie's Saloon as he sipped his beer. "It's chipped."

A well-endowed nude reclined on a red velvet piece of Victorian furniture that he thought was called a fainting couch. Rumor had it that a local woman named Sadie had posed for the mural, but because the painting was more than a century old, the rumor was unconfirmed.

"Sadie's not the only thing needing a little TLC around here." Ike Plunkett was still behind the bar, which was reassuring.

Vince remembered Ike from four years ago, and although the bartender's hair was a little thinner and his glasses a little thicker, he looked virtually the same. That couldn't be said for the town of Bickford, though. Except for the general store and this historic hotel, the place was pretty much dead.

Come to think of it, he'd seen no evidence that anyone else was staying at the hotel besides him and the two friends who hadn't arrived yet. Even more troubling, the saloon was deserted, and that wasn't normal for a Friday afternoon. At the end of the day, cowboys in the Texas Panhandle enjoyed sipping a cold one. "I never realized how much the town depended on the Double J."

"I don't think any of us did until it was gone."

"You'd think by now somebody would have reopened it." Vince wouldn't mind working there again. Turned out he was good at wrangling greenhorns.

"Can't." Ike used a bar rag to wipe down the whiskey bottles lined up beneath an ornate mirror behind the bar. "Somebody torched it, probably for the insurance, and the land's tied up in a big legal hassle."

"Sorry to hear that." Vince polished off his beer and signaled for another. He was thirsty after the long drive from Fort Worth.

"Not half as sorry as we are."

"No, probably not." But he *was* sorry, and disappointed, too. He'd talked his buddies Mac Foster and Travis Langdon into having a reunion, figuring they could party in Bickford like they had during the three years they'd all worked for the Double J Guest Ranch. "I don't suppose you have live music this weekend?"

"We haven't had a band in here for a long time. Can't afford to pay 'em."

"That's depressing."

"Tell me about it."

"Oh, well. At least you have beer." Vince lifted his bottle in the direction of the mural. "And Sadie! After a few of these, I might decide to repaint her nipple myself."

The street door opened with the squeak of an unoiled hinge and Vince turned to see if Mac or Travis had come straight into the saloon instead of stopping by the hotel desk to check in like he had.

His smile of welcome faltered when Georgina Bickford walked through the door. He took some comfort in noticing that she seemed as disoriented by his presence as he was by hers. That made no sense, really. It wasn't like they had a history, although he'd tried his damnedest to create one.

His fabled charm hadn't worked on her and she'd never gone out with him. Maybe that was why he'd thought of her so often since then. She was the one girl he'd never been able to impress.

She didn't look particularly impressed to see him now, either. "Hello, Vince."

"Hello, Georgie." He remembered that cool voice of hers, but at least she hadn't forgotten his name. After four years, that said something. He wasn't convinced it said something positive, though. A name could stick in a person's mind for both good reasons and bad.

"I'm surprised to see you here." She approached slowly, as if he had yellow caution tape draped around his bar-stool. "Just passing through?"

"Not exactly." He thumbed back his hat so he could see her better. She'd gotten prettier, but she'd always been great to look at with her big brown eyes and honey-colored hair. When he'd first started working at the Double J, he'd asked around and had learned that she'd left college to run the general store after her dad died. He'd tried to be friendly, but she'd never given him the time of day.

She frowned. "If you're looking for work, there's not much to be had, I'm afraid."

"So I gather." He hesitated. Oh, what the hell. "Can I buy you a drink?"

"No, thank you."

Shot down again, damn it.

"Georgie's first drink is always on the house." Ike sent a glance of compassion Vince's way as he placed a glass of red wine on the bar. "All of the council members get one free drink per day. Bickford Hotel policy. It's the least we can do when they have such a thankless job."

"You're on the town council?" Then he wished he hadn't sounded so surprised. "I mean, I'm sure you're well-qualified and all. I just . . ."

She appeared to take pity on him. "It's okay. I'm the youngest member, but I also run the second biggest revenue producer in town, so it's logical for me to be on the council." She smiled. "It wasn't a tough race. No one ran against me."

Hey, a smile. Progress.

"They wouldn't have dared run against you," Ike said. "What can I get you from the kitchen?"

"Does Henry have any barbecued pork back there?"

"I believe he does."

"Then a barbecued pork sandwich would be great. Thanks, Ike."

The bartender glanced at Vince. "Want to order some food? We still have Henry Blaylock cooking for us. Don't know if you remember, but he's terrific."

"I do remember Henry's food. Good stuff. But I'll wait for Mac and Travis to get here before I order."

"Fair enough." Ike opened the hinged section of the bar and walked back toward the kitchen.

"Mac and Travis?" Georgie picked up her wineglass but remained standing beside the bar instead of hopping up on a stool. "The same Mac and Travis who used to work for the Double J?"

"You have a good memory." She hadn't dated those old boys, either. Vince, Mac, and Travis had been the cutups of the group, and Georgie didn't approve of cutups. She'd made that clear soon after they'd met, and he doubted that she'd changed.

She took a sip of her wine. "Are you having some kind of Double J reunion?"

"In a way, but it's just the three of us."

Her brown eyes lit with curiosity. "And you're meeting here, in Bickford?"

"That's the plan." He liked her haircut, which was a little shorter than he remembered. It used to hang past her shoulders, but now it was chin length. The new cut made her look more sophisticated. Sexier.

"Why meet here?"

He shrugged. "It's where we used to hang out, but I didn't realize the place had gone . . . uh, that it's not the same."

"If you were about to say it's gone to hell in a hand-basket, you'd be on target. If you want to have a fun time, y'all might want to head somewhere else. Go on up to Amarillo, maybe."

"It'll be okay." He didn't remember her being quite so curvy the last time he'd seen her. She filled out the Bickford General Store's hunter-green T-shirt, although he was careful not to be caught ogling. He'd noticed that her jeans fit mighty nice, too. Not that it made any difference whether she was a knockout or not. She hadn't changed regarding him. She showed no interest whatsoever.

"I can't imagine what you'll find to do around here," she said. "Sadie's doesn't heat up like it used to on the weekend. Anastasia and I might be the last two single women under thirty in Bickford."

"What about Charmaine?" Seven years ago, when he was a new hire at the Double J, Georgie's stepsisters had been too young to go out dancing at Sadie's, but Charmaine, the older one, had snuck in one time and Georgie had marched her back home.

"She's working in Dallas. She'd party with you if she could, but she isn't here, and Anastasia's not into that. Besides, even if she was, there's no live music anymore."

"Yeah, Ike said it wasn't in the budget. No worries. I haven't seen Mac and Travis since we left the Double J. Maybe it's better this way. We can drink beer and catch up."

"For the entire weekend?" She sounded skeptical.

"Well, no. We'll do that at night, but during the day we'll head out and round up the Ghost. Ike says he's still—"

"You most certainly will not!" She set her wineglass down with a sharp *click* and faced him, sparks of anger in her eyes. "Don't y'all dare go out there and harass that poor horse for your own amusement!"

He blinked in confusion. The dappled gray stallion and his small band of wild horses used to be fair game, a challenge for the cowboys who worked at the Double J. Vince and his buddies hadn't succeeded in roping him, mostly because they'd never been able to devote an entire weekend to the project. Now they could.

But Georgie was obviously ready to rip him a new one on the subject of the wild stallion. "There is no reason on God's green earth why you should go after him! He's not hurting anything, especially now that so few horses live in the area. Back when the Double J was in operation, I admit he tried to raid the corral a couple of times, but those days are over. There are four horses boarded at Ed's stable, and they're all geldings. No mares. The Ghost leaves us alone and we leave him alone!"

"But—"

"Is that why you decided to rendezvous here? To go after that stallion?"

"Partly, yeah. We always talked about capturing him, but we never did. Now seems as good a time as any."

Her eyes glittered in defiance. "You won't find him."

"Oh, I think we will. We have two whole days to look."

Ike returned from the kitchen, and Georgie wheeled on him. "Did you tell Vince that the Ghost was still out there?"

Ike shrugged. "He asked. I wasn't going to lie to the man."

"Are you aware that Vince and his two cohorts are heading out on some macho quest to rope him?"

"I didn't know that." Ike looked at Vince. "You might want to reconsider. Georgie takes a special interest in those wild horses."

*Crap.* First he'd discovered that the town was deader than a doornail, and now Georgie Bickford was raining all over his wild horse roundup. Maybe she was right and they should take this party elsewhere, but he'd craved the small-town experience and he wouldn't get that in Amarillo or Lubbock.

Mac and Travis chose that moment to walk into the saloon. They'd shared a ride here because they both worked at a ranch outside Midland. They sauntered in with wide grins as if they owned the place. Vince left his barstool and went over to greet them. Much joking around and back-slapping followed. Vince couldn't believe how happy he was to see those old boys. Until they arrived, he'd been outnumbered.

Mac and Travis tipped their hats and said hello to Georgie, who replied without smiling.

"So where is everybody?" Mac glanced around. "Hey, Georgie. What's happened to this place?"

"We're experiencing an economic downturn." Georgie's jaw tightened. "I suggest you three mosey on to a place that's more suited to your needs."

"Nah, we don't need to do that," Travis said. "I assume Sadie's still serves beer."

"We do," Ike said.

"Then we're in business." Travis walked over to the bar and shook hands with Ike. "Good to see you. I'll have a longneck, like always."

"And I'll take my usual draft." Mac sat on a stool next to him.

"Coming up." Ike looked nervous, but he busied himself getting the beer.

Georgie cleared her throat. "I understand y'all are planning to round up the Ghost this weekend."

Mac nodded. "Yes, ma'am, we sure are. Isn't that right, Vince?"

For a split second Vince considered telling Mac there'd been a change of plans. Then his rebellious streak surfaced. By God, he'd organized this adventure and he'd see it through. There was no law against chasing after that horse. He met Georgie's flinty gaze. "That's right, Mac."

Georgie's mouth thinned. "Over my dead body."

Vince admired her spirit. He always had. But he couldn't let her get the upper hand.

"Don't go sacrificing yourself like that, darlin'."

She balled her hands into fists. "Do *not* call me—"

"I promise we won't hurt those horses one tiny bit." He turned to his partners in crime. "Isn't that right, boys?"

*"Boys."* She poured a boatload of scorn into the word. "What a perfect description. *Men* would not be involved

in causing distress to animals to stroke their outsized egos."

Travis stayed hunched over his beer, but Mac swiveled to face them. "Y'know, Vince, we don't *have* to round up the Ghost this weekend. Maybe we should just—"

"We're gonna round him up." Vince kept his tone mild and conversational, but his gaze locked on Georgie's. "There's no law against it."

Georgie held her ground and matched him stare for stare.

"Georgie?" Ike's tone was deferential, as if he didn't want her unleashing her wrath on him.

She gentled her voice. "What, Ike?"

"Your dinner's ready."

"Thank you. I'd like to sit in the far corner, please."

"I'll set you up over there, then."

Vince adjusted the fit of his black Stetson. "Seems like your meal's being served. You wouldn't want to let that barbecue get cold."

"I don't intend to do that. But this is not over." Turning on her heel, she marched straight to the table where Ike was laying out her silverware on either side of her steaming plate.

"I don't think you have to worry about those old boys," Ike said to Georgie in an undertone.

She settled herself in a chair facing the three cowboys at the bar. "Why not?" Oh, how Vince infuriated her! Her girlfriend Janet, who'd since married and moved away, used to rave about his *electric blue eyes* and *sinfully sexy mouth*. Right now Georgie would love to wipe that arrogant grin off his face with a solid right hook to his manly jaw.

Ike kept his voice low. "They all like to drink, and they

haven't seen each other for a long time. They'll be swapping stories 'til all hours of the night. I predict they'll be too hungover to go traipsing around the countryside tomorrow."

"Maybe. But they'll be here the next day, too."

Ike shrugged. "By then they'll have talked themselves out of it. I think they'd rather party than chase horses."

"Maybe." She wasn't convinced.

"You'll see." He glanced at her half-full glass. "Want more wine?"

"Yes, thanks. I think I'll hang around awhile."

"Suit yourself. But I wouldn't worry if I were you." Ike returned to his post behind the bar.

Soon after that Mac ordered up another round and Travis promised to get the next one. So maybe Ike had it right, after all. The last time these three had been in Sadie's, they'd worked off the effects of their alcohol intake by dancing.

Between the single women who'd driven in from the Double J and the eligible females in Bickford, the cowboys from the ranch had been in demand on the dance floor, especially this particular bunch. Georgie couldn't lie—she'd loved dancing with all three of them, especially Vince, who had a natural sense of rhythm. But she'd never encouraged him to think she was interested in being anything besides his dance partner.

Janet had told her she was nuts not to go out with him when he'd asked. But at some point they'd had a brief conversation about goals, and he'd admitted to having only one—to enjoy life as it came. That philosophy was fine for a Saturday night of dancing, but she'd had no interest in dating someone who was so unfocused. She'd been picky then and she was picky now.

Her pickiness was moot these days, though. The town's population of datable men, focused or not, had migrated to areas where jobs were available. Georgie didn't particularly want to be celibate, but circumstances had given her little choice.

She didn't approve of Vince's weekend plan and she would thwart it to the best of her ability. Yet, hypocritical though it might be, she took some guilty pleasure in seeing three virile cowboys at the bar for a change. Because they had their backs turned, she could look without getting caught, and that trio of tight buns perched on neighboring barstools gladdened her starved hormones.

The old guys who played poker here almost every night were adorable and dear. She'd known them all her life. But she couldn't deny that Vince and his two friends brought with them a blast of testosterone that had been absent from Sadie's for several years. She'd have to be sexually numb not to feel it.

Vince had always been the acknowledged leader of the group. He had charisma to burn. Mac, his brown hair cut short and his dark eyes perpetually full of the devil, had been Vince's second-in-command. Travis, younger than both of them, used to play the role of kid brother. He seemed to have grown up, though. His blond hair had darkened and his green eyes had lost their innocence.

Mac delivered the punch line of a story she couldn't hear and Vince doubled over in laughter. That was another thing she'd missed—the laughter of men her age. Damn these three guys for their misbegotten plan to chase after the Ghost. If they'd come to hang out and talk, she might have enjoyed having them around.

Ike brought her a second glass of wine. He tipped his

head toward Vince and company. "Told you. They'll keep this up until I close the bar."

"When is that these days?"

"Normally? The poker game ends about eleven and the place is deserted by eleven thirty, so I shut 'er down."

"Could you do me a huge favor and stay as long as they want?"

"I will, but I won't be doing it just for you. We haven't seen cowboys in here spending money on drinks in a long time. Steve and Myra would want me to take advantage of that."

"I suppose they would." She certainly didn't begrudge the Jensons whatever revenue this reunion brought in. Steve and Myra were great, and they'd hung on here at the Bickford Hotel by carefully managing every dime.

"Three rooms rented is more than we've had since that group of rock hounds came through two months ago. Steve told me to make sure these guys had a good time this weekend. They might pass the word on to others that this was a nice place for a getaway."

Georgie straightened. "I hope that doesn't include encouraging them in this crazy scheme to round up the wild horses."

"I can't say. Steve knows they planned to do some riding, but I don't think they told him they were after the Ghost. I doubt they told anybody until you came in tonight asking what their plans were."

"Maybe it'll never become an issue if they stay drunk for two days. That would be good for everyone, right?"

"I suppose so. Well, not Ed. He could get some income if they rent horses from his stable."

Georgie considered the situation. "And I can't ask him not to when he could use the money like everyone else."

She sighed. "I guess if they end up following through on their plan, I'll have to figure out some other way to make sure they don't capture the Ghost."

Ike patted her shoulder. "Like I said, they likely won't feel like going, but even if they do, they won't be the sharpest tools in the shed after all that alcohol consumption. The Ghost is cagey. He'll be fine."

"I hope so. Anyway, you'd better get over there. I don't want those cowboys going thirsty."

"They won't. Not on my watch." Ike winked at her before heading back to set up the next round.

Georgie watched as Vince drained his beer bottle, his tanned throat moving in a deep swallow. She took note of his strong hands and the muscled forearms he'd bared when he'd folded back the cuffs of his Western shirt. She remembered the gleam of defiance in his blue eyes when she'd told him not to go after the Ghost. Despite how much he drank tonight, she'd do well not to underestimate Vince Durant.

# CHAPTER 2

Vince tried to block out Georgie's presence because she was damned distracting. He could feel her judgmental gaze boring into his back, and as a result he was drinking more than he should and pretending that Mac's and Travis's stories were more hysterical than they actually were. Fortunately the beer helped calm his nerves and made the stories funnier. Great invention.

He raised his bottle. "Gentlemen, I propose a toast. To the inventor of this tasty beverage. I'm betting there was a cowboy involved."

"You'd lose that bet." Mac picked up the glass in front of him and studied its contents. "Beer was the preferred drink of the pharaohs, my friend."

Travis laughed. "Yeah, right. You're making that shit up like you always do."

Ike leaned on the bar. "Actually, he's right. Beer's ten thousand years old, at least."

"It is?" Vince narrowed his eyes at Mac. "How'd you know that?"

"I read." Mac looked extremely proud of himself. "You should try it sometime, Vince."

"Hey, I read! Just never ran across that factoid."

"Me, either," Travis said. "Pharaohs drank beer. Who knew? Speaking of which, did I ever show you guys my Egyptian dance routine?"

"Unfortunately." Mac rolled his eyes. "Several times."

"Well, it's been a few years since you've seen it. I think I should refresh your memory."

"Don't feel obligated on our account," Vince said.

"You're both jealous because you can't bend your arms right." Travis climbed off his stool and angled one arm in front and one in back as he strutted along and bobbed his head while humming "Walk Like an Egyptian."

Ike laughed so hard he had to take off his glasses and wipe his eyes. "That's good, Travis. Real good. Especially wearing a cowboy hat."

"Don't encourage him," Mac said, "or he'll be doing that all night."

"Hey." Travis reclaimed his stool. "You're the one who brought up the pharaoh subject. I'm just elaborating on the theme. I didn't realize beer is such a noble drink."

"It is that," Mac said. "The Egyptians considered it sacred."

Travis grinned. "In that case, maybe I should do another dance. Want to see me dance again?"

"No, we want to see you drink." Vince finished off his bottle. "Another, if you please, Ike."

"I sure as hell consider beer sacred." Travis shoved his empty bottle across the bar. "Hit me again, Ike."

"You bet." Ike seemed quite cheerful about serving up the beer.

Vince thought about the sorry state of Bickford. So what if they all drank a little more than they should tonight? It was a celebration and the town could use the money.

"Don't know if you came across the *Mayflower* in your beer-related research, Mac." Ike set a bottle in front of Vince and Travis.

"His *research*?" Travis chortled with glee. "Vince, did you know we had a scholar among us?"

"A beer scholar at that." Vince nodded. "Probably has a Ph.B."

Travis smirked. "Yeah, *B* for bullshit."

"Never mind the village idiots." Mac looked at Ike. "What about the *Mayflower*?"

"The Pilgrims landed on Plymouth Rock mostly because they were running out of beer." Ike had a twinkle in his eye.

Travis stared at him. "That can't be right. I'll bet ten bucks you're making that up." He slapped two fives on the bar.

"You're on." Ike fished out his wallet and put a ten on top of Travis's two fives.

"I'm betting Ike's right." Mac added another two fives. "Vince, which way you leaning?"

"Beer on the *Mayflower*?" He added a ten to the pile. "I'm with Travis on this one. Can't picture those folks in the gray outfits knocking back the booze. How do we settle it?"

"We have to Google it." Ike glanced around the group. "Who has Internet on his phone? I left mine at home."

"Old phone, here." Travis held his up. "I'm a poor cowhand."

Mac shook his head. "I have basic service."

"Me, too." Vince shrugged. "Guess we're SOL." He started to retrieve his bet.

"Not so fast," Ike said. "Georgie has Internet on her phone."

As all three cowboys swiveled their stools around to face Georgie's table, Vince wondered if she'd refuse to look up the info for them. Probably not, though. The Georgie he remembered had liked being a source of knowledge. According to what he'd heard, she would have preferred to stay in school, but she'd had to drop out to save her late father's cherished general store from going belly-up. Apparently her stepmother was no help.

Ike came out from behind the bar and approached Georgie's table. "We need to settle a bet. Would you look something up on your phone, please?"

"For you, Ike, I'd be happy to." She smiled and pulled her phone out of the pocket of her jeans. "You want to know if the Pilgrims had beer on the *Mayflower*, right?" She tapped the information into her phone.

Ike nodded. "Right."

So she'd been following their conversation. Vince wondered if she'd been listening in hopes she could figure out a way to upset their plans. He wasn't about to allow that.

Georgie consulted her phone. "So who's betting on the Pilgrims having beer on board?"

"Me and Mac," Ike said. "I know I read it somewhere."

"According to this, they did." Georgie held up her phone. "They decided to land because they were out of supplies, chiefly beer. Apparently beer didn't go bad on a long voyage, while water did."

Mac hopped off his stool and snatched a startled Georgie out of her chair. "Thank you, sweet lady!" He swung her around in a brief victory dance. "You brought the light of reason to dispel the darkness of ignorance."

"Oh, hell." Travis glanced at Vince. "It's getting deep in here."

"No kidding." Watching Mac dance with Georgie brought back memories of Saturday nights when he'd been the one holding her like that. They'd danced well together and had seemed to anticipate each other's moves. She'd never said he was her favorite partner, but he'd known it, anyway. Those days were long gone, though, and he'd do well to forget about them.

Travis swiveled back toward the bar. "After all that talk about beer, I could use another one."

"Me, too." Vince turned his back on the sight of Mac escorting Georgie to her chair.

Then Mac added insult to injury by returning to his stool and leaning close to Vince. "You're playing this all wrong, buddy. You'd catch more flies with honey, if you get my meaning."

Vince's jaw tightened. "She won't be a problem."

"You could guarantee that with a different approach." Mac picked up his beer.

Vince wasn't so sure about that. He still wondered what she'd meant by that *over my dead body* comment. It continued to gnaw at him as he tried to imagine what stunt she might pull to keep them from going after the Ghost. He'd have to be on his guard. He'd always known she was smart.

She'd mentioned that Ed's riding stable only had four horses in it. He maybe ought to see if three of them were available before he let any more time go by. With her considerable influence in this town, she could fix it so he and his buddies had no transportation out to the maze of canyons where the Ghost kept his little band.

Reaching in his pocket, he pulled out his phone. It

didn't have Internet, but it suited him just fine. "Ike, you got a number for Ed's stable?"

"I do." Ike reached under the counter, pulled out a card, and pushed it toward Vince. "That's his cell. He's probably at supper, but he keeps his phone on."

"I hate to interrupt his meal, but I want to make sure we have some horses to ride tomorrow."

"Right." Ike's gaze flicked over Vince's shoulder to where Georgie had returned to eating her barbecue and drinking her wine.

As Vince dialed Ed's number, Mac leaned toward him. "You could hold off 'til tomorrow morning."

"I don't think so. He only has four horses."

"Yeah, but there are zero tourists in town, in case you hadn't noticed."

"Besides us."

"We're not tourists. We're cowboys."

"Without horses." Vince turned away as Ed answered. The stable owner sounded as if he had a mouthful of food.

Vince identified himself and apologized for interrupting Ed's dinner before launching into his request. "Mac Foster and Travis Langdon are here with me, and we'd like to rent three of your horses for tomorrow."

"Absolutely!" Ed quickly swallowed. "When?"

Vince considered that. The best time to locate any wild animal was early morning. "Six thirty."

Beside him, Mac groaned.

"Hang on, Ed." Vince grinned at Mac. "Make it six forty-five."

Mac shook his head. "I always knew you were a sadistic SOB."

"Six forty-five it is, then," Ed confirmed. "I'll have 'em saddled and ready."

"Great. We'll be there." Vince disconnected the phone. "We're all set. Ed seemed real glad for the business."

"I'm sure he is." Mac scowled at him. "But what's this crack-of-dawn routine? I thought we were on vacation."

"No, Mac," Travis said. "We're on a quest. Isn't that right, Vince?"

"That's a perfect description. And you don't start a quest at noon. Anybody knows that. You start at dawn."

Travis raised his beer bottle. "To the quest."

"To the quest!" Vince leaned over and tapped Travis's bottle with his. "Mac? You in?"

Mac grimaced and raised his glass with a decided lack of enthusiasm. "To the quest."

From the direction of Georgie's table came a snort of disgust. Well, let her be disgusted. He had the horses reserved and come morning, they'd head out. He couldn't think of any way she could stop them.

The impromptu dance with Mac had flustered Georgie. She wasn't used to being swirled into a dance without warning. Such a thing hadn't happened to her in years, not since the Double J cowhands had left town.

Her heart continued to race after Mac returned her to her seat and her half-finished meal. Mac didn't interest her, either. None of them did. But she'd forgotten how lovely it was to be caught up in strong arms and whisked around the floor, even without the benefit of music.

She'd forgotten how much she'd enjoyed the company of virile men, too. These three cowboys weren't her cup of tea, not by a long shot, but they certainly were . . . male. Exceedingly so. She gulped her wine.

What a fine mess she'd created for herself. By staying in Bickford and attempting to help save the town from total ruin, she'd suppressed hormonal urges that any typical twenty-eight-year-old woman would welcome. Doing that had been easy when no attractive, single men were in the vicinity.

When the cowboys left town Sunday night, the number of single guys her age would drop to zero once again. She'd been so busy worrying about the store and the town that she hadn't stopped to think that if things continued as they were, she could end up dateless for some time to come. She was willing to sacrifice a lot for the future of Bickford, but she hadn't intended to sacrifice her sex life.

Anastasia didn't have anybody to date in Bickford, either, but she didn't seem all that concerned about it. Georgie's stepmother, Evelyn, wouldn't want Anastasia to end up with someone from Bickford, anyway. She'd been trying to convince Anastasia to go live with Charmaine in Dallas so they could both find wealthy husbands, but Anastasia had resisted the plan.

Despite her art school training, she seemed content to help out at the store. Unfortunately she was such a dreamer that Georgie hesitated to leave her alone there. She'd once flooded the back room when she'd forgotten about the water running in the sink, and another time she'd almost burned the place down with a scented candle she'd set under a hand towel.

Georgie had finished her dinner and was about to leave when Clyde Abbott, the eightysomething mayor of Bickford and a dear friend, walked into the saloon. If she'd been paying attention to the time, she would have expected him. He was always the first to arrive for the nightly poker game.

Short and plump, he'd been married to his wife, Inez, for sixty years. She was thin and a good six inches taller than Clyde. They adored each other and attributed their happy marriage to giving each other plenty of space. Clyde played poker with his cronies every night and Inez watched crime drama on TV.

Clyde surveyed the three men sitting at the bar before making his way over to Georgie's table and pulling out a chair. "Those boys look familiar," he said in a low voice. "Did they work at the Double J?"

Georgie nodded and quietly gave him a rundown. Clyde was the only member of the council besides her who wasn't partially deaf. That allowed them to talk about the newcomers without being heard. She filled him in on the cowboys' plan to round up the Ghost and Ike's belief that they'd be too hungover to manage it.

Clyde kept glancing at the newcomers as she talked. When she was finished, he focused his attention on her. "I'm sure this upsets you."

"Yep."

"Let's think about this logically, Georgie." Clyde's recent cataract surgery meant he didn't have to wear glasses. His gaze was sharp and clear. "Your Ghost may be a little slower, but he's smarter, too."

"I hope so." She appreciated Clyde's understanding more than she could say. Of all the people in town, he and Anastasia were the only two with some idea of what the horses meant to her. "And he's not *my* Ghost. I don't have any claim to him."

"Nobody does, which is the point. But he's your project, so that's all I meant. I'm inclined to think Ike is right and this problem will take care of itself."

"They've rented three of Ed's horses. Vince did that a little while ago. They're supposed to pick them up at six forty-five."

Raucous laughter erupted from the trio perched on the barstools.

Clyde lifted his bushy white eyebrows. "Hear that?"

"I know, but—"

"It's the sound of happy cowboys tanked up on beer. They won't be in any shape to round up a slow-moving armadillo at six forty-five in the morning, let alone a spirited animal like the Ghost. You can relax, Georgie. Your wild stallion is safe."

"Okay, Clyde. I bow to your experience in these matters."

"And we mustn't forget that as long as they're here, they're spending money in Bickford. We get precious few visitors these days."

She sighed. "I know. I briefly thought about asking Ed not to provide them with horses, but Ed, like everybody around here, needs the money."

"We all do—that's for sure. Steve told me he'd rented three rooms this weekend, and I nearly fell over. I didn't recognize the names, but now that I see them, I recognize the faces. Whenever those three came into town, the bar tabs at Sadie's doubled. They were a draw."

"Guess so."

He gazed at the men sitting at the bar. "I'd sure love to have those days back."

"Without an operation like the Double J, I don't know how we can generate the same kind of excitement."

"I'm well aware of that. Inez, bless her heart, keeps suggesting that we have a bake sale, or enlist all the women in town to make quilts and sell those. I don't know how to tell her that those wouldn't generate the kind of revenue required. We need something more dramatic than that if we expect to turn things around."

"I know, and I've been racking my brain to come up with proposals for Monday night's meeting."

He turned to her, his expression eager. "And?"

"Nada."

His shoulders slumped. "Yeah, me, either. There has to be an answer, but I'll be damned if I can come up with one."

"I don't know how Steve and Myra manage to keep the hotel afloat," Georgie said. "With the general store I can count on the people in town to buy basic supplies. It's not a lot of income, but it has to be better than sitting with empty hotel rooms night after night."

"They wouldn't make it except for the saloon, and the guys and I do our part with the poker game every night. We usually order plenty of drinks and snacks. What, with our retirement income, we're the richest folks in town." He glanced toward the bar again. "These cowboys showing up will give Steve a temporary boost. Sure, it's not enough to save the day, but it keeps him solvent for a little longer."

"You're right, and I don't want to bite the hand that feeds us, so to speak, but couldn't they just stay here and drink and forget about chasing the Ghost?"

Clyde smiled at her. "I was their age once, and it doesn't seem that long ago. I was full of piss and vinegar, just like them."

"I'm sure you were." Georgie wasn't about to laugh, even though the thought of portly Clyde being a rabble-rouser was tough to imagine. His reasoned approach to life was what she cherished about him, but he was past eighty. He'd probably come to that wisdom gradually.

"Anyway, my advice is to relax and trust that the Ghost is a whole lot smarter than those young bucks, especially when they've spent the night sucking up beer and he's spent the night sucking up oxygen in the wide-open spaces. His head will be much clearer than theirs come morning."

Georgie chuckled. "You make a valid point."

"I should hope so. I'm the mayor." He smiled at her. "And speaking of that, if you'll excuse me, I need to go over and welcome those cowboys to Bickford." He pushed back his chair and stood. "We want them to know we're glad they came for a visit."

Instantly Georgie felt contrite. "Clyde, I have to warn you that I didn't make them feel welcome. In fact, I probably did the exact opposite."

"Why is that? What did you say?"

"I was somewhat forceful about my concerns for the wild horses, and when Vince insisted on his course of action I said . . ." Heat rose in her cheeks. "I said *over my dead body.*"

Clyde blinked, and then he began to laugh. "Georgie, I wouldn't be your age again for anything."

She had a feeling she'd been insulted. In this community, she was a little touchy about her relative youth. "What's my age got to do with it?"

"You're as passionate and determined to keep the cowboys from disturbing the Ghost as they are to have their big adventure. You each take your unshakable positions and charge forward, butting heads like mountain goats. I have a nostalgic fondness for those days but I would never want to relive them."

Now Georgie was certain that she'd been insulted. "Are you saying I'm just like those cowboys over there?"

"In the sense that you're as hot-blooded and ready for battle? Yes, I'm saying that. I'm glad they're here. It's put roses in your cheeks."

Georgie sat in stunned silence as Clyde walked over

and reintroduced himself to Vince, Mac, and Travis. She was not anything like them! Age-wise, yes, but temperament? No way. She was mature and reasonable, while they were immature and reckless.

She couldn't begrudge the town the money the cowboys spent here this weekend, but she'd rather they hadn't shown up at all. Yet even as she thought that, she realized it wasn't true. She hadn't felt this alive in months, maybe even years. If she could keep them from rounding up the stallion, then their visit would be a win for everyone.

# CHAPTER 3

Before he'd fallen into bed at God-knows-what-hour, Vince had set the alarm clock sitting on his nightstand. He vaguely remembered thinking he'd get about four hours' sleep, or maybe it was only three. His math skills hadn't been at their best after drinking so many beers that he'd lost count.

He couldn't even blame Georgie for the amount of alcohol he'd consumed. She'd left about the time the mayor had come over to welcome them to Bickford. After that, things were kind of a blur. More old guys had shown up, and a poker game had materialized.

Four years ago Sadie's had been all about music and dancing, but now that was gone and poker games with senior citizens had taken its place. But Vince, Mac, and Travis were nothing if not flexible. They'd fallen right in with the poker crowd.

The poker game didn't explain the late night, though, because the old guys had left by eleven. Sensible cowboys with a six forty-five ETA at the stables would have hit the sack, but no. Mac had suggested tequila shots, and the discussion had devolved into autopsies of their failed relationships.

Mac had the highest body count. He'd wooed and lost six women since they'd left the Double J. Vince could claim three, and Travis only had one. He'd been involved with a married woman and had finally broken it off not long before coming to Bickford.

Vince had listened in amazement. Travis had claimed that she was the love of his life and that she'd promised to leave her husband for him. In the end, he'd figured out that she had never intended to do that.

She had a luxurious lifestyle through her marriage and a red-hot lover on the side. She'd never been serious about leaving her sugar daddy. Which sucked for poor Travis.

Vince had further concluded that Travis wouldn't have revealed any of that if he hadn't put away at least ten beers and an untold number of tequila shots. Poor kid. He wasn't a kid any longer, especially after having his dreams crushed, but even so, the guy had taken it in the shorts and he was obviously torn up about it. Vince felt sorry for him.

When the alarm jangled at six fifteen, however, Vince felt sorry for himself. What the hell had he been thinking? He'd known they'd probably stay up late drinking and yet he'd been goaded by Georgie's challenge into renting horses so they could head out at sunrise because he didn't want her to interfere with his grand plan.

It didn't sound so damned grand now. But he hauled himself out of bed and staggered to the bathroom to splash cold water on his face. The horses would be saddled and patiently waiting for riders to show up, and Ed expected an all-day rental fee. A true cowboy didn't leave saddled horses standing around, nor did he stiff a guy who made his living providing mounts for those who didn't have them.

The hotel had a little breakfast room for guests. Mac and Travis had made it there ahead of him and were slugging back coffee and staring vacantly at plates loaded with food they probably wouldn't eat. Just the thought of bacon and eggs made Vince's stomach pitch.

He wondered if he looked as much like a desperado as his buddies. He hadn't shaved, either, and he couldn't guarantee his shirt was buttoned up right. Travis's definitely was not. Mac had opted to wear a pullover sweatshirt, which was not acceptable cowboy attire, but Vince understood the impulse to put on something that didn't require coordination.

Vince sat without saying anything and poured himself coffee from the pot on the table. He was about halfway through his first cup when Mac spoke.

"Here's my idea." His voice sounded as if he'd swallowed barbed wire.

Travis pressed shaky fingers to his temples. "Could you talk a little softer?"

As if too miserable to argue, Mac obligingly lowered his voice. "We go over to Ed's, pay him for a full day, and help him unsaddle the horses."

Vince gazed at him. The idea had merit, but he didn't want to give up completely. Then Georgie would win. Besides, rounding up the Ghost had been the main activity for this weekend, the source of stories for the bar and for the next reunion.

He cleared his throat, which felt about the way Mac's had sounded. "So we'll go out tomorrow morning?"

"Hell, I don't know if I'll be recovered by tomorrow

morning. I haven't had that much booze since I made myself sick as a dog on my twenty-first birthday."

"I've *never* had that much." Travis's face was the color of the white linen tablecloth.

Myra, who cooked breakfast every morning for the hotel guests, bustled up to the table. "You boys haven't touched your breakfast! Now eat up. I'm putting together a sack lunch for the trail. Do you want chicken salad or tuna salad on your sandwiches? Or some of each?"

"No, thanks." Travis's face went from white to green and he bolted from the table.

Myra frowned as she stared after him. "My goodness." She brought her attention back to Mac and Vince. "If he doesn't like chicken or tuna, I could whip up some ham salad."

"It's not that, ma'am," Vince said. "Travis had a little too much to drink last night and he's not feeling well."

Myra surveyed Vince and Mac. "Now that you mention it, you boys don't look a whole lot better than your friend. You might want to reconsider that trail ride."

Vince decided retreat was in order so they could live to fight another day. "I think we will take that suggestion, ma'am." He pushed back his chair. "Thanks for the coffee."

"You're welcome. Just go on back to bed, both of you."

Mac stood, too. "I promise we'll do that, ma'am, right after we walk down to the stable and pay Ed for his trouble."

"Never mind about that. I can call him. It'll be fine."

Mac looked tempted.

"Thank you," Vince said, "but this is something we need to take care of. Ed expected the money and we intend to get it to him. The fresh air will do us good." He glanced at Mac. "And while we're at it, we'll reserve the horses for tomorrow morning."

Mac's eyebrows lifted, but he didn't say anything. He touched his fingers to the brim of his hat. "Thank you for the coffee, ma'am. Sorry we wasted the food. Be sure and put it on my bill." He left money on the table for a tip.

"I wouldn't dream of it. Get yourself jackets before you go outside. It's nippy out there."

Vince looked at Mac and could tell he was thinking the same thing. If the two of them climbed the stairs to their rooms to fetch jackets, they'd never make it back down again. "We'll be okay," Vince said.

But when they stepped out on the hotel's front porch, he sucked in a breath. "Damn. She was right. Must be no more'n forty degrees out here."

"We'll walk fast." Mac crossed the wooden porch and took the steps with care, as if worried that he might trip and fall down them.

"I don't think you're capable of walking fast, old man." Vince clattered down the steps and had to stop at the bottom while his vision cleared and the rocks stopped tumbling in his brain. "Whoa."

"Yeah." Mac fell into step beside him as they started down the sidewalk toward the stable. Fortunately it was only about two blocks away, a little beyond what people used to call the Bickford House where Georgie lived with her stepmother and stepsister.

"Remind me not to suggest tequila shots tonight," Mac said.

"I will." Vince started to nod his head and then thought better of it. "We would've been fine if we'd stuck to the beer, but adding those shots was the killer."

"Do you suppose Travis will wonder whether we went without him?"

"I think Travis is praying that we left without him. That boy was in bad shape."

"I know." Mac took a deep breath. "But one good thing, he got that stuff off his chest."

"And we won't bring it up again."

"Nope." Mac looked to his right as they passed a boarded-up storefront. "That used to be an antiques store, didn't it?"

"That's what I remember. And beyond that was an ice-cream parlor."

"Right." Mac's voice was beginning to sound more normal. "Used to make damned tasty hot fudge sundaes."

"Not anymore."

"It's sad, you know? It was a quaint little town. Nice people. Good-looking women."

Vince couldn't help but smile, in spite of his aching head. "The town's dying and you're mourning the loss of the women. That's so you, Mac."

"What can I say? I consider women to be one of the benefits of being born a man."

"Six in the past four years?" Vince had been drunk, but not too drunk to be floored by that number.

"I actually fudged on that."

"There were *more*? Holy shit, Mac."

"No, fewer. In two cases, we broke up and then we got back together later on. I counted them both twice, because it seemed almost like two separate affairs since each time I saw someone else in between."

"It's a wonder you can keep them straight, or that you get anything else done."

"I have a healthy sex drive, that's all. Besides, you admitted to having three different women, so technically I'm only one up on you."

Vince realized that made some kind of crazy sense. "Guess so."

"Plus, as I recall, you had quite the time with the ladies of Bickford, yourself. When I walked into Sadie's and Georgie was there, I wondered if she was one of the reasons you wanted to come back here this weekend."

Bull's-eye. But Vince wasn't about to admit that he'd never forgotten Georgie. "Not really. I figured she'd be married with a couple of kids by now."

"Instead she's single and cuter than ever."

Vince wouldn't have used the word *cute* to describe Georgie. Beautiful and sexy, yes. A maddening challenge, definitely. But certainly not *cute*.

"You don't agree?" Mac glanced over at him. "I always pegged her as your type."

"Well, she's not. And more to the point, I'm not hers, either."

Mac's chuckle was followed by a soft groan of pain. "Remind me not to laugh. It hurts. But let the record show that you're still hung up on Georgie and frustrated by her lack of interest."

"Am not."

"Yes, you are. I'm sure this isn't news to you, but insisting on this roundup isn't helping your cause any. I'm ready to call it quits, and Travis could be talked out of it, so why not forget the whole thing? You'd stand a much better chance with her if you abandoned this so-called quest."

Vince's temples throbbed, but he'd had a hangover before, and it would be gone eventually. "You don't have to go if you don't want to. But with or without you and

Travis, I'm heading out there tomorrow morning with a rope and a plan."

Mac blew out a breath. "Then I'll go with you, if for no other reason than to keep you from making an ass of yourself."

*Too late.* But Vince kept that thought under his hat.

Georgie opened the store as usual at nine, and once she'd unlocked the doors and turned on the cash register, she surrendered to the impulse that had nagged her ever since waking up. She called Ed's stable. "Vince Durant rented three of your horses last night for a trail ride he was taking with his friends," she said. "Did they get off okay?" *Please say no.*

"Turns out they didn't go."

Georgie did a quick fist pump. Then she remembered that Ed might have been affected financially by the cancellation. "I'm sorry if you lost money, Ed."

"Actually, I didn't. Vince and Mac walked down here first thing and gave me the whole amount in cash. Said it was the least they could do. Then they helped me unsaddle the horses. They were real sorry about making me saddle them for nothing, so I gave them a discount for tomorrow morning, same time."

"That was nice of you." Damn it. They weren't giving up. She'd so hoped for that.

"Can't see any reason not to, with the generosity they showed me today. We talked about the Double J, and what a shame it was that it shut down, and then the fire. They'd love to come back to this area and work, but without the Double J, there's no way for them to do that."

She realized he'd only mentioned Vince and Mac. "Only two of them walked down?"

"Yeah. They said their friend really tied one on last night and was in his hotel room recovering. To be honest, those two didn't look particularly chipper, either. Judging from the bloodshot eyes and shakiness, they made the right decision to cancel their ride for today. I don't have a cancellation policy, although I should, I guess. They didn't have to pay me, but they did. They're welcome back here, anytime."

"I'm glad they treated you right, Ed." She wondered if she'd be lucky enough to have them all drink heavily again tonight. Then her worries would be over. They'd done it once, so why not repeat themselves? Both Clyde and Ike had been confident the cowboys would choose partying over riding out to capture a wild horse.

She had her usual trickle of customers that morning, and most of them were curious about the unfamiliar trucks parked in front of the Bickford Hotel. Ike's wife, Raina, came in around ten and reported that Ike was still dead to the world after staying up until three serving drinks.

"It was for a good cause," Georgie said. "I'm sure you don't like having him stay out that late, but because he kept the bar open, those cowboys didn't feel like chasing after the Ghost this morning. I'm grateful. I'm hoping he's willing to keep the bar open tonight, too."

"Oh, I'm sure he is." A slight woman with short brown hair, Raina was a piano teacher who had no pupils now that the population had taken a nosedive. "I saw the pile of tips he dumped on the dresser before he went to bed. All things considered, he's happy to serve them for as long as they want."

"I'm glad they were appreciative." Georgie had to admit that Vince and his friends had shown the proper consideration for the people who'd willingly provided them whatever they'd wanted. Now if they'd only extend that consideration to the herd of wild horses, she'd be thrilled.

Anastasia, her jet-black hair pulled back into a no-nonsense ponytail, came in at noon and brought Georgie some lunch. Typical of her, she hadn't heard anything about three cowboys coming to town and partying until the wee small hours in Sadie's Saloon.

After Georgie filled her in, she shrugged. "So?"

"I wouldn't care about it, either, except they'd planned to ride out today and rope the Ghost."

"Oh!" Anastasia's hazel eyes widened. "You didn't say *that*. They can't capture him. That's just wrong."

"I know." Georgie dug into the bowl of warm chili Anastasia had brought. "Thanks for this. It tastes great."

"And stupid."

"No, it doesn't taste stupid. You make wonderful chili."

Anastasia waved an impatient hand. "I meant capturing the Ghost is stupid. And mean. Where are these guys, anyway? I want to talk to them."

"Probably still sleeping it off. According to Ed at the stable, they walked down there before seven this morning to pay him and cancel the ride. He said they looked like death warmed over."

"Serves them right. They're not welcome here if all they can think to do is get drunk and chase after those horses."

"Unfortunately they are welcome here." But Georgie's heart warmed at her stepsister's loyalty to the Ghost and his herd. "They're bringing in money that everyone needs. Ed got paid, even though the horses didn't go out, and Raina said Ike had an awesome night of tips. The hotel has three guests who'll be spending more money before they leave town. We can't afford to turn our nose up at any of that."

"I guess not." She brightened. "If they go out, they might not find them. From what you've said, the Ghost is a tricky character."

"He is, at that. He—" The bell jangled as the door to the store opened. She quickly shoved her chili bowl under the counter as Vince walked in looking as if he'd somewhat recovered from his drinking bout. He'd obviously shaved and showered, and although his expression was a little drawn, his gaze was steady.

She wondered why he was here, but she was determined to be more polite than she had been last evening. She had to remember that he was bringing money into the town. He might even plan to spend some in her store. "Good afternoon, Vince."

Anastasia had turned when the bell had jingled. She walked forward and stuck out her hand. "I'm Anastasia Bickford, Georgie's sister."

"I remember you. I'm Vince Durant." He smiled as he shook her hand. "You were a teenager when I first got here, and then you went off to art school."

"Yep. Now I help Georgie in the store."

"I'm sure she appreciates that."

"I'm not the handiest person around. But I try."

Georgie felt a rush of love for Anastasia, whose artist's soul couldn't quite grasp mundane tasks but was brilliant at translating reality into light-filled watercolors and realistic charcoal portraits. Unfortunately she hadn't been doing that much since returning from art school. Georgie sensed it was a private matter and was reluctant to pry.

She returned her attention to Vince. "Is there something you need?"

"A new packet of razors. Mine's dull as a table knife."

Georgie looked closer and noticed a little bit of dried blood on his chin. That was usually caused by a sharp blade, not a dull one, but she wouldn't argue if he wanted to spend money in her store. "The aisle on your left, about halfway down." She gestured in the direction of the toiletries.

"I'll show you." Anastasia led the way.

Georgie watched in amusement and wondered what her sister was up to. She heard Anastasia's low, intense murmurs as they stood together in the aisle containing men's toiletries, but her words weren't distinct enough to make out.

They returned to the counter and Georgie rang up his purchase.

Vince glanced around. "The store looks good."

"Fortunately the people in town still shop here for most things instead of driving to Amarillo, so I do okay. Not like before, but okay."

Vince hesitated. "For what it's worth, I'm sorry the town has fallen on hard times. Bickford's a nice place. I'd . . . I'd like to see it prosper."

She didn't want to be touched by his sincerity, but she couldn't help it. She loved this town and hated seeing it going downhill. "Thanks."

"Well, guess I'll get back to the hotel and see how my buddies are doing." He picked up the package of razors.

"Don't forget what I told you," Anastasia said.

Vince's mouth twitched. "Oh, I won't. I doubt I'll ever forget that. See you both later." He walked out of the store with a loose-hipped stride.

For a brief moment Georgie was caught up in the masculine appeal of that stride and the width of those broad shoulders. She understood now why that was—she was a woman who'd denied her sexual needs for too long. Vince in particular hadn't snagged her attention, but seeing him reminded her that all men weren't balding and middle-aged.

"That should take care of that," Anastasia said.

Georgie looked at her sister. "Take care of what?"

"The problem with the horses."

"Why? What did you tell him?"

"That the Ghost has turned into a dangerous renegade with a terrible temper."

"He has not! He's a sweetheart. Well, I assume he is. I haven't been up close and personal, but he's definitely shy."

Anastasia continued as if Georgie hadn't spoken. "I said he almost trampled the last person who tried to capture him and any man who goes after him must have a death wish."

"Anastasia! None of that's true!"

"I know." She grinned. "But Vince has been gone for several years. He doesn't know that."

# CHAPTER 4

Vince waited until he'd walked a fair distance from the general store before giving way to laughter. He didn't want Anastasia to know how miserably she'd failed to intimidate him. That would be mean.

He was still chuckling when he walked into Sadie's and discovered his two buddies sitting at a table looking much better than they had a few hours ago. The brims of their hats were tipped back. This morning they'd been pulled down to shield their bloodshot eyes.

They'd both shaved and Mac had ditched the sweat-shirt in favor of a chambray button-up. They were even taking nourishment. Instead of beer, each of them had a mug of coffee to go with his sandwich. They were the only two people in the saloon besides Ike, who was at his post behind the bar.

"Hey, Ike, sorry to keep you so late last night," Vince called to him as he pulled out a chair at Mac and Travis's table.

"No problem. I slept in. And thanks for your generosity."

"It's the least we could do."

"Want something to eat?"

As he sat down, Vince surveyed what his friends had. "What'd you two get?"

"We both ordered the chicken salad," Travis said around a mouthful. "Excellent."

"Works for me." Vince glanced in Ike's direction. "I'll take a chicken salad sandwich and some coffee, if you don't mind."

"Coming up."

"You're looking perky," Mac said. "What's so funny?"

"Do either of you remember Anastasia, Georgie's little sister?"

Mac picked up the remaining half of his sandwich. "Not really. I remember the other one, Charmaine, the blonde. She was hot."

"I remember Anastasia," Travis said. "A little plump, but pretty. She was in the ice-cream parlor one day when I went in. She was working hard to sketch the sundae she'd ordered before it melted. Doing a damned good job of it, too."

Ike arrived with a steaming mug of coffee and put it beside Vince. "Your order will be up in a jiffy."

"Thanks, Ike." Vince took a sip of the hot brew. Sadie's served great coffee.

"So what about Anastasia?" Travis pointed to the package of razors Vince had laid on the table when he'd arrived. "Obviously you made a trip to the general store. Was she there?"

"She was, and apparently she's as creative with storytelling as she is drawing pictures. You should've heard the whopper she told me about the Ghost. I had a tough time keeping a straight face."

Travis picked up his coffee and took a sip. "What'd she say?"

"That the Ghost had turned into some kind of devil horse that was out to kill any man who tried to rope him." Remembering Anastasia's dramatic warning had him grinning again.

"Maybe he has," Travis said. "Like in that book, *The Horse Whisperer*. At the end the stallion kills the guy."

"He does?" Mac sighed. "That's disappointing."

Travis glanced at him. "Why?"

"Because you loaned me that book."

"I did? I wondered who had it."

"I do, doofus, and you didn't mention anything about the guy dying at the end. I was into it, but I don't want to finish it if that happens. I don't like endings where the main character gets whacked."

"Then watch the movie, instead," Vince said. "He doesn't die in the movie."

"Maybe I'll do that. And next time—" Mac paused while Ike delivered Vince's sandwich. Then he picked up where he left off. "Next time, Travis, don't give me books where somebody dies at the end. I hate that."

Travis smiled. "I didn't know you were such a wuss."

"I'm not! I can read any scary thing you throw at me, as long as the main guy is alive at the end. He can be bloodied up some, but he has to be alive." Mac gave Travis a belligerent stare.

"Okay, Mr. I-require-a-happy-ending, I'll keep that in mind. But my point was that Anastasia could be telling the truth. It sometimes happens, you know?"

"It's not the truth." Vince picked up half of his sandwich. "She just wants to scare us out of rounding him up. I'm sure Georgie's told her about our plan and she's trying to do her part to discourage us." He took a bite of what turned out to be delicious chicken salad.

Mac hunkered down and lowered his voice. "Listen, Travis and I were talking earlier, and we both think we should forget about doing it."

Vince quickly chewed and swallowed. "No, we should not." He should never have left those two alone while he went to the general store. They could lose focus so easily. "We have a plan and we need to stick to the plan."

"Yeah, but Travis and I got to thinking. Suppose we rope him. Then what? I can't believe you want to try and lead him all the way back to town. Nobody around here wants to deal with him."

Vince decided against revealing his fantasy of parading the Ghost down Main Street because Mac was right. That wasn't the best idea in the world. "We take a picture to prove we roped him," he said.

"Take a picture with what?" Travis asked. "We don't have camera phones."

"We'll buy a disposable at the general store." Vince was making it up as he went along. In actuality he hadn't thought much about what would happen after they'd captured the Ghost. He'd never been much for long-range thinking. He was more of a spur-of-the-moment kind of guy.

"That's a lot of effort to go through for a damned picture," Mac said. "Especially when it's obvious Georgie and her sister are dead-set against us doing it."

"That's the very reason we should do it." Vince wasn't about to see his concept unravel just because Mac and Travis were losing their enthusiasm for it. "We can't let Georgie Bickford push us around."

Mac looked him in the eye. "Travis and I can. But then,

we're not the ones with an ax to grind when it comes to Georgie."

"I don't have an ax to grind."

"She's the one who got away," Travis said. "You never forget the one who got away."

"That's bullshit. Georgie's nothing to me. I just don't like the idea of her dictating what I can and can't do." He bit off a good-sized chunk of his sandwich. While he chewed and swallowed, he caught Mac and Travis exchanging a look. "I suppose you think I have a thing for her."

Mac pushed away his empty plate. "Consider the evidence. You're the one who wanted to get together here in Bickford. Why?"

"Because it's where we used to hang out. It had nothing to do with Georgie. As I mentioned earlier, she could have gotten married or moved away."

"And the only way for you to check on that was to come here in person. But you needed your posse with you." Travis picked up his last potato chip. "Case closed." He popped the chip in his mouth.

"That isn't how it was." But telltale warmth crept up Vince's neck. He concentrated on eating his sandwich while he gathered his thoughts.

Hell, if what they said was true, he hadn't even admitted it to himself. He thought back to when he'd come up with this idea. He'd wanted to see Bickford again and have some fun at Sadie's. Finally rounding up the Ghost after all these years had seemed like an excellent adventure for the three of them, something they could brag about over drinks at the saloon afterward.

But now that his friends had brought up Georgie, he realized that his most vivid memories of Bickford and this saloon included her. On the few Saturday nights she hadn't made it to Sadie's, the fun had gone right out of the evening for him. He also used to dream up reasons to shop at the general store, a habit he'd never questioned until now. He'd done it again today. He could have managed without that package of razors.

Yesterday when she'd walked in, he'd checked her ring finger. He'd tried to buy her a drink. He couldn't sidestep the truth of what his friends were saying. His motivation for coming here had been connected, either a little or a whole lot, to Georgie. How humiliating that they'd figured it out before he had.

Finally he'd run out of food and couldn't delay the discussion any longer. He appreciated the fact that Mac and Travis had remained silent while he faced a few unpleasant realizations. Good friends did that for a guy.

Glancing up from his plate, he spoke quietly. "Number one, anything said at this table never gets repeated. I don't care how drunk either of you are; you keep it zipped."

Mac grinned. "Could you be more specific? I'll keep my mouth shut, but I make no promises about—"

"Keep everything zipped, nimrod. Georgie's off-limits and Anastasia's not your type."

"You don't know that."

"I do know that. I saw her less than an hour ago, and she is so not your type."

Travis looked hopeful. "Is she my type? By my calculations she's about twenty-three now. That makes her only a few years younger than me. Besides, I always liked her name."

Vince shook his head. "She's not your type because

you're leaving tomorrow and she's a nice girl, not the kind you get involved with and then cut out on."

"Vince is right, and not just for that reason," Mac said. "You're coming off a bad breakup, so nobody's your type until you get your shit together."

Travis winced. "So I did spill my guts last night. I was afraid of that."

"Yeah, but that's not going anywhere, either." Vince kept his tone businesslike. Travis wouldn't appreciate sympathy.

"Definitely not." Mac sounded equally brisk. "We do, however, have a matter on the table that needs addressing. Are we going to go after that horse or not?"

Vince glanced toward the bar and noticed that Ike wasn't there. Maybe he'd gone back to the kitchen for some reason, which was lucky, because Vince didn't want him hearing this. "Let me explain before Ike comes back. The bottom line is, I can't allow Georgie to think she got the better of me on this deal."

Mac groaned. "Why can't you just let it go?"

"Because I can't, that's all. Let's just ride out first thing in the morning and find the herd. That's not so much to ask. We don't have to rope the Ghost, but I want to lay eyes on him one last time. I want to be able to say I did that much."

"I can understand that," Travis said. "You want to save face. God knows I understand the value of saving face."

"I guess I do, too," Mac said. "So we'll get up at the crack of dawn and do this damn thing."

"Which means no tequila shots tonight." Travis narrowed his eyes at both of them. "A few beers, okay, but don't either of you talk me into tequila shots."

Vince nodded. "Mac and I discussed that earlier. Just beer. We'll play a little poker with the old guys and hit the hay."

Travis pushed back his chair. "In the meantime, I think I'll take a walk around town, check things out."

"I'll go with you." Mac tucked his napkin beside his plate and reached for his wallet. "Just in case you were considering a visit to the general store to renew your acquaintance with Anastasia Bickford."

"Who says I was planning to do that?"

"Me. I saw that look in your eye. You're remembering the cute teenager and imagining how hot she might be now. I intend to save you from yourself. Vince, want to come along?"

"Nah. I was just there. I'll take a nap and rest up for the poker game."

"Good idea." Mac smiled. "I suppose it wouldn't be cool for you to wander into Georgie's store twice in the space of a couple of hours. She might get the wrong idea."

"Or the right idea." Travis dropped some money on the table. "See you later, lover boy."

"Cut it out. It's a dead issue because she has no interest in me. All I want is to leave town with my pride intact."

"We'll help you find that horse," Travis said, "but keeping your pride is a one-man job. You're in charge of that."

"Just help me come within spitting distance of him. I'll handle the rest."

Mac eyed him. "You really are planning to rope him, aren't you?"

"I haven't decided yet."

"It's a bad idea, Vince."

"We'll see."

Mac adjusted the fit of his Stetson. "You think on it while I go babysit Travis and Anastasia."

"I will." Vince sipped the last of his coffee as he watched them leave the saloon. If Georgie really had been his main focus, he could have driven to Bickford anytime in the past four years.

But Travis was right that he wouldn't have risked coming by himself with no excuse for the visit other than to see how she was doing. Bickford wasn't on a main road. People didn't pass through town on their way to either Amarillo or Lubbock, which was another reason the town was in financial trouble. If you arrived in Bickford, then that had been your destination from the get-go.

Apparently it had taken him this long to come up with a logical reason to travel here. His reason might be flimsy as hell, but the reunion and the Ghost had been better than nothing. And he'd needed his wingmen.

So far he'd confirmed that Georgie was as indifferent to him as she'd ever been. He could have accepted that more easily if he'd found her in high cotton, living her dream in beautiful downtown Bickford. Instead she was facing the potential end of the town she loved.

He assumed her ancestors had settled the place, but he'd never asked. If so, then her loyalty to the town probably ran deep. He'd never felt that way about any place he'd lived. His folks had relocated a fair bit because his dad had worked in the oil fields and he'd traveled to where the jobs were. Moving around was what Vince did best.

Gathering up the plates and silverware, he carried them over to the bar, where Ike was taking inventory in preparation for tonight.

Ike glanced up from his list. "Thanks. You didn't have to bus the table."

"Don't worry. I swiped the tips, too."

Ike chuckled. "You're entitled."

"Kidding. Be right back with the rest of the stuff and your cash." He returned to the table and picked up the money Travis and Mac had left. Then he added his share. He admired many things about his friends, including their generosity. Despite limited resources, they always paid their way and then some.

He deposited the money and the coffee mugs on the bar. Then he decided to plant some information to shore up his reputation as a force to be reckoned with. He wanted Ike to pass the news on to Georgie so she'd know the plan hadn't been scrapped. "Just an FYI while you're checking your supplies—we won't be drinking as much tonight. We're riding out first thing in the morning to find the Ghost."

Ike gazed at him. "You realize I'll have to report that to Georgie."

"I'm counting on it." Vince left the saloon feeling a little like the old boys in *High Noon.* Georgie had thrown down a challenge, and he'd be damned if he'd back away from it.

When Mac and Travis walked into the store, Georgie expected Vince to follow. When he didn't, she was surprised. And disappointed? Surely not. He was the testosterone-driven cowboy who thought chasing a wild stallion made him a hero.

She smiled at Mac and Travis. Yesterday Mac had seemed ready to give up on the idea of rounding up the Ghost, so obviously he wasn't as committed to the project as Vince. That earned him points in her book. "What can I help you with, gentlemen?"

Mac glanced around. "I've been thinking about getting one of those self-inflating air mattresses, the thermal kind that's supposed to keep the cold from seeping up from the ground."

Travis looked at him in surprise. "You have? I didn't know that."

"I don't tell you everything." Mac turned back to Georgie. "You have a mattress like that?"

"Sure, but . . ." She hesitated, torn between wanting the sale and knowing that the Bickford General Store wasn't Mac's cheapest option for such a thing. The average cowboy didn't make a lot of money. She suspected he was buying this mattress to help her out, and she appreciated that more than he knew.

Finally her conscience wouldn't let her do it without warning him first. "You'd get a better price in one of the big camping stores in Amarillo or Lubbock, or maybe even online."

"I know." He smiled. "I'd rather buy it from you."

Hidden behind the grocery aisle where she was stocking paper goods, Anastasia sighed in obvious delight. "That's the sweetest thing I've ever heard." Then she walked into view. "I don't know your name, mister, but I can tell your heart's as big as Texas."

Both men stood a little straighter as they gazed at Anastasia. Georgie hadn't given much thought to Anastasia's outfit, but seeing it through the eyes of two single cowboys gave her a new perspective. Anastasia wasn't overweight, at least not in Georgie's opinion. Evelyn thought Anastasia needed to diet, but Georgie disagreed. She was healthy and she looked good.

But dressed in a white knit shirt and snug jeans, she

might look a little too good. Her sensible ponytail now seemed sassy and provocative. Thank goodness both men were leaving tomorrow.

"Anastasia, these are Vince's friends, Mac Foster and Travis Langdon."

"I thought so. Pleased to meet y'all." But Anastasia seemed far more pleased to meet Mac than Travis, although she extended her hand to both of them because she'd been raised to be polite. Her adoring glances, though, were all directed at Mac. "Anyone who'd choose to make a purchase at the Bickford General Store instead of driving to a discount place surely wouldn't want to chase some poor horse around God's creation."

Mac looked flustered. "Uh . . ."

"Did Vince mention what I told him about the Ghost?"

Travis spoke right up. "Yes, ma'am. I'm willing to believe it, too."

"You should." Looking pleased, she glanced over at Mac. "How about you?"

"Anything's possible."

"Then I hope y'all talk Vince out of that plan. Now come on back and I'll show you where those mattresses are located."

"I might buy one, too," Travis said.

"Okay." Anastasia didn't seem to care one way or the other when it came to Travis's potential purchases. She sashayed back to the camping aisle with a sway to her hips that Georgie had never seen. "Will you need a single mattress or a double?"

"Single, ma'am. It's just me."

"Good. I mean, now I know which size to pull out."

Travis followed behind as if hoping Anastasia would

include him in the discussion, but that looked like a lost cause. Once they'd rounded the end of the aisle, Georgie couldn't see them anymore, but she could hear perfectly.

Anastasia's syrupy voice drifted from the camping aisle. "Do you sleep outside a lot, Mr. Foster?"

"Please call me Mac."

At his slightly deeper tone, Georgie rolled her eyes. Yep, he was flirting. He'd been quite a rogue in the past and undoubtedly hadn't changed. But Anastasia might convince him to stay away from the Ghost, which would be a plus.

If Mac had intended to be in town for longer than another twenty-four hours, then having him flirt with Anastasia might be cause for concern. But tomorrow he'd be headed back to wherever he'd come from. With luck, that was a long day's drive from here.

That left tonight, but Anastasia wasn't the type to wander over to the saloon. She'd likely stay home and read as she usually did. Georgie had decided against having dinner at Sadie's tonight, too. The less time either of them spent around these cowboys, the better.

She'd fallen into the habit of eating over at Sadie's because she avoided spending time with her stepmother. They couldn't seem to spend two minutes together without arguing about money. The will had given Evelyn control of everything, and she spent money as fast as Georgie made it. The life insurance from George Bickford's death was gone, which meant the store was the only source of income.

It would support them, except that Evelyn sent large sums to Charmaine to finance her lifestyle in Dallas. Georgie figured that Evelyn had mortgaged the stately Victorian that had been in the Bickford family for more than a hundred years. The thought that they might lose that house made Georgie sick to her stomach.

Evelyn could also mortgage the store if she wanted to. Georgie hoped to hell she hadn't, but finding that out was impossible. Evelyn kept the key to George Bickford's home office, and she never left the door unlocked.

As Mac and Anastasia continued to flirt in the camping aisle, Georgie couldn't help smiling. Evelyn would be horrified if she knew that her daughter was making eyes at a dirt-poor cowhand. Marrying off both daughters to wealthy men was her plan to get out of Bickford.

Georgie wished Charmaine would hurry up and snag a rich husband, because then Evelyn would probably move to Dallas. Considered in that light, the money going to Charmaine for salon visits and designer clothes might be well spent if it worked to relocate Evelyn. Charmaine had a decent chance at success in her husband hunt. Her training as a model gave her poise, and her business degree made her a savvy personal shopper for the rich and famous.

Georgie's cell phone rang. She scooped it out from under the counter and checked the readout. "Hey, Ike. What's up?"

"Just so you know, those boys are riding out at dawn to find the Ghost. Vince told me, and when I mentioned that I would be reporting to you, he said he was counting on it."

"I see." Georgie lowered her voice. "If my sister has her way, he might have to go alone. She's trying to sweet-talk Mac and Travis out of it."

"She is?"

"Surprised the heck out of me, too. I've never seen her turn on the charm with any guy, but she took a shine to Mac. Maybe she'll influence him, and Travis, too."

"I don't know. Those guys are loyal to each other. I think if Vince goes, they'll tag along."

Georgie sighed. "If that happens, I'll be prepared."

Her comment was met with silence. "Georgie," Ike said at last, "I don't want you doing anything stupid."

"They're the ones who are doing something stupid."

"I just don't want you getting hurt."

"I won't, I promise. But don't expect me for dinner tonight. Knowing Vince's intentions, the less I see of him, the better."

"If you say so."

"I think it's best. Thanks for keeping me informed." She disconnected the call.

In her heart of hearts, she realized that she'd handled this situation poorly from the get-go, but she didn't know how to change the dynamics now. Instead of getting upset with Vince when he'd announced his boneheaded plan, she should have calmly told him that it was not in the best interest of the horses. That might not have worked, but it would have had a better chance of success than the path she had taken.

By getting all riled up and then issuing a challenge, she'd put him in a corner and forced him to defend his manly pride, especially when some of the exchange had been in front of his friends. She was a smart lady. She should have known that her knee-jerk reaction wouldn't be helpful.

On some level she had known it and hadn't cared. She was spoiling for a fight with somebody, and Vince just might oblige her. As her father used to say, the fat was in the fire. Too late to backtrack.

The store was closed on Sundays, so if Vince and his friends followed through, she'd be free to saddle Prince and ride out to defend the Ghost. Thanks to her father's mentoring, she was fully prepared to do that.

# CHAPTER 5

Georgie locked up the store at five after what had turned out to be a profitable day thanks to Mac and Travis. Apparently buying camping supplies had turned into a macho competition staged to impress Anastasia. Each cowboy had put a sizable dent in his credit card by the time they'd both walked out loaded down with mattresses, lanterns, and cookware.

After they'd left, Anastasia had peppered Georgie with questions about Mac, questions Georgie couldn't answer because she didn't know the guy all that well. So her sister had gone home to immortalize Mac on paper before his image faded from her mind. Her instant attraction to the tall cowboy was disconcerting.

Or maybe it was understandable, given the nunlike existence she and Georgie lived. Georgie didn't know how Anastasia behaved around single men her own age. There hadn't been any in Bickford since Anastasia had come home from art school a little over a year ago.

Funny how she'd fought so hard to get there, working to earn scholarships and arguing with her mother, who said the only men she'd meet would be starving artists. Privately Georgie wondered if a starving artist had broken Anastasia's tender heart while she was away at school. She'd returned a more subdued person who'd lost most of her enthusiasm for her work and hadn't pursued getting a job in her field. Instead she'd appointed herself Georgie's assistant at the store.

Georgie hadn't glimpsed her sister's old spark until this afternoon when she'd laid eyes on Mac. Regardless of how this turned out, seeing Anastasia excited enough to rush home and draw the guy's picture had been gratifying. But would that spark disappear when Mac drove away tomorrow?

If it did, Georgie vowed to figure out a way to solve this problem of two single twentysomething women in a town composed primarily of senior citizens. It wasn't good for either of them, but leaving wasn't an option, at least not for Georgie. Anastasia seemed fond of the town, too. The few times she had been inspired to work with her watercolors, she'd created some lovely scenes, many of them featuring either the historic hotel or the Victorian house she, Georgie, and Evelyn lived in.

The house was located at the far end of Main Street, two blocks from the Bickford Hotel. When it was built, it had been the grandest home in town. Actually, it still was. Georgie blessed her father for teaching her about home maintenance during the years after her mother died when only Georgie and her dad had lived there.

She couldn't have been much help at two or three, but she distinctly remembered helping him nail down a loose board on the porch when she was only four. By five she was pretty good with a paint brush, and by six she could

replace the stopper on a toilet tank and rewire a door-
bell. She'd been eight and quite the experienced handy-
girl when he'd married Evelyn.

The lessons hadn't been the same after that because
her father had tried to bring Charmaine and Anastasia
up to speed. He'd believed every woman should know
basic home maintenance, but Evelyn had told him that
was nonsense and so Charmaine hadn't been interested,
either. Anastasia had tried, but she'd been dreamy even
back then. She'd forget what she was doing and dump
over a bucket of paint or spill a box of nails.

She hadn't changed. She'd desperately wanted to help
Georgie paint the clapboards and gingerbread trim last
October. Her work had been perfect, but she'd fallen off
the ladder twice and Georgie had been sick with worry
each time. Finally she'd assigned her sister to ground-
floor painting, only.

The house looked great, though. In early evening the
outside color was still visible as lights began to glow from
behind the lace-curtained windows. Georgie loved the slate
blue that Anastasia had picked out. When combined with
the white trim, it gave the two-story Victorian a crisp, clean
facade. Anastasia had added another subtle touch to the
spindle posts holding up the porch roof. They were painted
white, but each indentation was defined by a slim line of
slate blue. Classy.

As always, Georgie climbed the porch steps with a
mixture of love and frustration. The house was home, but
it didn't belong to her. Instead it belonged to a woman
who didn't give a damn about it. Without Georgie around
to replace washers in faucets and fix loose shingles on the
roof, the place would be in trouble. An old house needed
upkeep. The effort was well worth it, in Georgie's estima-

tion, but then again, she cherished the history contained within these walls.

The front door, with its oval glass insert, had been hung when she was seven during her father's campaign to make the house more energy efficient. The campaign was ongoing even now. Georgie longed to replace the upstairs windows but she'd have to get permission from Evelyn, who'd already said it wasn't necessary. Evelyn had agreed to the paint because the store got it at a discount and the labor had been free. Windows would cost much more.

As Georgie walked into the hall, a reality show blared from the plasma TV Evelyn had bought recently. The screen was huge and ruined the look of the dainty parlor, but Georgie had nothing to say about that, either. She didn't have to glance in the room to know that Evelyn would be sitting there with a pitcher of martinis.

Anastasia bounded down the stairs dressed in her best jeans and a shirt decorated in sequins. She had a jacket in one hand and a rolled piece of paper in the other. She paused to stare at Georgie. "I thought you'd be at Sadie's! I was going to meet you over there."

Georgie stared right back. "Who are you and what have you done with my sister?"

She laughed. "I know, right? I never go to Sadie's, but I want to give Mac this." She unrolled the paper. "What do you think?"

Georgie gazed at Mac, perfectly captured in charcoal from the tilt of his hat to the slight smile lifting the corners of his mouth. "Amazing. I almost expect him to start telling a joke. You're so talented."

"Thanks, but it's easy when I have the right subject. This practically drew itself. I sat down, picked up a piece of charcoal, and before I knew it, there he was." She looked at the sketch and uncertainty crept into her voice for the first time. "I hope he likes it."

"Are you kidding? He'll be flattered out of his mind. Vince and Travis will be jealous and want you to draw them, too."

"You think?"

"I don't think. I know. If Mac has a portrait of himself, they won't want to leave here without one, too."

"Should I take my sketch pad? I wouldn't mind doing one of each of them. That would be kind of fun, actually."

"Yes, take it. I'll come with you."

"Cool." She started back upstairs and Georgie followed.

"While you get your stuff, I'll change into something more festive. After all, it's Saturday night!"

"It is!" Anastasia ducked into her room. "Meet you on the front porch in ten minutes."

"You got it." Georgie hurried down the hall and into her room at the back of the house. Anastasia's shy eagerness touched her heart. This might turn into the artistic kick in the pants her sister needed to start drawing again on a regular basis. If only they had tourists in town the way they used to, she would have a built-in customer base for her charcoal portraits.

They didn't have that, but for one night, her sister could shine, and even better, she seemed excited about doing that. The arrival of those three cowboys was shaking things up. Considering the melancholy atmosphere that had taken hold of the town and its residents, a little shake-up was a good thing. The issue of the Ghost and his herd hadn't gone away, but Georgie was willing to set that aside for now and focus on Anastasia's renewed creativity.

Ten minutes wasn't much time to transform from a

shop clerk to a fun-loving cowgirl, but Georgie made the most of every second. She opened her closet and took out her jeans with rhinestones on the pockets. After wiggling into them, she pulled on red boots she'd bought ages ago for dancing. Then she unhooked a red silk shirt from its hanger and put that on.

A quick brush through her hair, a refresh of her lipstick and blush, and she was ready to go. She grabbed a jean jacket and tucked some money in her pocket. How long had it been since she'd headed to Sadie's knowing that some good-looking cowboys were there? Years. Not since Vince had left.

She missed those days. Not Vince, of course, but the fun that had swirled around him. He'd created an atmosphere of celebration the moment he'd walked into the saloon. His grin had said plainly *let's get this party started.*

Too bad he'd come up with this dumb plan to capture the Ghost, but maybe going to Sadie's wasn't a bad idea in that respect, either. She'd approached the problem like a soldier marching into battle, but Anastasia was having better luck by being friendly. What if a few charcoal portraits mellowed the guys out so they decided not to round up any horses in the morning? Much as she longed to duke it out with Vince, settling things peacefully would be better.

Walking down the sidewalk with Anastasia reminded her of old times with Janet. Yet her little sister wasn't Janet, and the street was dark and deserted except for the streetlamps and the lights of the hotel at the far end of town. Four years ago the shops would have been busy at this hour. Georgie used to keep the general store open until nine, and then Janet would show up and they'd head toward Sadie's. The sidewalk had been crowded with well-heeled Double J guests looking for souvenirs or a bite to eat.

"I'm glad we're doing this," Anastasia said. "I've always felt sort of cheated because I was too young to go when you used to party with the cowboys, and when I was finally old enough, it was all gone."

"I know. I wonder if anyone in town realized how precarious our situation was, depending on the Double J the way we did. The town should have figured out how to attract tourists on its own and grow our reputation as a quaint little vacation spot. But no one thought of that, and I have no idea how to make it happen now."

"Yeah, it's like, *come to Bickford and be depressed by all the boarded-up storefronts.* I'm sure people would sign up for that."

"It does seem sort of hopeless, but I've decided one thing about you and me."

"We're getting matching tattoos?"

*"No."* She laughed. "What made you think of that?"

"I've always wanted to get a tattoo, but I'd be chicken to get it by myself. I almost— Well, never mind."

"Hey, you can't start a sentence with *I almost* and then drop it." Georgie had a pretty good idea what this was all about and thought maybe now was the time for Anastasia to unburden herself.

"I almost got matching tattoos with this guy at art school."

"Was he a rat fink bastard?"

"As it turns out."

Georgie put her arm around her sister's shoulders and gave her a quick hug. "Sorry."

"At least I found out before I got the tattoo. Those

suckers are horrible to get rid of, from what I've heard. If you and I did it, I wouldn't worry about wanting to laser it off someday."

"Thank you. That's a real compliment."

"I meant it to be." She hesitated. "And for the record, Charmaine thinks you're pretty cool, too."

"She *does*? I thought I was nothing but a pain in the ass to her."

"Oh, she resented the hell out of you for a lot of years, especially when you marched her home from Sadie's that night. She was spitting nails. But now that she's older, she realizes that having us and Mom move in must have been rough on you."

Georgie was stunned. And ashamed of herself for thinking that Charmaine was in Dallas sucking up money without a single thought to how that affected everyone else. "I . . . I haven't given Charmaine enough credit, I guess."

"Don't go giving her too much credit. She's agreed to Mom's program of trapping some rich dude, and she loves the salon appointments and the cool clothes. That's Charmaine. Always has been, always will be. But still, she understands you're the glue holding things together."

"That's . . . nice to hear." Knowing that Charmaine felt that way brought a lump to her throat. A little embarrassed by her reaction, she turned the comment into a joke. "Are you saying this is a sticky situation?"

"Yeah." Anastasia grinned at her. "And it's your fault, considering you're the glue and all."

"Maybe we need a vat of Goo-Gone so everyone can get unstuck."

"Nope, I'm glad I'm stuck with you, and so's Charmaine. I love Mom, but she shouldn't be in charge of the money. Your dad screwed up by leaving everything to her. He should have left it to you."

Georgie knew how that would have turned out. Evelyn would have challenged the will. "That might have created another set of problems. Plus, I wouldn't be sending Charmaine money to finance your mother's plan."

"I know." Anastasia blew out a gusty sigh. "I told her Charmaine would have to sacrifice herself, because I won't. The whole concept creeps me out. It's so nineteenth century."

"But if Charmaine's fine with it and she finds herself a millionaire, then—"

"Mom's hoping for a billionaire."

"Oh, jeez."

"Yeah. But she'd settle for a millionaire."

"Okay, either way, if Charmaine comes through, your mom can move to Dallas. I know she hates it here."

"And you'd get your house back," Anastasia said quietly.

"No, that's not what I meant." But it actually was. She had to be more careful about telegraphing how much she wanted her stepmother out of that house. Despite Evelyn's flaws, Anastasia loved her. If Evelyn moved away, Anastasia might go with her. That would kind of suck.

"It's okay, Georgie. I get it. You have all the responsibility and none of the power."

Georgie shrugged. "Oh, well. Can't do anything about that at this very moment, so let's forget about it for now." She gestured toward the door that led into Sadie's Saloon. "Besides, we're here."

"I know, and I'm nervous as hell. Maybe this wasn't such a good idea, after all."

"Coming down for a drink or showing Mac your drawing?"

"Both, but mostly showing him my work. I'm having second thoughts about that."

Georgie turned to face her. "I don't want to push you into anything, but I can guarantee that all three of those cowboys will be impressed. How long has it been since you've shown your work to anyone besides your immediate family?"

"Not since I left art school."

"You got out of the habit, so of course you're nervous. But what good is talent if it's not shared?"

Anastasia smiled. "You sound like one of my professors. Okay, I'll do it, as long as we walked down here and I have you as backup."

"I'll be right there, but just remember how much you loved drawing that picture and how eager you were to give it to him right after it was finished. If he'd been standing at the bottom of the stairs in our house, you would have handed it over immediately. But now you've had a chance to think about it and you've got cold feet. That's only natural."

"And speaking of cold feet, it's chilly out here! Let's go in where it's warm."

"Exactly. But promise you'll show him the picture right away. Don't put it off, or you might change your mind."

"Damn, Georgie. You know me too well. Okay, right away, the minute we get in there." Taking a deep breath, she opened the door.

As Georgie followed her inside, she noticed that the cowboys sat at the bar in the same order they'd taken the night before, with Travis closest to the door, Mac in the middle, and Vince on the far side. They all glanced toward the door in unison and wore matching expressions of astonishment, as if the moment had been choreographed. Georgie worked hard to keep from laughing.

Ike looked surprised, too, but he recovered more quickly than the others. "Welcome, ladies! I didn't expect the pleasure of your company tonight. Have a seat wherever you like. What can I get you?"

"Red wine for me," Georgie said.

"A draft for me." Anastasia set down her messenger bag and pulled out the sketch. "But first I have something for Mac, if he wants it." She held it toward him.

Mac's eyes widened as he carefully took the sheet of paper. Then he sucked in a breath. "Damn!"

"Let's see." Vince left his stool and peered over Mac's shoulder. "Wow. That's incredible."

"It is." Travis shook his head. "You are one lucky SOB, Mac Foster, getting something that awesome."

Mac lifted his gaze. "I don't know what to say, Anastasia. This is the best thing anyone's ever given me."

Georgie could have kissed him. When she glanced over at Anastasia, her little sister sparkled brighter than the chandelier hanging in the hotel lobby. In that moment, Georgie decided that dealing with these cowboys might be worth the trouble, after all.

# CHAPTER 6

Vince found Georgie's obvious pride in her stepsister touching. No doubt Georgie hadn't wanted to come down to Sadie's tonight knowing she'd likely run into him, but she'd done it for Anastasia's sake. That took selflessness and strength of character, two things he admired.

But Georgie wasn't just proud of Anastasia. She was fiercely protective, too. She'd tried to disguise it, but Vince was paying attention and he'd caught her intense expression prior to Mac's first comment. Woe to that cowboy if he hadn't made a big deal out of the drawing. Vince wouldn't have wanted to be in his boots.

Having Georgie on your side would be . . . amazing. Her loyalties ran deep. Bickford might be crumbling around her, but she wouldn't give up until she was the last person left. She was like a captain who had pledged to go down with the ship. She might not be impressed with him, but he sure as hell was impressed with her.

Once Mac recovered from the shock of discovering that Anastasia had drawn his picture, he paid for her draft beer and insisted that he'd buy her dinner, too. Vince couldn't get a bead on how Mac felt about Anastasia, but she seemed to have a gigantic crush on him. That might not be such a great thing. Mac was several years older and had a history of failed relationships.

Meanwhile Travis, poor guy, couldn't take his eyes off Anastasia. All they needed to make this a true fustercluck was for Georgie to become interested in Travis. That would guarantee nobody would end up happy. Fortunately Georgie wasn't casting longing glances in Travis's direction.

So far the Bickford sisters and Vince's group were the only ones in the saloon. Anastasia's drawing had created a bond, so when Mac suggested they push a couple of tables together before ordering dinner, everyone agreed. Mac held a chair at the head of the table for the new celebrity and sat down on her right. Travis grabbed the place to her left.

Three chairs remained—one at the far end, one next to Mac, and one next to Travis. Georgie took the end chair and Vince sat next to Mac. That put him closer to Georgie than she might have liked, but he couldn't help that. He did his best to ignore her nearness and the inevitable brush of their knees under the table.

Ike took their orders and relayed them to Henry in the kitchen. Then he made sure they all had drinks and brought out chips and salsa.

Studiously avoiding looking at Georgie, Vince kept his attention on his other dinner companions. He tried to block out the rhythm of her breathing, but that was fruitless. Nothing new there. He could admit it to himself now—she'd always turned him on.

Mac continued to hold on to his portrait. "I need a

safe place for this. Maybe I should take it up to my room so it doesn't get food on it."

"Or I can put it back in my messenger bag for the time being." Anastasia unhooked her bag from the back of her chair and set it on her lap.

"That works."

"I'll tuck it inside my sketch book so it won't get creased." She pulled out the tablet.

"You have more paper?" Travis gazed at the sketchbook.

"Yes." Anastasia slipped Mac's portrait inside the back cover of the sketchbook. "Why?"

"Well, I . . . you probably wouldn't want to do this, but I was wondering if you'd—"

"Sketch you?"

"Yes, ma'am. If it wouldn't be too much trouble."

Anastasia looked pleased as punch. "Of course not. I'd love to."

"I don't know, Travis." Mac frowned. "Her dinner will be showing up soon. You don't want to be bothering her while she's trying to eat."

Vince ducked his head to hide a smile. Mac liked being the only one with a portrait. Thank God for some comic relief from his two crazy friends. He'd never seen them compete for the same woman before. This could be entertaining and keep his mind off Georgie.

"It's not a problem," Anastasia said. "I work pretty fast. I'll get it done before the food comes, I'll bet. Then after we eat, I can sketch Vince if he wants."

"Me?" He blinked, caught off guard by the suggestion and not sure how he felt about having someone draw his picture. It could be kind of embarrassing to sit there while she did it. He started to tell her never mind when he noticed the eagerness in her expression. Instantly he reversed direction. "I would be honored. Thank you."

"Great!" She pushed back her chair and propped her open sketchbook on her bent knee. "Travis, I think I'll do yours in profile. You have a great nose."

"I do?" He peered at the sketchbook.

"A classic nose. But don't look at what I'm doing. Face Mac. Look over his shoulder. That's good. And hold still."

"A classic nose." Travis grinned. "Like the pharaohs."

Mac groaned. "Now you've done it, Anastasia. I'll be hearing about that classic nose all the way back to Midland."

"Anastasia needs to see my Egyptian dance. It matches my nose."

Vince laughed. Watching Travis's turn on the hot seat was fun. Travis obviously loved the attention and he was working it, doing his best to gain an edge over Mac, who'd looked like the frontrunner at first. Now Vince wasn't so sure. Travis had a way with women.

Travis and Mac traded inventive insults that made Anastasia crack up, but she kept drawing. She was obviously a pro at this. He wondered if she was using her talent for anything besides sketching visiting cowboys. He wasn't looking forward to his turn, but he'd do it. She was a sweet kid and he wouldn't hurt her feelings for the world.

A light touch on his arm surprised the hell out of him. He turned toward Georgie, astonished that she'd do that. The sensation of her fingertips on his forearm lingered, tantalizing him.

"Thank you," she murmured.

Her soft, sexy voice made him think of things he

shouldn't, such as what she'd feel like beneath him on a cushy mattress, something he'd probably never know. He didn't have to ask her what she was thanking him for. This was all about her sister. Apparently she'd caught his hesitation before he'd agreed to the portrait.

He gave a little shrug. "No problem."

Georgie continued to keep her voice low as she leaned closer. "I haven't seen her so excited about her work in a long time."

And speaking of excitement . . . Vince breathed in the scent of wildflowers. Whatever perfume Georgie had worn last time he'd seen her must still be her favorite. One whiff of it affected his heart rate and carried him back in time. They used to dance the night away in this saloon, but no matter how much he'd flirted with her, she'd never agreed to hang out with him except on the dance floor.

Sitting at the dinner table with her was a first, but it hadn't been her choice. She was only here because of Anastasia. In fact, she was only talking to him because of her sister's artwork.

Okay, he could discuss that. He mirrored her action, leaning forward. This close he could see the gold flecks in her brown eyes. Her mouth had always driven him crazy—so plump and inviting. Considering the lack of eligible men in town, he wondered when she'd last been kissed. "What's happened with her art?"

"She graduated from art school, but since then she hasn't been motivated to do much. If we still had tourists in town, I know she could sell her watercolors. She could even set up a booth somewhere to do quick sketches like these."

Vince nodded, although he struggled to pay attention.

Instead he watched the seductive movement of her mouth as she talked. He got the gist, though. Georgie thought, given an influx of tourists, Anastasia could draw portraits and make money at it. She was probably right. A lot of people loved having someone draw their picture. He wasn't one of those people, but at least nobody else was in the saloon right now so he'd have relative privacy for his sitting.

"I just wish I knew a way to bring back the tourist traffic. We need businesses that would attract people, and who would look at Bickford and see an opportunity to make money?"

"I don't know, Georgie." He said her name on purpose to make the exchange seem more intimate and personal. If he could wave a magic wand and restore the town to its former glory, he'd do it, partly for the good of all, but mostly for her. "It's a damned shame."

"It is." She held his gaze.

He'd never had such a long time to stare into her eyes, and he discovered something fascinating. The longer they looked at each other, the faster her breathing became. Could she be attracted to him after all? Her eyes darkened in a way that usually meant one of two things—either a woman wanted him or she was ready to clean his clock.

If they'd been talking about the Ghost, he'd think Georgie was working up to a good fight, but they'd been discussing the revitalization of Bickford. He couldn't escape the conclusion that Georgie, despite all her behavior to the contrary, found him sexually attractive. That was a revelation.

He smiled. "Listen, I wonder if—"

"Vince." Her voice vibrated with emotion. "Is there

any way . . ." She paused to take a breath. "Is there any way I can convince you to—"

"Dinner's ready!" Ike deposited plates in front of them, which ended the charged connection and cut off whatever Georgie had been about to say.

Unfortunately Vince could guess what that had been. Georgie might have some erotic feelings for him, but that didn't mean she'd forgotten about those horses. He didn't want to discuss them with her, because he was going out there tomorrow, whether she wanted him to or not. This was a wild stallion they were talking about, not some fragile creature that would keel over from fright if three cowboys showed up.

The Ghost was no shy guy. He'd successfully lured a mare out of the Double J pasture on a moonlit night Vince remembered well. The wranglers had heard a commotion and had poured out of the bunkhouse in time to see the mare clear the fence and take off with the stallion.

Vince, Mac, Travis, and a couple of others had given chase but they'd had no luck catching them. In the days that followed, they'd tracked the herd, but they'd never been able to get close enough to retrieve the mare. The loss of the mare didn't matter anymore, but Vince was curious to see if the Ghost was as magnificent as he remembered. Something about that animal called to him. He wasn't leaving Bickford without tracking him down.

Yeah, he itched to rope him and feel that wildness and power humming through the braided hemp. He craved a contest with that muscular stallion. But he might decide against doing that.

Thrilling though the prospect might be, roping the Ghost was pretty stupid and potentially dangerous. Guaranteed that Anastasia had made up her fantastic story about the stallion going rogue and Vince didn't believe a word of it. But roping any unpredictable two-thousand-pound animal was risky.

Still, he didn't want to make any promises to Georgie about what would or wouldn't happen in the morning. He wanted the freedom to act in the moment, the way the Ghost did. Tomorrow would be an adventure, and he didn't want to be bound by anything or anyone, including the very enticing Georgie Bickford.

Georgie remembered now why she'd never allowed herself to spend quiet moments with Vince Durant. Dancing a spirited two-step with him had proven to her that he was one potent cowboy. But as long as she'd remained a moving target, he'd never been able to get a bead on her and she'd kept herself safe from his mesmerizing sexuality.

Sitting at this table where he was too damned close, where their knees sometimes touched by accident, where she had no excuse to twirl away, she was caught by his magnetism. She'd done her best to concentrate on the issues at hand—Anastasia's art, Bickford's future, and the Ghost's freedom. But underneath those concerns lurked images of tangled sheets and slick bodies. Judging from the smoky sensuality in his blue eyes, Vince was thinking of the same thing.

She wanted to blame it on her circumstances, but that was a cop-out. Vince had always posed this kind of danger. She might be more susceptible to him now, but he'd tempted her years ago even when she'd known he wasn't right for her. He was no more right for her tonight than he'd ever been, but logic had nothing to do with the heat she felt when he was this close.

Maybe it was better that Ike had interrupted her before she could ask Vince to stay away from the Ghost. If he'd agreed, if he'd continued to look into her eyes with sex on his mind, she would have been lost. She might have done something she'd bitterly regret, like show up outside his hotel room tonight.

If she did something that bold, he'd invite her in. She didn't doubt that for a minute. And he'd be a wonderful lover if the gossip had been true. She had no reason to suppose it hadn't been.

But she wasn't looking for a night with a cowboy who had no plans for his life other than riding over the next hill to see what was on the other side. She didn't know how in hell to keep Bickford from sinking into oblivion, but somehow she'd do it. That was her goal and would remain her focus.

Vince didn't fit into that scenario. He might have stirred up buried urges, but he was leaving tomorrow. One night of hot sex would only make her want something that wasn't likely to happen again in the near future. She had enough frustration in her life without adding more.

Anastasia had finished Travis's portrait, and he left his plate untouched as he raved on about how great it was. Mac asked her to pull out his picture so he could study it some more. As both men lavished praise on Anastasia, she looked happier than Georgie had ever seen her. This was what she deserved, to be surrounded by people who valued her talent. If they happened to be hot cowboys, that was a bonus.

Georgie hoped the glow would last for a while after

the three men left, because she needed to come up with a game plan for her sister's art. Maybe she should check out art galleries within driving distance to see if any of them would carry Anastasia's work. She didn't know how her sister would feel about that, but something had to be done. Anastasia was wasting away in this little town and the arrival of Vince and his friends had proven it.

About the time everyone had finished dinner, the senior citizen brigade arrived for the nightly poker game. Among them was one of Georgie's favorites. Frank Bryson, a retired lawyer, was about the same age as Clyde, the eighty-something mayor of Bickford.

Frank and his wife, Sue, had bought a house in Bickford twenty-five years ago after staying at the Double J and falling in love with the area. They'd been one of several retired couples who'd babysat for Georgie after her mother died. Like many of his friends in Bickford, Frank had accepted that property values had plummeted, but he and Sue couldn't face the idea of moving.

The poker players gathered around the table while Travis and Mac showed off their portraits.

Frank glanced at Vince. "Where's yours?"

"I haven't done his yet," Anastasia said. "It's his turn right now."

"Great!" Frank clapped his hands together. "We get to see an artist at work. Don't mind us. Go ahead and immortalize this joker. Then we'll all play cards."

Georgie peeked over at Vince. He hadn't wanted to do this in the first place and now he'd have an audience.

Anastasia, high on her success, was oblivious to Vince's discomfort. "Vince, why don't you change places with Travis? The lighting's good where he's sitting. And take off your hat. You have wonderful hair. I love drawing good hair."

Vince cleared his throat, and Georgie braced for his refusal. She couldn't blame him. She wouldn't relish this kind of attention, either.

To her surprise, he pushed back his chair and stood. Then he took off his hat and handed it to her. "Would you please keep an eye on this?"

"Sure." She was too startled to do anything but take it. As she clutched the black Stetson, she felt somehow connected to him. A cowboy's hat was precious, and he'd entrusted his to her. She told herself not to overthink it.

Vince ran his fingers through his hair as he walked toward the seat Travis had just vacated. The anxiety in his expression reminded Georgie of someone taking the witness stand in a trial. Her estimation of him went up a notch. She wouldn't have thought that he'd do anything he didn't really want to do, and yet here he was, posing for a portrait because it would make Anastasia happy.

· Anastasia busied herself opening her sketchpad and picking up her charcoal while she answered questions about her technique from the older men gathered around her. At last she glanced up at Vince and her movements stilled. "You look nervous."

"I am."

Georgie's heart squeezed. She hadn't wanted to feel attracted to this guy, and she definitely didn't want to feel compassion for him.

"You don't have to do it," Anastasia said. "Really, you don't."

Vince took a deep breath. "I want to." Grabbing the chair, he spun it around and straddled the seat. "Go for it."

Georgie gulped. Damn, he was sexy.

Anastasia sat with her charcoal poised over the pad. "Are you sure?"

"I'm sure." His gaze briefly touched Georgie's. "Better to do something you regret than not do it and regret it later."

She got the message. He was going after the Ghost. But if he intended to rope that horse, he'd have to get past her first.

# CHAPTER 7

Vince didn't need an alarm to get him up the next morning. He was pumped. He'd seen the look in Georgie's eyes when he'd made that comment about regret over things not done. She'd known what he was talking about, and the fire in her eyes had said it all.

After she and Anastasia had left Sadie's, he'd found out from Ike that the general store was usually closed on Sunday. That left Georgie free to do whatever it was she had in mind. Sure as the world she intended to interfere with his Ghost hunt.

He was damned curious to find out what she'd do, too. Tracking the Ghost would be exciting all by itself, but add in Georgie trying to sabotage the effort and it promised to be an interesting day. He relished the challenge. He needed to blow off some steam. If he couldn't have good loving from Georgie, he'd settle for a good fight, instead.

The aroma of coffee drifted up the stairs as he finished dressing. Myra Jenson must be on the job making breakfast for her three guests, and this time they'd actually eat it. They'd all gone light on the beer last night and they'd turned down Ike's offer of tequila shots. Vince had been mighty suspicious of that offer, especially when Ike had said the first one would be on the house. Georgie might have asked him to push the booze in hopes they'd all get plastered again and be unfit to ride.

Come to think of it, that might have been the plan Friday night, too, and all three of them had cooperated beautifully. Seeing one another again after so long had been reason enough to keep drinking and talking long into the night. Vince didn't really regret it, but today would be a different story. Today he was primed and ready to go.

He was the first one at the breakfast table. He'd chosen a seat and poured himself a cup of coffee by the time Travis and Mac showed up.

Mac surveyed Vince's outfit. "Chaps and a vest, huh? You got spurs on, too, cowboy?"

Vince extended his boot out from under the table. The spurs were blunt-tipped, but they had a satisfying jingle when he walked.

"Damn." Travis glanced down at his plaid Western shirt and jeans. "I'm underdressed. I didn't get the memo that we were pulling out all the stops for this ride."

"It's all practical," Vince said. "We'll undoubtedly run into some mesquite, and I don't relish getting thorns in my leg. The spurs are in case my horse needs a little extra encouragement to turn on the afterburners."

"I'll buy all that." Mac sat across from him, and Travis plopped down on the seat between them. "But the leather vest is purely for show, my friend."

"And warmth!" Vince wasn't about to admit that he was wearing the vest for Georgie's benefit, assuming she showed up out there today.

Mac tugged on his down-filled polyester vest. "No, *this*

is for warmth. It zips up, unlike that fancy-dancy number you're wearing with its fringe and shiny silver buttons. Did you polish those up before you drove over here on Friday?"

*"No."*

"Sure does look like it. Those shiny buttons will reflect the sun real good. Travis and I will have to watch out that we don't get blinded."

"Maybe those are his quest clothes." Travis poured himself a mug of coffee. He also wore a down-filled vest similar to Mac's.

Vince sighed. "Bite me. You're both just jealous because I'm wearing this extremely authentic and classic Western wear and you two look like you've been shopping at L.L.Bean."

"We'll see who's comfortable out there and who's freezing his ass off in his classic Western wear." Mac smiled at Myra Jenson as she arrived carrying two steaming plates full of scrambled eggs and ham. "I promise we'll do your breakfast justice this morning, ma'am."

"I'm glad." She set a plate in front of Mac and Vince. "I'll be right back with yours, young man."

"Thank you, ma'am." After she left, Travis muttered under his breath, "*Young man.* I'm twenty-eight, for God's sake."

"That makes you about fifty years younger than the majority of guys in town," Vince said. "If you stick around here, you'll always be considered a young man."

"Yeah, but she didn't call you two that, and you're only a couple years older than me. I can't help it if I just look young."

Mac grinned. "And I can't help it if Anastasia prefers a more mature man like yours truly."

"Ah, who cares if she does? I'm not saying that's true, mind you, but like Vince said, we're leaving today, so it doesn't matter."

Vince dug into his eggs. "What if we weren't leaving today? Would you two duke it out over that girl?"

"No, we would not." Travis paused to thank Myra for bringing his plate. "We'd settle it like gentlemen."

"We would?" Mac cut off a piece of ham. "You mean like pistols at dawn?"

Travis rolled his eyes. "We'd cut cards for her."

"Nope." Mac shook his head. "Why would I agree to that when I'm so clearly her first choice?"

"Says you. I'm the one with the classic nose. I don't remember her specifically mentioning any feature of your face."

"That's because the entire thing is awesome."

"Amazing." Vince speared another bite of ham. "I've never seen you two go after the same woman. Has this ever happened before, or are we in virgin territory?"

They both stared at him.

"Hold on. Let me rephrase that. I was referring to the situation, not the lady."

"Good to know." Mac returned to his breakfast. "For a minute there I thought you knew something I didn't, and I was ready to abandon the field to Travis. I don't mess around with virgins."

"Me, either," Travis said. "Way too much pressure."

"So to answer your question," Mac said, "Travis and I have never found ourselves in this position before. But let me state the blindingly obvious. Bickford contains two single women in our age bracket. You have dibs on one of them. That leaves Travis and me to squabble over the other one."

"I don't have dibs."

"Oh?" Mac's eyebrows lifted. "That's not what you said yesterday. I believe the phrase you used was—correct me if I'm wrong, Travis—*off-limits.*"

Travis nodded. "Yup. That's what he said, all right."

"Then I take it back. A guy can't declare a woman off-limits if she wouldn't have anything to do with him."

"I don't know." Mac shoved away his empty plate. "That getup might change her mind."

Travis chuckled. "So that's why you're all tricked out in fancy leather and spurs. Makes perfect sense to me, now. Think we'll be seeing her out there this morning?"

"Maybe." Vince was counting on it. "I don't know how she'd mess with our plans unless she shows up."

"I don't know how she'd mess with our plans even if she does show up," Mac said. "What's she going to do, erect a giant net around the area to keep us out?"

"I've wondered that myself," Vince said. "That's why I can't resist running a little test to see what happens." He drained his coffee cup. "You boys ready to ride?"

Mac pushed back his chair. "Let's do it." He stood and pulled money out of his wallet for a tip.

Vince took out his wallet, and Travis followed suit.

"It's a nice hotel," Travis said. "I hate that they don't get much business. I'd recommend it to people, but there's nothing to do besides drink and play poker."

"Yeah." Mac started toward the front door. "Didn't there used to be a little movie theater?"

"There was." Vince had asked Georgie to go see a movie with him and she'd refused. "And a bookstore with a coffee shop in it, and at least two places selling crafts and knickknacks."

"And a place that sold Native American jewelry," Travis said. "I bought a turquoise necklace for my mom. She still has it."

"All gone now," Mac said as they walked out on the hotel porch and down the steps. "I'm glad we're bringing some money into town, but I'm sure it's only a drop in the bucket." He started down the sidewalk toward the stables.

"Hang on a minute," Vince said. "I want to get something from my truck."

Mac turned around. "I hope you're not going after some big-ass belt buckle to complete your ensemble."

"No. I need to get my rope."

Travis groaned. "Don't bring your rope, Vince. If you bring your rope, you'll feel obliged to use your rope, and we've already decided that's a bad idea, right, Mac?"

"Yes. Travis and I took a vote and so it's two to one against your rope going along on this quest."

"What if we get in some situation where we need a rope?"

Mac spread his arms wide. "Like what, for God's sake?"

"Like . . . one of us gets thrown and rolls over the side of a cliff, and is hanging there holding on to a tree branch, and we need a rope to haul him back up."

"Right," Mac said. "Because that happens to me every damned time I go out riding. I can *never* stay on my horse, and wouldn't you know I often get thrown off right next to a cliff, and if somebody doesn't have a rope, I'm done for."

Travis grinned at him. "What a coincidence! I'm the same way! I've lost track of the number of times somebody's had to haul my butt out of a canyon using the rope they were considerate enough to bring along."

"All right, all right." Vince heaved a sigh. "I want to

bring it because if I don't, Georgie will know I was just bluffing."

"Which you are, right?" Travis peered at him.

"Pretty much."

Mac shook his head. "Okay, bring the damned rope, but I swear, if you get a hankering to throw a loop over that stallion, you're on your own, buddy. Travis and me, we'll just ride off and leave you attached to him and let you figure out what to do about it."

"That's fair." Vince walked around to the passenger side of his truck and took out the rope he'd stashed there. Looping it over his shoulder, he rejoined his friends.

"We have to walk past Georgie and Anastasia's house to get to the stable," Mac said. "I suppose you're hoping Georgie's looking out the window so she can see how cool you look."

"Hell, no, I'm not. What are we, in junior high?"

"It feels like it," Travis said. "With Mac and me trying to get the same girl and you parading past your girlfriend's house looking all studly."

"She's not my girlfriend."

"See?" Travis laughed. "Then it's exactly like junior high. You're walking past the house of the girl you like, but she doesn't like you back, but you're hoping to impress her with your outfit so she'll start liking you."

"You are both totally whacked." But as they all passed the Bickford House, Vince stared straight ahead. No way would he want Georgie to see him looking over there. Yeah, it was kind of like junior high, after all.

Georgie waited by the parlor window until the three cowboys had gone on to the stable. She did her best to ignore the way Vince's chaps and leather vest added to his hotness factor. She'd never seen him dressed that way because he'd always come into town with his dancing clothes on. Today he was every inch the rugged cowboy and it stirred her blood.

The rope looped over his shoulder stirred her blood in an entirely different way. It made her mad as hell. That rope was a red flag signaling his intentions, and no matter how good he looked to her, he was still the enemy.

And she had her battle plan. Picking up the coiled stock whip from the delicate table next to the Victorian love seat, she walked out of the parlor and down the hallway to the kitchen. Fortunately no one was awake yet besides her and she could slip out the kitchen door without anyone knowing.

She'd left a short note for Anastasia explaining that she'd gone out to see the wild horses. Anastasia would know there was more to it than that, but she wouldn't say anything to Evelyn. Even if she did, Evelyn wouldn't care. Georgie's comings and goings had never been of interest to her. Years ago that had mattered, but now Georgie just shrugged it off.

A crisp morning breeze swirled around her as she walked across the backyard to the small barn and paddock where she kept Prince, the gelding she'd had for eighteen years. He'd been five when her father had bought him. Now he was a mature twenty-three, and she intended to keep him for at least another eighteen years. She'd known several horses who'd lived past forty.

He was the only horse in the small barn. The other three stalls were empty. After her father's death, Georgie had reluctantly agreed to sell his horse, especially when the buyer turned out to be someone looking for therapeutic riding horses. It had been for the best. Georgie had struggled to keep both horses exercised, and Evelyn had complained about the expense because neither she nor her daughters rode.

Prince stood saddled and waiting for her in the paddock where she'd left him twenty minutes ago. He was used to her early-morning rides. Wild horses, like most wild animals, were more active first thing in the morning.

After tying the stock whip to the saddle, she mounted up. "Okay, Prince. Let's go raise some hell."

Prince snorted as if he understood perfectly. Sometimes she thought he did. After eighteen years, he was tuned to her moods. His solid presence had comforted her more than anything or anyone in the months following her father's death.

These days, whenever she was frustrated by Evelyn or the sad state of the town, she'd take Prince out for a short ride and return feeling a hundred percent better. She'd named him Prince when she was ten and going through her Cinderella phase. It was still a fitting name.

A dense grove of mesquite grew along a dry wash about twenty yards from the trail that led into the hills and canyons outside Bickford. The terrain was similar to neighboring Palo Duro Canyon State Park, but not as spectacular and therefore not as well-traveled. When the Double J had been in operation, guests used to brag about the undiscovered beauty of the area.

The Double J had been a perfect match for the town. It had brought in enough people to keep local shops in business, but not so many that the permanent residents felt overrun by the visitors.

Many of the guests had returned year after year, and Georgie still got Christmas cards from some of them. They always asked if anyone had decided to rebuild the

Double J, and Georgie had promised to let them know if that ever happened. After four years of the land being tied up in court, she doubted a new ranch ever would be built.

Guiding Prince carefully through the thorny mesquite branches, she found a spot where she was hidden but could still see the trailhead. Heart thumping, she waited.

Prince stood like a statue. Only the slight flick of his ears and an occasional swish of his tail would alert anyone, and Georgie didn't expect Vince and his friends to be looking for someone hidden in the trees. They'd be getting the feel of their unfamiliar mounts and discussing their strategy.

Georgie had the advantage. She'd been riding Prince for years and she knew the landscape better than anyone else in Bickford. Not many of the residents took trail rides anymore. Four of them still owned horses, which they boarded with Ed for convenience. Ed cut them a deal because they allowed the horses to be rented out, which had worked well until tourism had disappeared. Now Ed had the bad end of that arrangement.

Male laughter preceded the arrival of the cowboys. Georgie leaned forward and stroked Prince's silky neck. "Be very quiet, Prince," she murmured. "Don't greet those horses."

She didn't think he would. He seemed to understand when silence was golden. Her excursions out to see the Ghost and his herd had accustomed Prince to observing without making noise. That training would help now.

Before she could see any of the men, she heard Mac's voice. "She drew my portrait first. That's all that needs to be said."

"She was practicing on you so she could do a better

job on mine," was Travis's cocky reply. "You were a re-hearsal, a test case."

"If that's so," Mac said, "then she must be crazy about Vince, because she saved him for last."

"Leave me out of this." Vince came into view as he guided his horse around a bend in the trail. Ed had put him on Cinder, a coal black gelding nearly a hand taller than Prince. Of all the horses in Ed's stable, Cinder was the fastest.

Georgie wondered if Vince had requested the most spirited horse. Given his mission, she wouldn't be surprised.

Travis rode behind Vince on Duke, a thirty-year-old palomino who held himself like a parade horse despite his age. "Now that you mention it, you didn't seem so eager to have her draw you," Travis said. "Why didn't you just tell her no?"

"Because she's a sweetheart and refusing to do it might have been a slap in the face. Besides, she's a good artist. She deserves respect for that."

"That's for sure." Mac brought up the rear on Jasper, a muscular roan with good manners and decent speed. "She needs to do something with her talent. Her work belongs in a gallery."

Although Georgie wasn't happy about the activity these three had chosen for this morning, she was grati-fied by what they were saying about her sister's artistic ability. Anastasia was still enraptured with Mac, although she'd confided on the way home from Sadie's that she thought Travis was cute, too. Young, but cute.

After Georgie had gone to bed, she'd heard the faint sound of Anastasia humming. She always did that when she sketched, so Georgie had to assume she was adding more portraits of the three cowboys to her portfolio. Well, good. Charcoal renderings of cowboys might be just the thing to catch a gallery owner's notice.

While blessing Mac and Travis for making Anastasia feel like a star, Georgie was thankful they'd both be gone in a matter of hours. Her sister didn't need to get tangled up with either of them. She had a future as an artist if she'd reach out and grab it. Georgie was determined to help her.

"But that aside, we all know why you let her draw your picture, Vince," Mac said.

"Yeah, because I just told you."

"That might be part of it, but mostly you were hoping to earn points with Georgie. Am I right or am I right?"

Georgie strained to hear Vince's answer, but the riders had moved out of range. Damn it. Just when the conversation was getting really interesting, she'd missed a key element.

Oh, well. She wasn't here on this cool spring morning to learn Vince's intentions toward her. His intentions toward the Ghost were far more important right now. Making sure the stock whip was secure, she edged out of the shelter of the mesquite trees.

If these men had been greenhorns, she wouldn't worry, because they'd never find the wild horses. But they were seasoned cowhands who'd had the good sense to go looking at the right time of day. They were heading straight for the little creek where the Ghost liked to water his herd every morning.

She'd told Vince on Friday that he'd never find the horses, but she hadn't believed it then and she didn't believe it now. They'd find the Ghost, and when they did, she intended to be right on their heels, creating chaos.

# CHAPTER 8

Vince hadn't expected to love the trail ride so much. He'd forgotten how beautiful the hills and canyons were outside of Bickford. They weren't quite as showy as Palo Duro, but they'd been easily accessed from the ranch, which would have made them perfect for trail rides.

Unfortunately, the Double J's owners hadn't wanted their guests straying outside the fenced property, an area they monitored for hazards. They'd said their pampered clientele wouldn't be interested in long, sweaty rides that might bring them into contact with snakes, coyotes, and cougars.

As Vince passed the fork in the trail, he glanced over toward a barbed-wire fence that marked the edge of what used to be Double J property. Someone had posted a huge No Trespassing sign.

"Damn shame," Travis said.

"Yep." Vince continued on down the trail.

"Hey, Vince," Travis called out.

"What?" He reined in his horse and turned to look at Travis.

"Maybe we should ride over there and see what's left of the ranch buildings."

Vince had to smile. That was so Travis, to ignore a posted sign. "In the first place, there's a super-sized notice telling us to stay out."

"So what?"

"In the second place, I don't want to take the time, and in the third place, it would be depressing as hell."

Mac had come up behind Travis. "I agree with Vince. The Double J was a really nice ranch, and I don't want to look at the charred remains."

"I was just curious." Travis shrugged. "But come to think of it, you probably couldn't handle it, Mac. It would be just like finding out the guy dies at the end of *The Horse Whisperer.* You'd get all choked up."

"I would *not* get all—"

"We're not going." Vince started back down the trail. "Or at least I'm not. You two can sit there and argue all day if you want."

"Couple of pansies," Travis muttered as he fell in behind Vince.

"I'm not a pansy," Mac said. "I'm an optimist."

Travis continued to debate the issue with him as Vince led the way into the canyon. Their destination was a little creek they all remembered, although the name of it had escaped them. They'd agreed that the horses were most likely to be there this time of day.

Vince maintained a steady pace, but he kept Cinder down to a walk because he wanted a chance to look around. He didn't think they'd be lucky enough to see the horses yet. They were still too close to town for that. But he'd spotted a couple of coyotes moving stealthily through the underbrush, no doubt stalking cottontails.

Higher up, patches of juniper and cedar softened the look of a rocky cliff. A breeze carried their piney fragrance down to him and he breathed deep. They rode past forks in the trail where an alternate route wound up to the rim through a series of switchbacks. He'd taken those a few times on his days off. The rim of the undulating canyon walls offered spectacular views, especially at sunset.

The arguing had finally ceased, as if his friends had also been captured by their surroundings. Travis pointed out a red-tailed hawk circling overhead, and Vince stopped so they could let a bobcat stroll across the trail several yards in front of them. The bobcat made the horses a little jittery, so Vince waited until it was long gone before continuing on. After that, they all remained silent until Mac spoke Vince's name, a note of warning in his voice.

Vince drew Cinder to a halt and turned in his saddle. "What?"

"Someone's following us."

Vince listened. "I don't hear anything."

"They probably stopped when we did and now they're waiting for us to go on. Or I should say *she*. We all know who it is."

Vince sighed. "Yeah, I guess we do." He gazed at Mac and Travis. "We have three of Ed's four horses, and according to Ed, the good people of Bickford hardly ever ride, especially this far out."

"Just Georgie." Travis glanced back at the winding path. "What do you want to do?"

Knowing she was back there armed with a plan made Vince's blood pump a little faster. But he didn't want his friends to know that, so he shrugged as if he didn't give a damn what she was up to. "It's a free country. She can tag along after us if she wants to. Let's just go on."

Mac nodded. "That's what I was thinking, too."

"Then let's do it." Travis tugged at the brim of his Stetson. "We're burning daylight." When Mac laughed, Travis turned to him. "It's a great line!"

"Oh, it's a terrific line." Mac grinned at him. "Wish I'd said it, but you beat me to the punch."

"Come on, you jokers." Vince nudged Cinder into a trot. "Let's go find us some wild horses."

Behind him, Travis urged Duke into a trot, too. "Shouldn't we go slower in case we suddenly come up on them?"

"Um, yeah, I guess so." Vince eased back on the reins. He had to laugh at himself. Now that he knew Georgie was back there, he'd instinctively wanted to head out at a more energetic pace instead of moseying along like a tourist.

But he didn't know for sure where the horses might be, and now that they were a ways from town and deeper into the canyon, the horses could be anywhere. His knowledge of herd behavior told him they'd likely be down by the creek, but maybe not. He needed to start concentrating on what lay ahead instead of who rode behind.

Again, nobody was talking, but that had less to do with enjoying the scenery and more to do with Georgie being back there possibly eavesdropping. The atmosphere among the three riders was no longer relaxed. Vince tried to listen for Georgie, but he couldn't distinguish the hoofbeats of a fourth rider from the two immediately behind him.

Finally, when the trail widened out, he moved to the left and motioned for Travis to come up beside him. "I want you to take the lead for a while. I'm gonna drop back behind Mac."

"It's a little spooky, having her follow us," Travis said.

"I know. Wish I knew what she was up to."

"Keeping you from bothering those horses. That's what she's up to."

"I know that, but I mean specifically how she plans to do it."

Travis smiled. "What if she intends to rope *you*? That would make life interesting."

"Huh." Vince rolled his shoulders as if shrugging off the idea as impossible. But it wasn't. Georgie was a capable woman who knew things like plumbing and carpentry. He'd heard about that from her friend Janet. And she could ride, too. Stood to reason she could also swing a rope. "I hope she doesn't have something like that in mind. I don't want her interfering, but I don't want her getting hurt, either."

"Maybe you're the one who would get hurt."

"Only if I'm making sure nothing happens to her. I don't know if she's thought this through. She should just leave us alone to do this thing."

"Yeah, but she feels strongly about it, Vince."

"Well, so do I. I have every right to be out here if I want to."

"I never did think to ask, but how come you're so intent on finding the Ghost this weekend?"

Vince hadn't known the answer a few days ago, but he'd given the matter some thought, and now he did. "I haven't seen him since we left and I miss that. I realized recently that he's like a symbol to me."

"What kind of symbol?"

"He represents freedom. He can come and go as he pleases, and that's how I am, how I want to be. He's in charge of his world. Nobody tells him what to do."

"So why rope him? If you like that he's free, roping him makes no sense because you'll take that away."

In spite of knowing Georgie probably couldn't hear him, Vince kept his voice down. "You're right, and that's why I won't. A part of me wants to because it would be great to feel all that power at the end of my rope, you know?"

Travis nodded. "I see what you're saying, but it wouldn't be worth the trouble, and the horse would hate it."

"Yeah, he would. It would be wrong to put him through that."

"If you're hankering for an adrenaline rush, you'd be better off getting yourself a motorcycle."

"And I might. That's a good idea, Travis."

"So you brought the rope why?"

"Aw, hell, Travis," Vince muttered. "You know why I had to bring that rope."

"So Georgie would think you were dead set on following through with your plan?"

"Bingo."

"Look, I don't blame you. A man has to protect his rep, especially if a woman keeps brushing him off like she does with you."

"That's what I'm thinking. Anyway, right now I'd just like to be able to gauge for myself how far back she is. For all I know, she's given up and Mac hasn't noticed."

Travis laughed. "She's not the giving-up type."

"Yeah, you're right." Vince dropped back beside Mac.

"I caught some of that," Mac said. "So you want to bring up the rear and listen for her?"

"Assuming she's still back there."

"Oh, she is. She's keeping the same distance between us. When we broke into a trot, so did she. Now she's walking again."

"Unsettling."

"Not to me. I'm not the one planning to rope the stallion she's protecting."

Vince leaned toward Mac. "Look, I'm not doing it, okay?"

"Not even in the heat of the moment? I mean, you brought the damned rope. You might not be able to resist the temptation."

"I can resist."

"Now, see, if you'd told her that, she might not be tailing us."

"I know."

"But you wanted to keep her guessing."

Vince nodded.

"And prolong this little fight you have going on."

"Pretty stupid, huh?"

"Not if you've been carrying a torch ever since you left town and you aren't any further along now than you were back then. Considering that, it makes perfect sense."

Vince cringed. "Keep it down, will you? Sound can carry out here. And echo."

"So I take it you don't want me shouting *Vince loves Georgie* to see if I can make it echo?"

"Damn it, Mac. I don't *love* her. I just—"

"Yeah, yeah, I know what you *just*. Drop on back and listen for the lady." He shook his head. "Poor sap."

Vince didn't have a response for that so he reined in his horse and let Mac go ahead of him. He *was* a sap. And he probably would have given up on Georgie if he didn't think—hell, if he didn't *know*—that she was sexually attracted to him. The way she'd looked at him last night at dinner had been practically X-rated.

Of course, his situation with Georgie was sort of like his situation with the Ghost. If he succeeded in getting her into bed, then what? Well, other than the obvious immediate activities that would take place.

But he hadn't considered what would be the next step after they'd thoroughly worn each other out. And he wouldn't worry about it now, either. No use planning what would happen as a result of something that probably never would happen.

He let Travis and Mac pull away from him so he could concentrate on the sounds behind him. At first he mostly heard birds chirping and the wind through the branches of the mesquite trees that created a thicket on either side of the trail. Then he pulled Cinder to a halt and finally picked up the soft thud of hooves on dirt, and the sharper crack of a hoof coming down on a rock in the road.

If she was that close, he could call out to her and she'd hear him. He could wheel Cinder around and ride straight at her. Would she turn and run? No, she'd stand her ground and insist that he should head back.

He wasn't planning on heading back, so he wouldn't confront her. He'd continue to bring up the rear, though, where he could listen for her and know that she was still behind them. They'd taken the game this far, so they might as well finish it so he could find out what she had up her sleeve.

Urging Cinder into a trot, he heard her do the same with her horse. When he slowed, she slowed. He amused himself that way for about two hundred yards, which caused Mac to turn around in his saddle with a *what the hell* expression on his face.

"Testing out Cinder's gait."

"I see." Mac shook his head and faced forward again.

Soon after that, Vince heard the ripple of water over stones. The creek tumbled downhill and included several small but musical waterfalls. Vince suddenly remembered the name of it—Sing-Song Creek.

Cottonwoods, which were taller than other trees in the area, grew along its banks. He could see the tops of them now. Soon the trail would enter a small meadow that provided a perfect grazing spot. His pulse quickened. The herd might not be there, but he had a strong hunch they would be.

Before they reached the meadow, Travis held up his hand to signal a stop. Mac moved up beside him and Vince pulled in behind both of them.

Travis turned in his saddle and lowered his voice. "I think I heard a horse nicker and it was coming from the meadow."

"It's gotta be them," Vince said.

"I agree." Mac looked back at him. "How do you want to play this?"

Vince gauged the direction of the breeze. "For now, we're downwind, so they shouldn't be able to smell us, but they might have heard us. Maybe if we move slowly out into the meadow, they won't spook, at least not right away."

"I wonder if that mare's still with them," Travis said. "The one he stole from the Double J."

"Jezebel," Mac said. "I'd probably recognize her. White socks on three legs and a wide blaze down her face. Anyway, you should head out first, Vince. This is mostly your show. We'll take our cues from whatever you decide to do."

Vince fingered the rope tied to his saddle.

Mac caught him doing it. "Don't, buddy. Seriously, there's no good reason to and a ton of reasons not to."

"I know. I just have this urge to get close to him, and I probably can't unless I rope him."

Travis glanced at Mac. "Vince identifies with the Ghost."

"Great. Wonderful. But you should have brought a camera instead of a rope."

"Cameras are for bird-watchers."

Mac sighed. "I see that gleam in your eye. I swear you're going to get us in trouble yet."

"With Georgie, you mean," Travis added.

"Yep. That lady's fierce. I really don't want any of us to tangle with her."

"I won't rope the Ghost," Vince said. "I promise."

"Okay, then." Mac picked up his Stetson by the crown and settled it more firmly on his head. "Your word is good enough for me. I hope the Ghost cooperates and you get up close and personal."

As Vince took the lead again, he hoped so, too. He doubted he'd be back this way again, and he wanted a memory of that stallion to carry around with him in his travels. He gave one last thought to Georgie somewhere behind them waiting to see what they'd do, or more accurately, what he'd do.

He wasn't sure, exactly, except that he wouldn't uncoil his rope. Cinder's ears pricked forward as the mesquite trees gave way gradually to a meadow about half the size of a football field. The herd was there. They'd obviously been grazing, but now their heads were up and their ears pointed in Vince's direction.

Heart thudding, Vince searched for the stallion among the horses. He counted eleven, a mixture of bays, buck-

CRAZY FOR THE COWBOY    101

skins, and one dappled gray yearling. But the stallion wasn't with them.

He nudged Cinder into the meadow. The horses watched him and the lead mare began to circle, tightening the parameters of the herd. Vince glanced to his left as Travis and Mac reached the edge of the meadow.

Where was the Ghost? Vince surveyed the area and finally thought to look behind him. There he was, standing on a slight rise overlooking the meadow. His nostrils flared as he looked in Vince's direction.

A shiver of excitement ran down Vince's spine. As if playing a giant game of chess, he guided Cinder forward, putting his horse between the Ghost and his herd. The stallion tossed his head and looked from Vince to the eleven horses in the meadow.

Vince kept moving slowly into position. The Ghost would be compelled to rejoin his herd, especially in the face of this intrusion. When he did, he'd have to pass in front of Vince. And Vince would get his wish for a close encounter with the horse that had become his personal totem.

The Ghost pawed the ground as if debating his options. Then with a loud snort, he bolted for the herd, trumpeting orders as he ran. The wild horses responded, hooves pounding as they headed for the creek and leaped to the other side.

Cinder shied, obviously not liking the idea of standing his ground as the stallion charged toward them. But Vince kept a firm hold on the reins and stayed in the saddle as he watched, mesmerized by the strength and power of a horse who played by his own rules.

The Ghost swerved to avoid the horse and rider in his

path, while Cinder pranced and snorted in protest. Vince got exactly the view he'd been hoping for. He held his breath as his gaze locked with the Ghost's. For a split second he felt a thrilling connection with the stallion's wild energy.

But a sharp *crack* followed by a loud *whoop* turned out to be the final straw for Cinder. He bucked, and bucked hard. Vince used every bit of riding skill he possessed and managed to hold on. The crack sounded again, and there came Georgie, whooping and hollering as she wielded a stock whip with the confidence of Zorro.

The ground shook as the Ghost thundered past him and followed his herd, leaping the creek with ease. Then he raced away, going deeper into the canyon. Once they were gone and Georgie stopped cracking her whip, Cinder settled down and stopped bucking.

Breathing hard, Vince stared at her. "What in hell was *that*?"

She sucked in air as she coiled her whip and looped it over the saddle horn. Her hat hung by its string and her hair had been whipped into a tangle by the wind. Her expression was pure defiance. "You were too close. I had to make sure you didn't . . ." Her attention moved to the rope still tied neatly to his saddle. "I couldn't take any chances."

Travis rode up. "Listen, Georgie, Vince wasn't—"

"Being responsible," Vince said. She'd charged to the rescue because he'd given her every indication he would rope the stallion, and he didn't want to minimize what she'd done to protect that horse.

"That's for damn sure." Georgie glared at him. "And now Prince and I are going home." Back straight, she left the meadow and started back down the trail.

Travis scratched the back of his head. "Why didn't you tell her that you never were going to rope that horse?"

"Because I led her to believe I was. Essentially it's my fault that she felt she had to act. I can't let her think it was for nothing." What a jerk he'd been, too.

"I don't get it."

"That's okay, Travis." Vince gave him a weary smile. "There's nothing to get. I'm an idiot."

Mac approached on Jasper. "Don't try and figure that boy out, Travis. He got himself fixated on Georgie years ago and he's not over it yet."

"It's not a one-way proposition." Vince felt obliged to explain that he wasn't pining after someone who didn't give a shit. "She's interested, or she was last night. Probably not anymore."

Mac shoved his hat back with his thumb. "You could always try eating crow. That sometimes works."

"I'm not sure it would with Georgie."

"You should try it, though," Travis said. "Grovel for a while, and then see if she'll let you kiss her."

"I doubt that will ever happen, either."

"You never know." Travis grinned. "If she kisses you back, you're golden. If she bites your tongue, then you have to accept that she doesn't want you, after all."

Mac laughed. "Spoken like a man who's been bitten a few times."

"Only once, and I seriously miscalculated that time. She was flirting with me to make some other guy jealous, only I didn't understand that until I put my tongue in her mouth. I was a lot younger then. I'd have sense enough to know better now."

"So what's our takeaway?" Mac leaned back in his saddle.

Vince shrugged. "Damned if I know."

"Pay attention, Vince," Travis said. "First, apologize; then try a kiss and see what happens. But wait a few seconds to see how she reacts to the mouth-to-mouth before you go for the tongue action. A damaged tongue plays hell with your enjoyment of beer."

"I'll take all that under consideration."

"You'll have to work fast, though," Travis continued. "We're checking out today."

Vince had been thinking about that. "I might not. Unlike you two, I'm between jobs. I have a little put aside, so I could afford to stay on. Then it wouldn't look so much like I'm running away after this little incident."

Mac nodded. "And if you let her cool down, you might be able to get in a kiss, after all."

"I don't know about that, but I might be able to get in that apology." Vince thought that of the two, the apology was more important. He might have no chance with Georgie, but he hated thinking that her last image of him would be their confrontation in the meadow, one that he'd created by his boneheaded stubborn pride. He would tell her that if she'd give him the chance.

# CHAPTER 9

Georgie treated Prince to a thorough brushing and an apple after she brought him back to his paddock, and all the while she tried to decipher what had been going on with Vince and that stallion. She'd been right on the heels of those three cowboys and had ridden out behind them into the meadow. One look at Vince as he'd placed himself between the Ghost and the herd had launched her into action.

She'd been convinced he'd set himself up to rope the stallion, but after all was said and done, his rope was still tied to his saddle. If he'd intended to throw a loop, he would have had it ready as he approached. She hadn't taken time to notice whether he had the rope in his hand or not.

If he hadn't planned to rope the horse, what had he been doing out there? She would never know, because she wouldn't be seeing him again. She had a list of maintenance issues to tackle that would keep her busy all day and maybe prevent her from dwelling on Vince Durant.

Both Evelyn and Anastasia were still asleep when she went back into the house. Evelyn typically slept in, and

Anastasia had probably stayed up late sketching. Georgie ate a quick breakfast and started in on her chores.

She was oiling the hinges on the front door when Anastasia, still wearing her nightgown, came looking for her.

"Travis just called. He wondered if we'd like to come and have lunch with them at Sadie's before they leave."

Georgie looked at her. "Are you sure he meant both of us?"

"That's what he said."

"Did he happen to mention anything about what happened this morning?"

"No." Anastasia's eyes widened. "The Ghost! Did they go out there?"

"They did. And so did I."

"Oh, my God. What happened?"

Georgie gave her an abbreviated version. "Now I don't know if Vince meant to rope him or not. Either way, he's on my shit list."

"On mine, too!" Her shoulders drooped. "I guess my story didn't work, then."

"That's okay. I had a feeling he'd ride out there no matter what, and he took his rope. I saw him carrying it down to the stable. Cowboys don't usually take a rope unless they're going to use it."

"And you really went after him with your whip?"

"Not close enough to touch either him or Cinder. I was going for the loud noise and the intimidation factor."

"Wow." Anastasia put a hand to her chest. "I've seen you crack that whip. You're very intimidating." She gazed at Georgie a moment longer. "I'll call Travis back and tell him we can't make it."

"Hey, you should go. You might get more inspiration." She smiled. "I heard you humming last night."

"Did I keep you awake?"

"No." Thoughts of Vince were to blame for that. What an infuriating man, but at least he'd be gone soon. "And even if it did, I wouldn't care. I love that you're excited about drawing again."

"Me, too."

"Seriously, go to lunch with them. It'd be fun for you."

"But they defied you about those horses. That's not nice."

"It's mostly Vince's doing. I think Mac and Travis would have abandoned the idea in a heartbeat. If you want to be mad at someone, you can be mad at him, but I'm sure Mac and Travis would love to see you one more time."

"I'd love to see them, too. Okay, I'll go, but I'll give Vince the hairy eyeball."

Georgie laughed, which felt good after the tension of the morning. "You do that. Wish I could be a mouse in the corner. I'll bet you do a great hairy eyeball."

"I do. Check this out." She lowered her head, and when she raised it again, her gaze was filled with loathing.

"Yikes! Remind me never to tick you off! I feel like somebody just walked over my grave."

Anastasia smiled. "After that guy dumped me at art school, I practiced my hairy eyeball in the mirror for days and finally got the perfect opportunity to use it on him at the coffee shop where we used to hang out. He started shaking, and then he got up and left. Left his double-shot latte, too, so I drank it."

"Way to go! Now that I know you're armed and ready, you have my blessing to go down to Sadie's and do your worst. Vince deserves whatever he gets. I can't wait to hear about it."

"I'll give you a full report."

Georgie hesitated. Anastasia was twenty-three and could certainly take care of herself as she'd just demonstrated. Still, Georgie worried about a potential letdown after the guys took off. They might throw out some meaningless comment about coming back soon.

"Spit it out, sis." Anastasia crossed her arms. "Something's on your mind."

"I just want to say that . . . these three guys might never come back."

"I know. That's okay."

"You really seemed to like Mac."

"I did. I do. But he and Travis work on a ranch outside Midland. They can't exactly pop up here anytime they feel like it. Don't worry. It's not like I'm in love or anything. It was fun to flirt a little."

"But you and I need to get out more. Maybe we should drive into Amarillo once in a while, see if there are any good places to dance."

"You're right. We should. I mean, there's Charmaine partying hearty in Dallas, while we sit here sucking our thumbs."

"Exactly!"

Anastasia studied her. "Are you sure you don't want to come to lunch? You have an hour to practice your hairy eyeball. Trust me, it's extremely gratifying to watch them quaking in their boots."

"I admit it's tempting, but I think you'll have a better time if I don't go. And I have a long list of things I promised myself I'd get done today."

"Then I'm going to hit the shower. You're welcome to change your mind anytime between now and the time I leave."

"Thanks."

But she didn't change her mind, not even when Anastasia called her into her room to look at the sketches she'd made last night. Instead of individual portraits, she'd created scenes of the cowboys joking with each other. She'd captured their personalities so well—Vince's charm, Mac's irreverence, and Travis's sweetness.

Georgie exclaimed over all of the sketches. "Please don't say you're giving these away, too."

"No. I thought I'd take them so they could see, but I'm keeping them."

"Good."

"Sure you don't want to come with me?"

"Thanks, but no, thanks." She gave her sister a hug and sent her on her way. She could spend time with the other two, but she wasn't up to seeing Vince again. He aroused too many conflicting emotions in her. Once he left town, she'd be able to breathe easy and her heart would settle into its normal steady beat. She was looking forward to that.

Three hours later she was on her hands and knees securing a loose baseboard in Charmaine's old bedroom when Anastasia came dashing up the stairs calling her name.

"What?" She put down her tools and hurried into the hall. "What's wrong?"

Anastasia clutched her messenger bag in both hands as she gulped for air. "Travis and Mac just left."

"Are you upset? I thought you were okay about—"

"I'm fine with it. No worries about them." She stared at Georgie. "But . . . you're not going to like this."

Georgie had a premonition of impending doom. "What am I not going to like?"

"Vince . . . Vince has decided to stay on a few more days."

Georgie's heart, the one she'd hoped would resume its normal steadiness today, started to pound. "Why in hell would he do that?"

"I think it's mostly because he wants to talk to you."

"But I don't want to talk to him!"

"I told him I was pretty sure you didn't, but he's booked himself into the hotel for a few more nights, anyway."

"Didn't you give him the hairy eyeball?"

"I did! Right after I found out he was staying, and he must be tougher than my ex-boyfriend, because he didn't shake or anything. He did sort of swallow, so I think it bothered him a little, but he's still staying. He wants to apologize."

"I don't want his damned apology. I want him gone."

"Then I can only think of one thing to do, Georgie."

"Will it get me tossed in jail?"

"No."

"Then whatever it is, I'll do it. I'll try anything."

"I figured out the hairy eyeball doesn't work as well when you're delivering it by proxy, which is what I tried today. You need to deliver it in person." She gazed at Georgie. "I advise you to drop everything and start practicing."

Vince sat in Sadie's at one of the tables drinking ginger ale. He didn't know if Georgie would respond to the request he'd sent via her sister. But if a miracle happened and she came down sometime this afternoon or tonight, he couldn't be toasted when she arrived.

Because he hadn't anticipated this situation, he had

nothing to do while he waited. Ike had taken pity on him and had found him some old newspapers to read. The news wasn't current anymore, but he enjoyed the other stuff, the advice columns and such.

He could use one of those advice columnists with him right now. He'd ask them the best way to apologize for totally screwing up a situation without coming across as weak. Travis had mentioned groveling, but Vince didn't think that was a good idea. Any woman who knew how to use a stock whip wouldn't respect a man who groveled.

Finally, because he couldn't sit still another second, he picked up his empty glass and walked over to the bar to talk with Ike. The bartender had spent a lot of his time this afternoon in the kitchen because apparently there was a problem with the deep fat fryer, and the poker players were big on having fries with their beer.

"Is it fixed, yet?"

"I think so, at least for now," Ike said. "Somebody needs to drive up to Amarillo tomorrow and buy a new one, though. This baby's on its last legs." He glanced at Vince's empty glass. "More ginger ale?"

"To tell you the truth, I can't stomach another glass. I'm done with sugary fizz. I'd switch to beer, but sure as the world Georgie will come waltzing in the door the minute I do."

"Then have a beer if that's what it'll take. One beer won't hurt anything."

"I know, but it's the principle of the thing. I don't want to be knocking back booze when she comes in. It sends the wrong message."

Ike leaned on the bar. "What sort of message do you want to send?"

"That's the thing I've been sitting over there trying to decide. Have you ever been in deep shit with Raina?"

"Too many times to count, my friend."

"Excellent. Well, I don't mean that it's excellent you've been in trouble with her, but maybe you can help me out. How do I get out of the doghouse and still keep my self-respect?"

"That's a million-dollar question."

Vince smiled. "And all I have on me is a few twenties and a major credit card."

"In that case, let me give you a cheap answer to your expensive question. Are you sincerely sorry for what happened out there?"

"More than I can say."

"Then look right at her and tell her that. Put your heart into it. Make it simple and straightforward. Then wait to see how she reacts."

"Sounds easy enough. What then?"

"That depends on what she does. If her expression softens up a little, great. You may be able to coax her into liking you again. If she dumps a pitcher of beer on your head, then she's still mad as hell."

"Right there's the problem. You just said that I might coax her into liking me *again*. I don't think she liked me in the first place. At least Raina likes you sometimes. Georgie's never really liked me."

"I'm not sure that's true."

Someone in the kitchen called Ike's name and he pushed away from the bar. "I'd better go see what the problem is. Maybe the fryer isn't fixed, after all."

"Before you go, what do you mean, you're not sure that's true?"

"I think Georgie likes you. In fact, I think she likes you a little too much for her own comfort."

"Now, see, that's what I think!"

"Then keep that in your mind while you're dealing with her." Ike walked back to the kitchen.

Yeah, right. That advice assumed he'd get to deal with her at all. She had complete control over that. He sighed and walked back to his table and the pile of old newspapers. Maybe he should break down and have a beer when Ike came back.

He'd pretty much made that decision when the street door to Sadie's opened and Georgie walked in. One look at her expression and he knew he was in for it. But at least she was here.

She'd worn a silky white blouse, snug jeans, and the same red boots she'd had on last night. If only she'd been smiling, he'd think that she'd dressed nice for him. But she wasn't smiling. Instead she looked as if she could cheerfully string him up by his balls.

He stood and tugged on the brim of his hat.

She walked straight over to his table and glared at him. "You have some nerve, Vince Durant."

"I couldn't just leave."

"That's too bad, because that's all I want you to do. Just leave."

Vince was glad nobody else was around, including Ike. Dislike rolled off Georgie in waves. It was embarrassing how much she disliked him. He couldn't remember ever being disliked this strongly in his life. Except for that powerful glare she'd given him when she'd first walked in, she wouldn't even look him in the face.

He took a deep breath in hopes that it would calm him

for what he wanted, what he needed, to say. "Would you please sit down?"

"I'd prefer to stand."

"Okay." He couldn't very well force her into a chair. "Then would you at least look at me?"

She lifted her gaze.

The anger in her brown eyes nearly knocked him over. It certainly took his breath away, which meant his apology was going to sound weird, as if he'd been running. "I'm sorry, Georgie." He braved the hot fury in her eyes and focused on them with all the sincerity in his heart. "I did a really dumb thing this morning."

Her reaction was subtle, but the tightness around her eyes and mouth eased. "That's for sure."

He imagined that her voice wasn't quite as hard as it had been before, but maybe that was wishful thinking. "I have good memories of this place . . . and of you. I hate to think I ruined them today."

She swallowed.

"I can't take back what happened. I could try to explain, but I don't suppose you'd want to hear it."

"Not really."

"All right, then." He remembered Ike had said to apologize and then wait to see what happened next. So he stood there without speaking. Maybe she'd turn around and walk out. And that would be the end of that.

"I'm curious about one thing."

His pulse quickened. Instead of walking out, she'd asked a leading question. "What's that?"

"Why did you take your rope?"

Trust Georgie to ask that. He was afraid the truth would destroy whatever slight progress he'd made, but she deserved no less. "I wanted you to think I'd use it."

"But you weren't going to?"

"No."

"Damn you, Vince Durant! You tricked me!"

"Yes, and I have no excuse. Stupid pride. That's all it was." But he noticed that instead of stomping out the door, she stayed where she was and kept on looking at him. That was something.

Finally she seemed to reach a conclusion. "So taking that rope was just male vanity."

"Yes."

She blew out a breath. "At least you admit it. I'll give you points for that."

"You will?"

Her mouth relaxed a little more. The corners twitched as if she might be holding back a smile.

He hoped to hell that she wasn't secretly laughing at him, but maybe that was better than the glare she'd given him to start with. He seemed to be ahead of the game, so he chose to stay quiet and not take the chance he'd somehow stick his foot in his mouth.

Sure enough, as the silence lengthened between them, the hostility gradually disappeared from her expression. "I can't believe you're still standing here in this saloon. You're supposed to be on your way back to . . . wherever you came from."

"Fort Worth."

"Is that where you work?"

He'd gentled a few horses in his day, and although he would never dare compare Georgie to a skittish mare, and certainly not out loud, he recognized that question as a slight movement forward, as if a shy animal had stretched its neck out to see what was being offered.

"Not now. I quit that job. I'm between jobs."

Her expression closed down again. "That's right. You like to stay on the move and keep your options open."

So that was part of her objection to him. If so, that was a big obstacle. Years ago he'd had an inkling that she disapproved of his unstructured approach to life, but her comment just now proved it. How interesting that she admired the Ghost, a creature who lived by his own rules.

He decided to take another risk. "Look, Georgie, we've both had a rough day, but I'd like to think that we've come to a truce of sorts."

"I suppose."

"Could we have one drink together, to toast the end of our feud?"

She took a long time to answer, and it looked as if a million thoughts were racing through her head. "I take it you're not leaving tonight, then?"

"No point. I haven't decided where I want to look for work yet. I need to make some plans before I head out."

"I suppose one drink wouldn't hurt."

He longed to do a fist pump, but that would destroy the cool facade he had going on. "Great. Ike should be back any minute. Let's have a seat."

He reached for a chair and pulled it out for her. When she sat down, he took the first easy breath he'd drawn in hours. Maybe some mistakes could be fixed, after all.

# CHAPTER 10

Curiosity had always been a source of joy and frustration for Georgie. She liked knowing what made things tick, and that included machinery, animals, and people. She'd considered a double major in psychology and mechanical engineering when she'd been in college, but that plan had gone down the drain when her father had died and she had been needed to run the store.

She'd had Vince pegged as a good-looking, carefree drifter who never planned ahead and seldom considered the consequences of his actions. She still thought that assessment was fairly accurate. But he'd surprised her several times today, and those surprises had aroused her curiosity.

Ike came out of the kitchen and did a classic double-take when he saw her sitting across the table from Vince. Then he covered it with his jovial bartender persona. "Georgie! I was hoping you'd come by tonight. Lasagna's on the menu."

Much as she loved lasagna, she didn't plan on sticking around for dinner. She'd headed down here before happy hour on purpose, hoping to catch Vince alone in the saloon. She'd expected him to be drinking, but he'd surprised her there, too.

"I won't be staying for dinner," she said.

"You'll be sorry if you don't." Ike beamed at her. "I got a taste of the sauce a while ago, and it's more outstanding than ever."

"I'm sure it is, but I need to get home soon."

"In the meantime, Ike," Vince said, "how about a couple of drinks? Beer for me, and . . . red wine for Georgie?" He glanced at her.

"That's fine." She was drinking with the enemy. Her time perfecting her hairy-eyeball glare had been wasted. Or maybe not. He'd looked plenty scared in the beginning and he might not have been so honest with her if she hadn't blasted him right off the bat.

She was sitting here, she told herself, to satisfy her curiosity. He'd mentioned that he had a reason for his obsession with the Ghost. Moments ago she'd been too furious to listen. But now she wanted to hear what he had to say, especially if he continued to be as honest as he had been about the rope.

She hadn't expected him to admit that he'd taken it to taunt her. Irritating as that was, it was flattering, in a way. He'd carried his rope down the street past her house in hopes she'd see him do it. And she had. She'd played right into that scenario by stationing herself at the parlor window in time to watch the three men pass by.

But sometime over the weekend Vince had figured out, or else had been convinced by his friends, that throwing a loop over the Ghost would be a very bad idea. To Georgie's astonishment, Vince had listened to the voice of reason. He just hadn't wanted her to know that.

How fascinating. Without brothers, and given the lack of virile young men in Bickford these days, she hadn't had much chance to study the workings of the male mind, especially a testosterone-fueled one. Apparently Vince had been showing off for her benefit. Definitely flattering. And a teensy bit arousing, although she didn't like admitting that.

"Where'd you learn to use a whip?"

Another surprise. She hadn't expected he'd want to talk about that humiliating incident. "My father taught me." She smiled as she remembered the practice sessions out in the backyard. "He was a big Zorro fan and he had a collection of whips. When I was a kid I wanted to be into whatever he was into."

Vince nudged his hat back with his thumb and he gazed at her. "Seeing you cracking that whip was . . . unexpected."

"That was the idea."

"You seemed to know what you were doing."

"I do, although I'm a little rusty. I used to be able to do tricks with it."

His blue eyes lit with interest. "Yeah? Like what?"

"My dad would hold out pieces of straw and I'd cut off the tips without hitting his hand. We actually put on demonstrations for the Double J guests once in a while. But I haven't practiced in a long time. I'm not sure if I could do it anymore."

Vince leaned forward and rested his forearms on the table. "I'd like to learn that."

His movement made her aware of his muscled forearms, tanned and sprinkled with dark hair. He'd rolled back the sleeves of his blue plaid Western shirt, a perfectly common thing for cowboys to do as the day warmed up. She'd never thought of it as a seductive move, and yet the sight of his arms resting easily on the table sent a message to parts of her that hadn't been awake in some time.

"You could—" She paused to clear her throat. "You could probably find a class somewhere. I can't remember how my dad learned, but he must have taken lessons before I was born because he was already very good at it when he started teaching me."

"How old were you then?"

"Six. I'd been begging him for at least a year to teach me how. He gave me my own whip for my birthday, but it was shorter than his, which bugged the heck out of me. I practiced and practiced until he finally allowed me to use one the same length as his."

Ike arrived with their drinks and a basket of fries. "The fryer works! I know you didn't order these, so they're on the house. We had to test out the fryer."

Georgie glanced up. "You've had trouble with it again? You should've called me."

Ike concentrated on setting down their drinks and depositing the basket of fries in the middle of the table. "I should have. I don't know why I didn't think of that."

"I don't, either. I'm the one who replaced the cord the last time it acted up. I'll bet the element's about to go." Then it occurred to her why Ike hadn't called. He'd known that Vince was hoping she'd show up so he could apologize. Summoning her down to repair a deep fryer would have been awkward under those circumstances.

"I'm driving up to Amarillo tomorrow to buy a new one so I have it when this one croaks," Ike said. "Let me know if you need anything from the big city." He winked at her. Calling Amarillo *the big city* was a joke in Bickford. It wasn't truly big, like Houston or Dallas, but compared to their town, it was huge.

"Let me get back to you on that. I may be driving up myself soon."

"I'd be glad to save you a trip if it's something I can get for you."

"Not really. I'm hoping I can talk Anastasia into going with me and taking her portfolio around to some of the galleries."

"Good!" Ike nodded in approval.

"That's a great idea," Vince said. "Has she shown you what she sketched last night after you two went home?"

"She did. I was worried she'd give them to y'all."

"We wouldn't have taken them if she'd tried. We figured out her work should be hanging in a gallery somewhere. We hauled out our portraits and got her signature. I'll bet they'll be worth something someday, not that any of us would part with them."

Ike glanced around the saloon. "If we had more traffic through here, I could display her work. I should probably do it, anyway, if she's willing. Some of the residents would buy it. The Double J guests would have snapped it up, though, and paid a pretty penny for it, too. Damned frustrating that we used to have the perfect setup for her, but she wasn't ready to go pro."

"She may not think she's ready yet," Georgie said. "But this weekend did wonders for her confidence. That's why I want to get her up to Amarillo before the effect wears off."

"That's a good plan," Ike said. "Well, give a holler when y'all need a refill."

"We'll do that." After Ike left, Vince raised his beer bottle. "To a truce."

"A truce." She touched her glass to his bottle, and their hands brushed in the process. She didn't like it. No, that wasn't true. She liked it too much.

In fact, sitting here with Vince was cozy and dangerous. It could lead to things that would be a huge mistake. "I'm only staying for one drink." She felt the need to counter his tacit agreement with Ike that they'd require refills. "Then I need to get home."

Vince sipped from his bottle and put it down, but he kept his hand wrapped around it. "You're going to turn down the lasagna after Ike's glowing recommendation?"

Now she was fixated on his hands as she wondered what a real touch would feel like instead of that casual brush of fingers during their toast. She really had gone without sex for way too long. She didn't want to do the math on that. It would be too depressing.

What had they been talking about? Oh, yes. Dinner. "The lasagna will be just as good the next time Henry makes it. I'm spoiled because I can eat here whenever I want. You can't, so you should definitely have some."

"Still trying to get rid of me?"

She looked into those blue eyes. Janet had been right. They were electric. "I can't see any reason for you to hang around Bickford. There's no work for you here."

"What if I just happen to like the place?"

"I can understand that. It's a nice area. But there's nothing for you to do. Your friends have left so you can't party with them anymore. There are no jobs available. Unless you can afford to go into permanent retirement here in Bickford, it's a dead end for you."

"I didn't say I wanted to *live* here. But I've missed the place and I have a little financial cushion, so I hate to pack up and leave right away when I don't have to."

She took a hefty swallow of her wine. She might need a refill, after all, if the conversation continued like this. Aware of Ike standing behind the bar, she lowered her voice. "I hope this doesn't have anything to do with me, because if it does, then . . ."

He lifted his eyebrows and smiled, and she completely lost her train of thought. She had no idea what she'd meant to say next. The louse waited, still smiling, while she struggled to finish her thought.

"Then that's a dead end, too." She gulped some more wine.

His voice was like velvet against her taut nerve endings. "Are you absolutely sure about that?"

She found the courage to look straight at him. "Yes." Damn, but his eyes were blue. His tan might make them seem bluer than they actually were, but the combination of those eyes and his easy smile worked on her, and he knew it.

He was better at this game than she was. He'd been better at it the last time he'd been here, and he'd been practicing ever since, while she'd effectively entered a convent. She was no match for him and she should get the hell out of there while she still could.

He continued to speak in a low, seductive tone. He hadn't used that tone on her before; if he had, their entire history might have been different. "Is that because you don't want me or because you don't approve of me?"

"Both." She finished off her wine.

Vince kept his gaze locked with hers. "Ike?"

"Coming up."

"No, I should go." She started to get up.

"Don't go yet."

"Why?"

"Because I haven't told you about the Ghost."

He was good, very good. It was the only thing he could have said that would cause her to sink back down to her chair.

"One red wine for the lady." Ike set the full glass in front of her.

"Thanks, Ike," Vince said.

"Yeah, thanks, Ike." She wasn't sure if thanks were in order or whose side the bartender was on right now. She looked at Vince. "Talk fast, because after I finish this glass of wine, I'm leaving."

And Georgie had said there was nothing to do in Bickford. Vince could imagine spending hours matching wits with her, and when they got tired of that, they could spend even more hours having great sex. She hadn't been entirely truthful when she'd answered him earlier. She might not approve of him, but that didn't stop her from wanting him.

She was strong, though, and determined not to end up in his bed. He wasn't arrogant enough to think he could override her objections. If he gave himself time to think about it, he might not want to, either. Oh, hell, yes he did, but it might not be right, just like roping the Ghost wasn't right. But, oh, she tempted him.

She took a sip of her wine and looked at him. "Well?"

God, she was saucy. He liked that so much. "As you know, I like to stay loose and keep my options open."

"I do know that, yes."

"Freedom to come and go as I please is important to me."

"Uh-huh."

"You think that's bullshit, don't you?"

She nodded. "Pretty much. But it's your life. If it works for you, then that's how you should keep things."

"I plan to."

"And that makes you and me complete opposites."

He couldn't resist. "They say opposites attract."

"Or else they're like oil and water. I'd go with that cliché if you're hunting for one. Anyway, we're veering off track here, and my wine will be gone before you know it. Then so will I. I suggest you cut to the chase."

"Okay." He drained his beer bottle. "I identify with the Ghost. He comes and goes as he pleases. He's a symbol of personal freedom, and I probably knew that subconsciously when I was here before, but it really came home to me this weekend."

"So you wanted to rope him? How messed up is that?"

"You're absolutely right. It's messed up."

She drew a mark in the air indicating she'd scored a point.

He dipped his head to acknowledge it. "But it's human nature to seek a connection with something you consider a symbol, or a totem. That's why some native tribes use eagle feathers in their ceremonies. They want to connect with that power."

"There's a huge difference between a feather and a two-thousand-pound wild stallion. You might want to choose the feather option next time you want a connection to something wild and free."

"I'm not into feathers unless I'm getting kinky with a woman in bed." He probably shouldn't have said that, but she provoked him until he had to be a little outrageous to balance the scales.

Excitement flashed briefly in her eyes before she

squelched it. She pretended to cover a yawn. "If that was supposed to get me hot, it didn't work."

He ducked his head so she wouldn't see him grinning. "I didn't expect it to."

"Yeah, you did. You're a world-class flirt, Vince, but you really should pick a town with more *options*, as you would say. I still don't understand why you'd want to spend any more time in Bickford."

"I called Ed earlier and asked him to have Cinder ready at six thirty in the morning. I'm going back out there."

She sat up straighter. "You'd better not be taking your rope."

"I won't, I promise. I've apologized to you. Now I want to apologize to the Ghost."

"Good luck with that. After what happened today, he'll stay hidden in the canyons for who knows how long."

"I figured he might, but I have all day. I can spend it exploring. I've always wanted to do that, but when I was working at the Double J, I didn't have the time."

She stared at him. "Are you saying that you might be here again tomorrow night, too?"

"Steve and Myra could use the money. I hear they need a new fryer."

She seemed to wrestle with that bit of information. She couldn't very well contradict him. The Jensons could use every penny that came in. When it came right down to it, she had nothing to say about whether he stayed or left. And he had a mind to stay.

Picking up her wine, she polished off her second glass and set it down on the table. "Are you doing this just to bug me?"

"No."

"Then why stick around?"

"I'm not sure I can answer that. It just feels like the right thing to do. That's why I like to keep my options open. When something feels wrong, I can leave. When something feels right, I can stay."

"For how long?"

"I don't know yet."

She heaved a sigh and pushed back her chair. "I don't understand you, Vince Durant."

"Get to know me a little better and you might."

"I don't think so. Thank you for the wine." She stood.

So did he, because he hadn't forgotten Travis's advice. "I'll walk you out."

"Please, don't bother. This isn't the kind of town where women need to be accompanied and watched over."

"I know. I'm going to walk you out anyway." He followed her to the door and held it open. "After you."

"Vince, this is ridiculous."

"Humor me." He stepped out onto the sidewalk. The temperature was perfect and the setting sun turned the sky the deep gold of her hair.

"I don't know if I dare humor you." She glanced up at him. "I can't figure out what you're up to, and that bothers me."

"It's simple, really. When I drove away from here, I felt as if I'd left some things unfinished."

"Like what?"

"Like this." He took off his hat and slipped his hand behind her head. She knew he was going to kiss her. He could see it in her eyes. He gave her a moment to say no, and when she didn't, he touched his mouth to hers.

But he remembered Travis's warning and kept his tongue to himself.

# CHAPTER 11

Georgie hadn't been fooled by Vince's maneuver. *I'll walk you out* had sounded like a ploy, and she'd planned to simply push him away if he tried to get too friendly. Sad to say, once his lips touched hers, she folded immediately. Game over.

As she'd noted earlier, he'd had years of kissing practice since they'd last met, while she'd cozied up to a cash register and lists of inventory instead of a hot cowboy. His mouth, the one Janet had been so infatuated with, was every bit as talented as it should be, given all those years he'd had to work on his technique. Awed by the way he took over, Georgie gladly surrendered to his superior knowledge. To borrow his phraseology, it seemed like the right thing to do.

He started slowly, the pressure of his lips light as the feathers he apparently disdained. When she didn't resist, he applied more pressure, delicious pressure, as it turned out. His mouth covered hers with assurance. He settled in, giving her a taste of what was to come with subtle movements of his lips against hers.

She savored the taste of beer and the salty tang of the

fries, and something else, something wild and untamed that promised adventure and excitement. Nothing about his kiss was steady or reassuring. Instead he challenged her to risk letting go of her safe haven for the excitement only he could provide.

Wrapping her arms around his neck, she clung to him with a moan of anticipation. She hadn't been kissed in so long, and never like this, never with a promise of pleasure so great that she'd sacrifice everything to have it.

He took the kiss deeper. A slow slide of his tongue heated her blood to the boiling point. Red alert . . . woman about to spontaneously combust. As his tongue lazily stroked the inside of her mouth, images of soft sheets and sweaty bodies flashed through her mind. She wiggled closer. Judging from the evidence, he was watching the same picture show.

He lifted his mouth a fraction from hers and took a shaky breath. "Come up to my room."

She was ready to go, eager to go, until the sound of someone clearing his throat shattered the moment. Pushing away from Vince, she whirled around to find they'd been joined by the mayor of Bickford.

"I'm so sorry to interrupt," Clyde said, "but I needed to ask you something about tomorrow night's meeting."

She had no clue what meeting he was talking about.

"The town council," he added helpfully.

"Oh! Of course! The council meeting. How could I forget?" Easy. Get in a lip-lock with Vince Durant, and she could kiss her brain good-bye.

"Myra usually takes the minutes, but she has to drive down to Lubbock tomorrow. You know her daughter and son-in-law are there with the baby, little Sophie."

"Yes, right." She had trouble remembering her own

name at the moment, let alone Myra and Steve Jenson's children and their first and therefore extremely precious grandchild.

"We need somebody to step in for her and take the minutes. Steve says he can't read his own handwriting and he's a lousy typist. Ed's nervous about his grammar and Ida . . . well, she might embellish things too much. I have to preside over the meeting, so that pretty much leaves you, if you don't mind doing it."

"I'd be happy to." Clyde had interrupted the best kiss of her life to ask her to take minutes for the council meeting tomorrow night? Maybe later she'd understand that was reasonable behavior, but right now she wanted to shake him until his dentures rattled.

"Good. Oh, and Vince?"

"Yes, sir?" Vince sounded a little ragged around the edges, and his hand trembled slightly as he put on his hat.

"You're welcome to come to the meeting, too. Only residents get to comment on the proceedings, but you might find it interesting. Democracy at the grassroots level, as it were. We meet in Sadie's at seven."

"Thank you. I'd like to come."

"I think you'll find it illuminating. Well, I'm off to lose my shirt at poker. Are you playing tonight, Vince?"

"Absolutely. Be there in a second."

After Clyde left, Georgie turned to him, her thoughts in a jumble. "What was that all about?"

"Saving your reputation."

"I beg your pardon?"

"At the very least he caught us kissing. He might have overheard me ask you up to my room. I hope not, but I'm taking no chances. I'll go back in there and play poker because obviously I can't be doing that and hauling you upstairs at the same time."

She nodded because what he said made sense. "Thank you." Then she remembered the rest of the conversation. "You're not really coming to the council meeting, are you?"

"Why not?" He smiled at her. "Grassroots democracy. Who could resist?"

"So you're definitely staying another night."

"Looks like it." He seemed pleased about that.

She was not. The longer he stayed, the more irresistible he'd become. She couldn't rely on timely interruptions to save her from herself, either. "This is crazy."

Stepping closer, he cupped her cheek. "Speaking of crazy, that was some kiss."

It had been, and she wanted to kiss him some more. She had plenty of reasons for not doing that, but she couldn't remember them when his warm, muscular body was inches from hers. Time to dial back her response and get the hell out of there. "I guess so."

"You *guess*? Lady, you were moaning."

"I . . . had a cramp in my toe." Kissing him had not been smart, not smart at all. But it had been damn hot. She was still vibrating.

He stared at her. "I don't believe you had a cramp in your toe. I think you were into that kiss. If I hadn't thought so, I wouldn't have asked you up to my room."

"I wouldn't have gone." *Liar, liar, pants on fire.* And were they ever. If Clyde hadn't interrupted them, she'd be in his hotel room right this minute and happy for the opportunity. She'd do well to remember the potent effect Vince had on her and stay out of kissing range.

"Too bad." He looked into her eyes. "Let me know if you ever change your mind."

"I won't. Good night, Vince. Thanks for the drinks."

"Anytime."

She turned away and started walking. She'd bet he was watching her. Having a handsome cowboy gaze after her with longing was a heady experience she hadn't had in a while, either. She probably enjoyed it more than she should.

So that was that. She'd satisfied her curiosity about kissing Vince Durant, and thanks to Clyde, she hadn't made the mistake of taking Vince up on his offer. It would have been a mistake, right? A night or two of hot sex wasn't what she wanted.

Well, okay, she wanted it, but when she wasn't in the middle of a sizzling kiss, she could assess the situation rationally. She understood why Vince was interested in her. During the time he'd lived here she'd played hard-to-get and his ego had been wounded. His only reason for hanging around now was to prove that he could have her, after all. If he succeeded, he'd check that off his list and move on.

Being an item on his checklist didn't appeal to her at all. She'd keep that concept in mind the next time he trained those blue eyes on her. He was tempting, especially to a woman who lived in a town filled with senior citizens. But she had her pride, too, and that would keep her out of trouble.

Vince played cards with the seniors and was in bed by eleven. He didn't sleep all that well for thinking about Georgie and how close he'd been to coaxing her up to his room. He really shouldn't continue to pursue her, but he couldn't seem to help himself.

As he tossed and turned on the queen-sized bed, he

thought about pheromones. He'd read about them a few years ago. Maybe that was part of the problem with Georgie—she gave them off and he sucked them in.

That made him want to do things like kiss her, which then made him want to do other things, like invite her up to his hotel room. And that was another issue. She'd let him kiss her. If she was so dead-set against him, why had she let him do that? This predicament was partly her fault, then, wasn't it?

He could solve the situation by getting in his truck and driving away in the morning. He'd pay for the rental of Cinder before he left, of course, but no one was making him hang around town, so why not go? Georgie had accepted his apology, which had been his main reason for staying.

He pictured himself checking out of the hotel first thing in the morning and settling his bill. Maybe he'd have breakfast, because Myra Jenson would have taken the time to fix it for him. Her husband, Steve, had played poker with the guys, and he'd mentioned that breakfast would be served as usual in the morning.

Steve had added that Vince would be on his own after that, because Myra would be down in Lubbock with their daughter and granddaughter. He'd apologized for the inconvenience but had offered what he'd planned to eat, cold cereal and coffee. Vince didn't have anything against cold cereal and coffee, but maybe it was a sign that it was time to leave town.

All right. He'd do that. Punching the pillow until he had it the way he wanted it, he settled down and closed his eyes. The minute he did, he pictured Georgie taking minutes at the council meeting. He'd miss seeing that. He'd miss observing grassroots democracy, too.

The mayor himself had invited him to attend the council

meeting tomorrow night. Georgie hadn't been happy about that. Despite the extreme heat of her kiss, a kiss that had melted every ounce of good sense he possessed, she still wanted him gone.

But she also plain wanted him, period. He couldn't remember the last time a woman had kissed him with such yearning. No red-blooded man, especially no red-blooded cowboy, could easily turn his back when a woman responded like that.

So he'd stay another night, just to see what happened. Maybe nothing would. Maybe all he'd get out of the deal was a long ride through the canyon on Cinder tomorrow and an education in grassroots democracy tomorrow night. But he'd be able to watch Georgie take the minutes. That would be a kick.

The following night Vince ate an excellent dinner of chicken-fried steak at Sadie's and was joined by Steve. A husky guy with a full head of white hair and bifocals, Steve turned out to be a good conversationalist. Vince kept hoping Georgie would show up, but apparently she'd decided to wait until the meeting was ready to start.

Vince asked how Steve and Myra ended up buying the hotel.

"I got an unexpected inheritance." Steve took a drink of his beer. "I'd managed hotels for years and always wanted to own a small one. The Bickford happened to be for sale fifteen years ago when I was looking around for something exactly like this. Back then it was a little gold mine. Now, not so much."

"Have you thought of selling it?"

Steve cut into his steak. "Myra and I've talked about it, but we love it here. We've made some good friends.

For a while after the Double J closed down, we were fine. People still came to stay at the hotel because the town hadn't started going downhill. But it turns out the little shops needed both the guest ranch and the hotel to stay in business. One by one, they closed up, which changed the atmosphere of the place. People stopped booking hotel rooms. Don't blame 'em."

"It's a damn shame, though."

Steve nodded as he finished chewing and swallowed. "But I honestly don't know how we can turn it around. The council members, of which I'm one, were asked to bring ideas to the meeting tonight. Inez, Clyde's wife, told me to suggest the quilt raffle again. We have some champion quilters in Bickford. But that's not a solution. We need something bigger and more dramatic."

"Yeah, you do." Vince thought about his ride through the canyon today. Gorgeous country, perfect for trail rides. He hadn't seen the Ghost, though. Georgie had been as right about that as she seemed to be about a lot of things. Yesterday had scared the stallion and he'd taken his herd into hiding.

Vince felt responsible for that, but he also knew the trauma would subside and the herd would come back to the pasture and the creek because it was such a perfect place for them. Their memory of yesterday would fade. If no one else upset them, they'd resume their normal pattern of meandering through the canyon.

He couldn't help thinking of an idea he'd had when he'd worked at the Double J. The ranch owners hadn't thought anyone would go for it, but Vince still liked the concept. Yet he didn't really need to get involved in the town's problems. He was an outsider, and he wanted to keep it that way.

A few minutes before seven, Georgie walked in. He happened to be looking in that direction, but he might have sensed her arrival even if he hadn't been turned that way. He felt connected to her by an invisible string. She might not have that sensation, but he sure did.

Tonight she wore a dark-green blouse tucked into her jeans and she'd slung a tote bag over her shoulder. She didn't look at him.

Ike busied himself collecting dinner dishes and taking drink orders.

"Excuse me," Steve said. "I need to help move tables. Been nice talking to you, Vince."

"Same here, Steve. Need any help?"

"Nah, I think we've got it. We're used to this routine."

Vince could see that. Ed arrived about that time and he, Clyde, and Steve put three tables together to create an official place for the council members to sit. Ed was a typical old cowboy and didn't pretend to be anything different. He came to the meeting in the same worn jeans and faded shirt Vince had seen him wearing this morning.

Vince understood why Steve, Clyde, Georgie, and Ed were on the council. Steve, Georgie, and Ed ran the only surviving businesses in town. Clyde was the mayor.

But Vince couldn't figure out why an ancient lady named Ida Harrington was part of the group. She'd walked into Sadie's wearing a sparkly Western shirt and bright red jeans. Her thinning hair was the color of the wine Georgie liked to drink. In fact, Ida ordered a glass of it the minute she stepped inside the door.

The other council members hovered around Ida, making sure she had the seat she wanted at the table, the wine she'd ordered, and some fries. Soon several baskets of fries appeared on the council table, along with glasses and two pitchers of beer. Vince had never been to a town council meeting, but Ida's wine and the pitchers of beer didn't seem right.

Apparently they were a normal part of the meeting, though, because Clyde poured a beer for each of the men. Ida finished her first glass of wine and signaled Ike for another, and the meeting hadn't even started. Georgie was the only teetotaler in the group.

Sadie's was more crowded than it had been all weekend. The residents turned out for these meetings. Every chair was filled and Ike was doing a brisk business behind the bar. Council meetings might be as lucrative as having three cowboys blow into town. Grassroots democracy was way more entertaining than Vince had expected.

But despite the beer and the relaxed attitude of everyone in the room, the meeting started exactly at seven on the dot. Vince glanced at the neon Budweiser clock behind the bar when Clyde brought the gavel down. Impressive.

Georgie had pulled a little computer out of her tote and began typing as Clyde opened the meeting. She looked capable and efficient. Vince settled in to watch her take minutes because, after all, he'd stayed partly for that purpose.

The beginning of the meeting was pretty boring. It involved approving the minutes from the last meeting, and there was some bickering between Ida and Clyde about wording. Eventually that was settled, and the treasurer's report followed. Steve was the treasurer, and his evaluation of the finances was met with moans and groans from the crowd.

Vince could understand. The town had no money and wasn't likely to get any soon. But Ida questioned several of the items in the budget. Steve treated her with great respect as he explained each issue, and she finally settled down.

A pleasant-looking couple had parked themselves at Vince's table after asking if the seats were taken. Vince leaned toward them. "Who is that woman?"

The guy lowered his voice. "Oldest person in town, at least ninety-five if she's a day. And loaded. She keeps hinting that she might give the town money, but so far, we haven't seen a dime."

"That's frustrating."

"Tell me about it. Not that she could solve our problems with a donation. We need more than cash. We need to create a reason for tourists to come here. I suppose she could be waiting for someone to suggest a project she's willing to underwrite."

Vince nodded. Sounded fair to him. But no wonder everyone catered to Ida. If they ever came up with a big idea, she'd be a great source of funding. Vince considered his concept and wondered if it would work for the town. But this wasn't his rodeo. He'd probably be better off not saying anything.

Beer, wine, and mixed drinks continued to flow. Both council members and residents who'd gathered for the meeting sipped on their beverage of choice. Georgie was still the only one with a glass of water.

Vince began to wonder if grassroots democracy meant everyone getting happy. It was good for Sadie's, and people didn't seem terribly upset that the town was nearly bankrupt. Maybe handling things this way wasn't such a bad idea.

Clyde finally got around to new business and asked council members for their input regarding programs to rejuvenate the town. None of them had anything to offer, not even Georgie, and Vince knew how smart she was. In a way, he was surprised she hadn't thought of his idea.

Maybe he should have given it to her yesterday so she could have presented it if she'd been of a mind to. But he hadn't done that. So now here he sat, with what he thought was a terrific idea burning a hole in his pocket.

Ida smacked her wineglass down on the table. "I can't believe *nobody* has come up with a plan. This is a community of hard workers, of good people, of intelligent people. All we need is a plan. Won't somebody *please* come up with a brainstorm? We can't let Bickford die!"

Vince stood. He had no business saying anything, but if everybody else was drawing a blank, then he couldn't in good conscience keep quiet. "I'm not a member of this community, so I have no right to speak, but I do have an idea." He avoided looking at Georgie, because she had the power to distract him, and he needed to keep his mind clear so he could explain this right.

Clyde glanced at him. "Ordinarily we only invite comments from those who live here, but we're desperate, Vince. If you have an idea, I, for one, would love to hear it."

"Me, too," Ida said. "And may I add that you're real pretty to look at, whoever you are."

Vince felt his face grow warm. Apparently he could be embarrassed by the comments of a ninetysomething lady. "Thank you, ma'am."

Ida smiled at him. "You're welcome, young man. Now say your piece."

Vince swallowed. Being the life of the party was one

thing. Speaking to a roomful of strangers about his idea was something else again. But he'd started this, so he might as well finish it.

"When I worked as a wrangler for the Double J, the guests were offered short trail rides on ranch property, never more than an hour at most. Otherwise they kept busy with swimming, massages, mud baths, stuff like that. In my opinion, they never got the true Western experience. They didn't see many wild animals and certainly not the Ghost and his herd. I told the ranch owners they should set up overnight rides into the canyon so people could try and spot the wild horses, but the owners weren't interested."

He snuck a look at Georgie. She was totally focused on him, but she didn't look upset, which was good. He'd wondered how she'd react to this, considering her love of those animals.

Feeling encouraged, he went on. "I still think it's a decent idea. Folks could camp out, have a chuck-wagon meal or two, pretend they were back in the Old West, and maybe catch sight of the horses sometime during their adventure. No guarantee of that, of course. It would be like whale watching, Western-style. That's it. I'm done." He took his seat.

The room erupted into excited conversation, and Clyde had to bang his gavel several times to restore order. "So, Vince, are you suggesting that the town could do this to increase tourism?"

"That's what I'm saying." Vince shrugged. "It might not work for you, but I think it's worth considering."

Ida beamed at him. "Sweetie, you're a genius. I love it."

# CHAPTER 12

Once again, Vince had surprised the heck out of Georgie. What he'd proposed was creative and far more likely to revive the town than anything that had been suggested so far. By contributing this idea, he'd turned his visit from a potential curse to a potential blessing.

Plus he'd looked so good doing it. She'd deliberately stayed away from Sadie's until five minutes prior to the meeting because she hadn't wanted to put herself in temptation's way. The minute she'd walked into the saloon, temptation had been sitting right there wearing a clean chambray shirt and a heart-melting smile. Vince was entirely too gorgeous for his own good.

A vivid memory of how those smiling lips had felt the night before almost made her run into a chair. She hoped nobody had noticed, especially not the man who'd wrecked her composure. She should never have kissed him in the first place, and damned if she didn't want to do it again.

Fortunately the meeting had required her to concentrate on her little laptop and take reasonable notes of the proceedings so she'd be able to produce decent minutes. But then Vince had made his excellent suggestion, and now she couldn't avoid looking at him because he was the man of the hour. Ida certainly thought so.

Not everyone agreed with Ida, though. Pandemonium followed her ringing endorsement of Vince's suggestion. Those who were in favor of his concept loudly proclaimed their enthusiasm for a plan that could save Bickford. The naysayers were equally loud as they cited the potential liability, the work involved, the lack of available horses, and most of all, the lack of qualified people to lead the trail rides.

Clyde finally got the crowd under control by whistling through his teeth. Georgie grinned. She hadn't known he could do that. Apparently no one else had, either. They stared in shock at their eightysomething mayor.

He shrugged. "Learned how to do that when I was a kid growing up in St. Louis."

"You sound like one of those guys on *Rawhide*," somebody called out. "You could be the trail boss!"

"No, I couldn't. I'd love to think I was up to it, but I'm not. Finding the right people to supervise the ride is critical."

The racket from the audience started up again, but this time Clyde's gavel was enough to silence it. "Either this stops or we'll clear the room. We need to discuss this in an orderly fashion." He surveyed the room with a piercing gaze. "Understood?"

When several people nodded in agreement, Clyde glanced at Ed. "You're qualified to be a trail boss, but you have a business to run."

"And when my arthritis acts up, I can't sit a horse for very long." Ed looked down the table at Georgie. "You could do it, but you also have a business to run, and besides, we'd need at least two people. I could maybe be the second person, but not the main person. We need someone younger than me for that."

When Frank Bryson stood and asked permission to speak, Georgie expected him to bring up legal issues. His many years as a lawyer made him a great resource, but she worried that in this case he'd throw a wet blanket over this promising idea.

Sure enough, he did. "An experienced trail boss is a must. I can't stress that enough, and I don't think we have who we need living here in Bickford. Georgie, you're an accomplished horsewoman, but you've never been responsible for a group of riders, some of whom might be first-timers. Much as I love you, you're not qualified for the job."

"You're right, Frank." She didn't take offense. Frank and Sue were like loving grandparents who wouldn't want her to bite off more than she could chew.

"I'm glad you agree. Because if someone gets hurt out there and they can prove we didn't have a qualified person in charge, the town could lose what's left of its shirt."

"And at the moment we've only got a couple of sleeves and a few buttons." Steve leaned back in his chair. "It's a cool concept, and at first glance it seems like a great idea, but we have to have the right personnel. And reliable horses. The four in your stable aren't enough, Ed."

"No, they're not. I have room for more animals, but I don't have any extra tack."

"Right," Clyde said. "And unless I'm mistaken, nobody has a chuck wagon sitting in the backyard, either. This wouldn't be a simple fix. It would take a considerable investment, and we could get ourselves into more trouble than we're already in."

"Yeah." Ed tugged on the brim of his battered straw

hat. "I carry liability, but I know every time I rent out a horse, I could get sued, no matter what disclaimer I have them sign beforehand. And that liability insurance is pricey. I probably don't have as much coverage as I should."

Georgie felt the excitement ebbing, and she couldn't bear to have this first glimmer of hope doused so quickly. "Hang on. Let's not talk ourselves out of this. I know it sounds like a lot of details to be worked out, but let's not get discouraged about the possibility before we find out whether it's feasible."

"Atta girl!" Ida punched her fist in the air. "I'll go you one better. I believe in this, so I'm prepared to make a business loan to the town for the purchase of a few more horses and the necessary tack. Oh, and a budget for promoting the thing."

"That's a generous offer," Clyde said, "but we don't want to get ahead of ourselves. No point in buying stuff until we have a trail boss."

"I was getting to that," Ida said. "When we find a qualified trail boss, I'll pay his or her salary for the first six months until we get this thing off the ground." She named a generous amount to be paid every two weeks. Then she looked at Vince. "If you want my opinion . . . hell, you'll get my opinion whether you want it or not. Ladies and gentleman, we have our trail boss sitting right over there." She pointed to Vince.

Georgie's pulse rate shot up. *Dear God, no.* But she couldn't argue with Ida's logic. Vince had dreamed up the idea so he must have a plan for how it would work. He'd been taking city slickers out on the trail for at least ten years. He was strong, healthy, and charismatic.

Plus he was currently out of a job and Ida was guaranteeing him a salary. With his preference for short-term employment, he might be all over her offer. When he rose from his chair, she wondered if he'd accept the job.

Technically he couldn't do that yet, because the council hadn't voted to adopt the plan. Still, if Vince seemed willing to be the trail boss, it might help convince the council members to vote in favor of the entire concept. She would vote that way herself, even though having him around would be a challenge for her. She held her breath.

Vince cleared his throat. "Much as I appreciate your confidence in me, ma'am, I'm not interested in taking that position."

Georgie exhaled.

"Say it isn't so!" Ida shook her head. "You would be so perfect!" She turned to Georgie. "A little birdie told me you were kissing this good-looking cowboy yesterday evening. Can't you convince him to take the job?"

Her face grew hot and she looked at Clyde. Surely he hadn't blabbed to Ida. That wasn't like him, and yet he'd been the only one on the scene.

"I wasn't the little birdie!" Clyde said.

"No, it wasn't you, Clyde," Ida said. "Actually it was more than one little birdie, but I never reveal my sources. This is a small town, and when two people are kissing on Main Street, it can't be considered a secret, can it?"

Georgie groaned and covered her face with her hands. Then she heard Vince speak her name and looked up.

He'd remained standing through all that. His color was high, too, and his troubled gaze was fixed on her. "It was my fault," he said, "and I'm sorry I've embarrassed you."

A soft sigh went up from the female members of the crowd.

"It's okay." She was still embarrassed, but she was impressed that he was willing to shoulder the responsibility for the kiss.

"Good grief, kids!" Ida clucked her tongue. "It was a kiss, not an X-rated peep show! Personally, I was glad to hear that we had a little PDA going on in Bickford. The town's become entirely too boring. But my point is, Georgie, would you please use your influence to change this boy's mind?"

Vince stuck his hands in the front pockets of his jeans. "With all due respect, ma'am, I won't change my mind. So I don't want y'all to go blaming Georgie if I refuse the job."

"We won't do that, son," Clyde said. "We're all mighty fond of Georgie around here. You don't have to worry about her taking any flak."

"Good. I'm glad to hear it." Vince lowered himself to his chair.

Clyde surveyed his council members. "Here's what I propose. We can approve a motion to move forward with this project contingent on finding a qualified trail boss. Do I have such a motion?"

Georgie made the motion and Steve seconded it. There was no discussion and the motion passed unanimously.

"Georgie, I'd like you to be in charge of finding us a trail boss. If Vince isn't interested, he might be able to recommend someone who is. And under the circumstances, we can't wait another month to hash this out. We'll need to meet again next Monday. I hope by then you'll have found someone."

"I hope so, too." At least it wouldn't be Vince. She had that much to be thankful for.

*     *     *

As soon as the meeting adjourned, Vince expected Georgie to make a beeline for the door, but instead she walked over to his table. He stood.

"Can I talk to you for a minute?"

"Sure." The couple who'd shared his table during the meeting had left. "Here?"

"Here's fine."

"Drink?"

"Love one."

He grinned. "I guess now you can allow yourself, huh?"

"I don't know how everybody else does it. My critical-thinking skills go down the drain after a glass or two of wine, a fact I clearly demonstrated last night."

He winced as he remembered how she'd covered her face during the meeting. "I'm sorry about that, Georgie. Well, that's not entirely true. I'm not sorry I kissed you, but that I made it so public. I should know better. I've lived in a lot of small towns."

"I'll bet. Vince, the travelin' man."

"That's me." He held out a chair for her. "Have a seat and I'll get you that drink. Ike's too busy to wait tables tonight." As he walked over to the bar, he thought about her comment that he was a travelin' man. She hadn't said it like it was a bad thing. Maybe that was because in this case, his tendency to move around had worked to her advantage.

She hadn't wanted him to take the job. He'd seen it in her face. He wouldn't have taken it, anyway, but he'd caught the quick flash of horror in her eyes before she'd composed herself. That had clinched it for him. No way in hell would he be the trail boss for this project, even if it had been his idea.

Just because he'd thought of it didn't mean he wanted

to be in charge. Taking folks out on an overnight trail ride wouldn't be a problem. He'd done that before at other ranches, but only when he'd been backed up by people who knew as much about the process as he did. He'd never run the whole show.

He probably understood more than anyone here, with the exception of Ed, what this undertaking involved. They'd want to purchase calm horses suitable for beginners and more spirited ones for those with riding skills. All four of the horses in Ed's stable were too high-strung for a beginner rider.

Ed had the expertise to pick out the tack, but he might not know how to plan a trail route if he wasn't in the habit of taking people out. An overnight campsite would have to be prepared in advance, complete with a fire circle and wood. Somebody with camping knowledge would need to organize the chuck wagon, the bedrolls, and the tents.

Vince could do those things if necessary. That wasn't really the part that bothered him. Being responsible for the success or failure of the whole shootin' match—that was what bothered him. He'd be a key man, someone everyone looked to for answers, someone difficult to replace. That was so not his style.

Moments later he carried his bottle of beer and Georgie's red wine back to the table. She'd fired up her laptop and was looking over her notes.

"Think you got everything that went on?" He set her wine down next to her and took a seat across the table from her. All things considered, he'd play it safe and not get too close.

"I think so, at least the gist of it. Myra summarizes instead of trying to capture every little detail, so that's what I'm doing."

"It's generous of you to give your time this way."

"I'm glad to do it. Everyone on the council is giving their time, too."

"Yeah, but I doubt any of them are as busy as you are. It looks to me as if you run that store pretty much by yourself."

"Anastasia helps me."

"I know, but she told us during lunch on Sunday that she's more of a liability than an asset. After she described a few of her accidents, I have to say she might be right about that."

Georgie smiled. "She's supportive, though. I don't know what I'd do without her. And if this trail-ride thing could work out and we get some tourist business in Bickford, Anastasia could sell her art. I know she could."

"I know she could, too." He felt a little guilty taking a free portrait. He actually did like it, but he wasn't sure what to do with it. Tacking it to the wall of whatever bunkhouse he landed in would not be smart. He'd never live that down.

Closing her laptop, Georgie picked up her wine. "Here's to you for offering us that idea. Ida's right. It's pure genius."

He shifted in his chair, uncomfortable with that level of praise. "I wouldn't say that."

"I would. I wanted to talk to you so I could get Mac and Travis's phone numbers."

"To offer them the job?"

"Right. Do you think either one of them would take it? Or better yet, both of them? They've had the same kind of guest ranch experience you have, and they know the area. I'd rather go for someone who's familiar with the town, the trails, and the wild horses."

"They might consider it, but . . ." He hated to shoot her down, but he thought chances were slim either of those old boys would say yes.

"What's the problem?"

"You'll be asking them to give up a steady job for something that might or might not work out. If it doesn't work out, they might be able to get their old jobs back, but probably not. The ranch owner would have replaced them by then."

"But it *will* work out. We just need to get it off the ground, and I have some thoughts about that. A few of the regulars from the Double J send me Christmas cards every year. I'll bet they'd book a trail ride for a chance to come back to this area for a few days."

"It's a start. Be sure and tell Mac and Travis that. It might make a difference."

"Okay, I will." She pulled her phone out of her tote. "Anytime you're ready."

"I have to look it up." He got out his phone. "This stored phone number thing has spoiled me. I don't memorize phone numbers anymore." He gave her both numbers.

She keyed them in and glanced up. "When's the best time to call them?"

"Now."

She hesitated. "I suppose you're right. During the day they'll be working on the ranch and might not be able to answer." She glanced around. "But I hate making phone calls in public places. It seems so rude. I'm going outside."

"I'll go with you."

"No, you won't. That's how we got in trouble last night. You sit right here while I go call them."

He blinked. "That sounded suspiciously like an order."

"It kind of was, Vince. Stay here, okay?"

He couldn't resist teasing her. "Afraid of me?"

She looked into his eyes. "In a word, yes."

That stung. He wasn't the kind of man who pounced on women, and he resented the implication that he was. "I'm perfectly capable of walking outside with you and not making a move. And I want to know what they say."

"I know you won't make a move."

"Then we can both walk out there." He pushed back his chair. "We'll leave our drinks here. Ike will understand that we're coming back. In fact, I can tell him that so he doesn't clear them away."

"Please don't come outside with me." She picked up her phone. "Hold the table."

"For God's sake, this is Sadie's. I don't have to hold the damned table. Nobody's going to take it away from us."

"Vince."

"What?"

"The combination of you, me, and twilight is way too tempting for me. I'd appreciate it if you'd stay where you are so that I can make my phone calls without getting distracted."

"Really?"

"Really."

He grinned. A guy had to be happy when he learned that he was irresistible. "Well, all righty, then."

# CHAPTER 13

Georgie wasn't pleased that she'd had to spell it out for Vince, but facts were facts. Fortunately Vince should be leaving tomorrow. He wouldn't want to stick around and risk getting roped into the new project somehow. He'd made it clear that all he'd intended to offer was the idea, and she was immensely grateful.

She called Mac first. Of the two, she saw him as more of a leader and therefore better suited for the job.

He answered right away and sounded surprised to hear from her. And a little worried. "Is Vince okay?"

"He's fine."

"And he's still there?"

"Yes, but he should be leaving soon. He gave me your phone number because I want to offer you a job." She quickly explained Vince's idea and told him how much Ida was willing to pay for the first six months.

"Did you ask Vince?"

"I did. He doesn't want to."

"Interesting. I would've thought he'd do it, especially considering it was his idea. Did you ask him why he doesn't want to?"

"No. I figured that was his business." And she'd been so relieved that she really hadn't cared why. "Will you do it?"

Mac hesitated. "That's good money, but what if the whole thing falls apart after six months?"

"It won't. I have contact info for some of the regular guests at the Double J, and we have money for advertising. I'll set up a website. I'll . . ." She thought quickly. "I'll get my sister in Dallas to talk it up. She knows a lot of people there, people with money. It'll work, Mac. I know it will."

"Maybe it will. I hope it does." Mac sighed. "I'd love to help, Georgie, but I just bought a new truck and the payments are a chunk of my salary here. I can't take the chance on quitting this job for something that might not work out. I love what I do, and I'd hate to have to wait tables or work construction because no ranch was hiring."

Georgie had no good response. It was a valid point and Vince had warned her that the lack of a guarantee could be a problem. "What about Travis? Do you think he'd take it?"

"You can ask him. He's right here."

Travis came on the phone. "Hey, Georgie! What's this you're trying to talk Mac into?"

She went through her pitch again and tried to make it as appealing as possible. She mentioned that he'd probably get a free room at the hotel, although she had no idea if Steve and Myra would agree to that. She thought they might, though.

"I heard what Mac told you," Travis said, "and my answer would be the same. I don't have a lot of savings, and if your deal went belly-up, I'm not sure if I'd be able to hire on back here, or anywhere. Like Mac said, jobs in our field aren't all that easy to come by."

"I understand." Georgie swallowed her disappointment. "I was so hoping we could find someone we already know, but I'm willing to take your recommendation if there's anyone else who would be interested in doing this."

"Most cowboys I know are staying put. Mac and I had to scrounge after we were laid off at the Double J, and we were both finally able to get on here."

"But will you ask around? Somebody might be excited about something a little different."

"They might, but I can't figure why Vince isn't doing it. He's never been worried about where his next job is coming from and he's got the personality for it. He has a way of making greenhorns feel ... I don't know ... confident, I guess. He's popular with them."

"I'm sure he is." Georgie glanced through the window of the saloon and noticed that Ida was sitting at Vince's table. The two of them seemed to be having a jolly time. "He didn't say why he doesn't want the job."

"I think you need to find out why. Maybe you can overcome his reasons, because he's your best bet."

"You're probably right, but he sounded like his mind was made up. Will you keep my number handy in case you hear of anybody?"

"Sure thing. I wish you luck with it, Georgie."

She thanked him and disconnected. Damn. Travis was right, but she didn't have to like it. If only he or Mac had taken the job! But they hadn't, and she couldn't blame them.

She believed this plan would work, but if it didn't, she and the town would be no worse off than before. Asking two cowboys to give up steady jobs they cherished to take a chance on an untried business venture wasn't fair. Vince, on the other hand, had no cherished job at the moment, so if this didn't work out, he'd be no worse off than before. In fact, he'd be better off because he would be well-paid for six months.

Yet he'd rejected the possibility. Much as she wished he'd leave and eliminate the temptation he presented, she had to get him to stay. But contrary to Ida's suggestion, she wouldn't use herself as bait. Just the opposite. If he agreed to accept the job, it would be with the understanding that nothing would go on between them.

Taking a deep breath, she walked back into Sadie's and over to the table where he and Ida were sharing a laugh. They both glanced over as she approached and Vince got up to pull out her chair.

"I adore this man," Ida said to Georgie as Vince resumed his seat. "If I were fifty years younger, I'd make a play for him myself. I would've made a hell of a cougar at forty-five. But I was married to Mr. Harrington at the time, and he would have taken a dim view of me having a boy toy." She sighed. "I always wondered what it would be like to rob the cradle."

"Don't give up the dream, Ida," Vince said. "Pick out a studly seventy-five-year-old."

"That's an excellent idea, except there are no unmarried seventy-five-year-olds in Bickford. Isn't that right, Georgie?"

"That's right, although if we can get this new project going, that could change."

Ida's eyes, already large behind her thick glasses, grew even larger. "You are so right! I hadn't thought of that. And don't use the *if* word, honey. Say *when* we get this new project going. The power of positive thinking is the only way to go."

"I agree." Georgie smiled brightly at Vince. "Does that mean Vince has agreed to be our trail boss?" Maybe Ida had done the work for her.

"He has not, much to my dismay. I even offered to increase his salary."

Georgie decided to put him on the spot. "So why not, Vince? Seems like this is tailor-made for you. You know the area and you're an experienced wrangler who's logged a bunch of trail-ride hours with dudes and dudettes."

Vince peered at her. "Mac and Travis turned you down, didn't they?"

"Yep, but they both said you were perfect for the job."

"No, I'm not." Vince took a swallow of his beer.

Ida clucked her tongue. "Of course you are. As Georgie pointed out, you have all the necessary qualifications and you're handsome as sin, besides."

"I wouldn't say that." He began to blush.

"You are so! You're the total package, the quintessential cowboy, complete with mile-wide shoulders, narrow hips, cute butt—"

"Come on, Ida. Stop it." His blush deepened.

"Don't *come on, Ida* me. I'm ninety-five years old and that gives me the right to be politically incorrect. Besides, I'm right, aren't I, Georgie? Doesn't he have the cutest butt you've ever seen?"

Georgie took a quick gulp of her wine. "Since I hope we'll be working together, I'd rather not say. I don't want to be sued for sexual harassment."

"See?" Ida glanced at Vince. "She does think so or she wouldn't have answered that way."

"Hold on a minute," Vince said. "You really want me

to take this job, Georgie? I thought that was the last thing in the world you wanted."

"Is that why you said you wouldn't do it?" Maybe it was that simple.

"It wasn't the whole reason, but it was a contributing factor."

Ida finished her wine. "I can sense you two will make more progress if I leave you alone."

"That's not true." And Georgie liked having her there as a chaperone. "Please stay."

Vince pushed back his chair. "I'll get you another glass of wine, Ida."

"No, I'm leaving." She stood and looked directly at Georgie. "Whether you realize it or not, this cowboy likes you, and I fully believe that you're the one to talk him into this."

"I'm not so sure, but I'll try."

"No, no." Ida wagged a finger at her. "There is no such thing as *try*. Mr. Harrington taught me that and he made a lot of money so he must have known a thing or two. Don't say you'll *try* to do something. Simply say you'll do it. And you will."

"All right." Georgie knew how much was riding on this for the town. "I'll do it."

Once Ida walked away, Vince muttered under his breath. "No, you won't."

"Look, I admit that at first I didn't want you to, but I've finally realized you're the only one who can."

"It's not right for me, Georgie."

"Why?" She looked into his eyes, which was always a dangerous proposition, but she had to figure out what was going on with him, and his eyes were extremely expressive.

At the moment they were filled with stubborn determination. "I don't want to be in charge of it."

"Well, you wouldn't be, exactly. The council will be involved."

"The way I look at it, I'd be indispensable, and I never want to be in a situation where I'm indispensable. Then I'm stuck there. I can't pack up and leave if I feel like it, because nobody can fill my shoes. I don't want that."

"Oh." She was beginning to get the picture. Only one fix occurred to her and it was risky. "Then how about this? I'll be your backup."

He frowned. "How would that work?"

"I'm not sure yet. I'm figuring this out as I go along. But basically you'd keep me in the loop on everything, which would be a good idea, anyway. But I'll pay close attention, and we can take practice rides, maybe with Ed when he's available, so you can teach me everything you can about how to do this right."

"You won't have time. You have the store."

"I'll shorten the hours. People can adjust. They really don't need me to be open eight hours a day, but they're used to it so that's what I've done. They'll understand that shorter hours are for the good of the project. And I'll ask Anastasia to help out more."

"But I'll still be in charge, and I don't want that."

She shook her head. "No, I'll be in charge. You'll be helping me. Maybe you'll be more important in the beginning, but as soon as you teach me what I need to know, you'd be free to bail at any time if you get claustrophobic."

"I don't know, Georgie." He stared down at the table, and when he looked up at her, those blue eyes hadn't softened much. "It'd be better all the way around if I just didn't get involved."

Desperate times called for desperate measures. "Vince, I'm begging you to take the job. We'll write up a contract with Frank's help that allows you to leave anytime you want. I'm just asking you to stay until I'm fully qualified to lead the rides."

"A contract? Hell, no. I've never signed a contract in my life and I don't intend to start now."

"Okay, no contract. A gentleman's agreement between you and me that you can take off whenever you want."

His eyes twinkled briefly. "Georgie, you're no gentleman."

"I realize that, but—"

"It's okay. Neither am I."

She caught the gleam in his eye and looked away. "You'll have to be if this is going to work. We'll be business partners, in a way, and I refuse to complicate this with anything like . . ."

He lowered his voice. "Sex?"

"Yeah." She took a shaky breath and lifted her gaze to his. "I want you to do this for the sake of the town, but I'm asking you to turn off the charm for my sake. Please. Can we have that understanding?"

He looked at her for a long time. "You have guts, Georgie Bickford."

"I love this town."

"I can see that. I don't understand it, but I respect it. I may well live to regret my decision, but I'll take the job. And I'll abide by your conditions."

Triumph made her giddy. "Oh, Vince, thank you!"

"Don't thank me yet." But judging from his smile, he was pleased with her reaction. "I haven't done anything."

"You will, though, and it'll be awesome." She couldn't stop grinning. She pictured the shops looking festive with new coats of paint, the hotel and Sadie's bustling with tourists, her sister's art going like hotcakes, and jobs being snatched up by those who'd reluctantly left town years ago.

"Just so we're clear that I'm only helping and you're in charge."

"Absolutely." She temporarily abandoned her fantasy and focused on him. "I'm a quick learner. You'll be amazed how fast I'll be qualified to take your place."

"Sounds like now you're in a rush to shuffle me out."

Huh? Was that regret she heard? "Only if that's what you want. From what you said, you want to minimize your commitment."

"I do. I definitely do." He finished his beer. "You know me. Always heading somewhere else."

Now that was the Vince she recognized. "Then I'll plan accordingly. If the concept goes gangbusters, maybe I'll consider hiring someone to take over the store so I can do the trail rides full-time with no restrictions." And then she'd have a safety net.

She rarely allowed herself to think about what could happen if her stepmother decided to sell the house and the store. It was too horrible to contemplate. But if she had the trail rides to fall back on, she could make a living here in Bickford. She might even find a way, with creative financing, to buy the house.

"I do have one request, though."

She gazed at him. "What's that?"

"If I'm going to be staying in town for a while, and if there's time in your schedule, would you teach me how to use a whip?"

"Um, sure." Considering how closely they'd have to

work together on the trail rides, one more shared activity shouldn't matter. And refusing would seem ungracious. Yet somehow the idea of teaching him to use a whip seemed . . . intimate. Well, she wouldn't allow it to be.

"Great. I'll never forget the way you charged into that clearing. It seemed like you were throwing bolts of lightning."

"That's what if feels like, too. It's fun." Her skin flushed with pleasure at the admiration in his eyes. He wasn't trying to be seductive, or at least she didn't think he was. Yet her resistance to him had never been very good to start with, and when he said things like that, she liked him far too much.

"It looked like fun. That's why I want to do it."

"Then we'll make the time." But during those lessons, she would *not* allow herself to stare into his eyes the way she was doing now. Seeking a distraction, she pulled her laptop out of her tote. "Now that you've agreed to do this, we need a plan of attack." She flipped open her laptop and turned it on. "What's first on the agenda?"

"On my end, finding horses. Since you have the computer, we should get together and see what animals are available within a hundred miles or so. Do you want to go with me to look at them?"

"Yes. We might need more down the line and I'll need to understand the criteria."

"Can you round up a trailer?"

"Ed has one that holds four. Let's see if he can go with us." She'd set up a chaperone whenever possible. The less time spent alone with Vince, the better. "How many horses are we talking about?"

"Seven or eight. We need to cap the rides at eight people, and if we can use a couple of the horses Ed's boarding, we'll be okay to start with. Eventually you'll need more so you can rotate them out in case you have medical issues with any of them, but might as well keep expenses down at first if we can."

His responses told her that he'd been thinking about this even though he'd rejected the leadership role. "I'm guessing after the horses comes the tack."

"Yep. But we might pick up some while we're buying the horses. If not, we'll go back online and see if we can find some used equipment. We'll need bridles, halters, saddles, all that stuff, but maybe Ed has some extras he can loan us."

Georgie leaned across the table and kept her voice down. "Economizing is good, but Ida has a substantial fortune, and no heirs. She's wanted to invest in a revitalization project for years, but we couldn't come up with something until you suggested this. I know you're not going to throw money out the window, but she'll expect you to get what you need."

"Probably." He smiled. "I like her."

"Then maybe we should take her along on some of these buying trips, too."

"Does she know anything about saddles and horses?"

"I doubt it. She lived in downtown Chicago until she moved here ten years ago after her husband died. She wanted to live somewhere completely different because her husband had never wanted to leave Chicago."

"Then I don't know how much help she'd be to us."

Georgie knew why she wanted Ida to ride along on those trips, but if she admitted that, he'd realize how worried she was about spending time alone with him. She'd have to get over that, though.

He'd agreed to her conditions, so from now on, the responsibility for keeping their relationship platonic was hers. She didn't take that responsibility lightly as she glanced at him sitting across the table from her. She remembered Ida's evaluation—handsome as sin, mile-wide shoulders, narrow hips, and a cute butt. When Ida was right, she was right.

# CHAPTER 14

Vince wondered what the hell he'd gotten himself into. He'd allowed Georgie's intense loyalty to her town to override his better judgment, and now he'd given his word that he'd do this thing. On top of that questionable decision, he'd agreed to behave like a gentleman at all times. Ida was paying him well, but it wasn't nearly enough to compensate him for extreme sexual frustration.

Watching Georgie's fingers flying over the keys as she took notes on her little computer taunted him with how those nimble fingers could work magic on his naked body. She'd never see that naked body, though, let alone touch it. He'd given his word on that, too. He might be a rogue in many ways, but once he promised something, he kept that promise.

Consequently he avoided promises in general, and he'd just made two of them in the space of five minutes. Apparently being around Georgie caused him to become temporarily insane. But as he reviewed the course of events, he realized he couldn't have chosen differently.

Once he'd presented his idea to the council, he'd set the wheels in motion. If he had it to do over again, would he keep his mouth shut? Probably not. He didn't love this town the way Georgie did. He doubted anyone loved this town the way she did. But he hated to see people floundering when he had a possible solution to their troubles. If he'd stayed silent and driven away tomorrow without saying a word about overnight trail rides to see the wild horses, the boarded-up town would have haunted him. Georgie's futile struggle to save it would have haunted him.

So here he was, watching her type and longing to kiss her and invite her up to his room again. He ached for this woman in a way he'd never ached for anyone. Stupid, stupid, stupid. He was about to spend six months in hell.

She glanced up from her computer. "Sadie's doesn't have Internet access or else I'd start searching for horses right now. I could do it on my phone, but we need to look at pictures, right?"

"Right." He was so busy noticing how her lashes framed her deep brown eyes that he barely came up with the right response.

"It's better to do that on the computer. How about we set a time for you to come over to the store? I have Wi-Fi there and we can browse to our hearts' content."

To her heart's content, maybe, but he didn't think his heart would be content for some time. "Okay. When do you want me there?"

"Let's say nine thirty. I don't have many shoppers then, which is why I think I can shorten the hours, no problem. I'm thinking ten to three for the new store hours. People here are all retired. They don't need me staying open any longer than that."

"Guess not." Her mouth was perfect, absolutely perfect. He'd thought so all along, but after kissing her yesterday evening, he knew for sure that her lower lip had the right amount of fullness to allow for a soft landing while he gently explored with his tongue . . . and now he was getting hard. Better ditch that train of thought ASAP.

"Let me see if the council members can come to the store about ten thirty so they can hear what we have going on so far. I wanted to have some preliminary plans before we called them together, but I think we have those." She gazed at him as if expecting him to say something.

"Yes. We definitely have preliminary plans." He'd chimed in a beat too late but that couldn't be helped, now.

"You're tired, aren't you? You probably need to go to bed."

Dear God, if she only knew how much he needed to go to bed—with her. "Yeah, I think so."

"Then let's call it a night." She turned off her computer and closed the lid. "I'm excited, Vince."

He wished she could be excited in a different way than what she meant. He shouldn't wish that, but he was only human. "Good. Me, too."

"You'll see. This will be wonderful. We're going to transform Bickford."

"That would be great." He wondered if she had any idea how beautiful she looked right now. She had a big heart, and her vision of the future included what was best for all. That selflessness gave her a glow that mesmerized him.

He wasn't as good and pure as Georgie, which was another reason they were so wrong for each other. She thought of others while he mostly thought of himself. But maybe some of her influence was rubbing off on him, because helping her get this project off the ground would mean making some sacrifices.

It felt sort of weird, too. He wasn't sure how good he'd be at self-sacrifice because it was so new to him. He should make sure that he taught her well, because he might hit a point where self-sacrifice didn't work for him anymore. If Georgie was trained to take over, then he could walk away with a clear conscience.

She tucked her laptop in her tote and stood. "We have a big day ahead of us tomorrow. We should both get some sleep."

He left his chair when she did. If she was going home, he had no reason to stay. "You're closing the store at three tomorrow afternoon, then?"

"That's my idea. I'll open at nine in the morning, like usual, and then I'll post the new hours so everyone who comes in will see them. The word will spread fast. It always does in Bickford."

He thought of their kiss, which had been common knowledge in less than twenty-four hours. "Kind of hard to sneak around in this town, isn't it?"

She nodded. "For me, it's difficult. For you, it would be impossible." She gazed up at him. "Were you thinking of trying to sneak around?"

He laughed as he fished some money out of his wallet. "Not anymore." He walked beside her toward the front door of the saloon.

She hooked her tote over her shoulder as she glanced at him. "You don't have to walk out with me. After all, you're already home."

"I want to walk out with you as a point of honor. You wouldn't let me do it before, but now we've set our boundaries, so we should be fine."

"Well, yeah, but . . ." An emotion shimmered in her eyes for a second and was gone. "It seems pointless."

"Actually, it isn't. I'm also going to walk you home. On the way you can tell me your plans for what will go on once the town's up and running again. I'm curious about what you envision. I know you've thought about it."

"You're right. I have."

He held the door for her and they stepped outside. "Brr. Chilly out here."

"The temperature really dropped. Too bad I decided not to bring a jacket."

"I know. I would've borrowed it."

She laughed. "Go back inside, Vince. We can talk about my dreams for the town another time."

"Manly men don't run inside because they're cold. They shake it off. Come on. We'll walk fast." He started off at a good clip. When she didn't follow, he turned back.

She stood in a pool of light given off by an ancient fixture over the door to the saloon. The way it settled on her golden hair made her look angelic, except for the goofy grin on her face. Angels didn't usually wear that expression.

She hurried toward him. "Sorry. I got distracted."

"Okay." After Ida's comment about his butt, he figured that was the distraction. He wasn't going to ask, though. They passed the boarded-up movie theater, so he asked about that instead.

"I would love to have the theater reopen," she said. "It wouldn't even need renovating. The last owners reupholstered the seats and put down new carpeting. But when they were losing money hand over fist, they closed it down."

"Same with the ice-cream parlor, I guess."

"Yes, and that was such a great combination. People

would go to the movies and then have ice cream afterward. Old-fashioned fun. This has to work, Vince."

"I think it will." But he was having trouble concentrating on the subject. Instead he thought about her standing back by the saloon ogling his butt. If she was going to do that on a regular basis, she'd add to the tension they'd both be under, so maybe he should ask about it, after all. "Back there, when you got distracted, were you ogling my butt?"

"Um, no. Not really."

"Don't lie to me about this. Ogling isn't going to help us behave ourselves. You weren't really behaving yourself if you were doing that, come to think of it."

"I promise I wasn't ogling."

"Then what the hell was so distracting?"

"I was just fascinated by . . . your walk."

That brought him to a screeching halt. "My *walk*? What about it?"

"Well, you were going fast."

"Because it's cold out."

"Right. But usually cowboys amble along."

"Unless it's cold. Then we get a move on. I still think you were ogling my butt."

"No, I swear I wasn't. It was in my field of vision, of course, but—"

"Aha!"

"But the thing is, you're slightly . . . bowlegged. It's very cute to watch you walk fast, especially from behind."

Vince groaned. "Remind me never to do that again. Even if I'm being chased by a damned bear, I will amble. Now let's amble on down to your house. We don't have much more to go, although it'll take a little longer now that we're ambling."

"See, that's why I didn't tell you." She fell into step beside him. "Now you're self-conscious about it."

"No man wants to be told he has a cute walk, Georgie. A steady pace? That's fine. A determined stride? Even better. But never, under any circumstances, does a man want to hear that he has a cute walk."

"You asked me!"

"I thought you were ogling my butt, and that had to stop."

"I wasn't, and I won't. I can't tell you to be a gentleman and then ogle your butt. That's a double standard."

"I'm glad we agree on that point."

"Now let's change the subject."

"Fine with me." He still thought she might have been checking him out while she watched his *cute walk*, but he'd let it drop.

Then he wouldn't have to admit that while they'd been standing there arguing, he'd noticed that the cold air had made her nipples hard enough to show through the fabric of her bra and her silky blouse. He'd looked away the minute he'd noticed, but he was currently replaying the image in his head. A guy could only be so good.

She pointed to her left. "One of these old shops would be perfect for Anastasia's studio. I'd like to see her have a space somewhere other than in the house. My stepmother isn't particularly supportive, and that has to affect her creativity."

"Her mother's not supportive? I don't get that when she's such a good artist."

"That's not the path Evelyn wants her to take. It's a long story, too long to go into right now, but my hope is that she can move into an actual studio, and something on Main Street would be great. That side of the street would probably give her the kind of light she needs, too."

"I wouldn't know the first thing about that." But he thought Anastasia was lucky to have Georgie looking out for her interests, especially if her own mother wasn't doing that.

"I only know a little, but I think one of these shops might be right for her. She could work in the back and have a place in front where she could display stuff. She could use the second floor for storing paintings, or maybe even live there if she wants to be more independent."

"Have you mentioned it to her?"

"Not yet. There's no point until we see whether the trail rides are successful. I will say that having you come on board gives me more confidence."

"But you didn't want me to do it at first. And don't deny that, because I saw your face when Ida told everybody I'd be perfect."

"I can't deny it." They'd reached the low gate at the end of the walkway to her house, and she turned toward him. "I was afraid if you stayed around here, I would eventually give in and . . . you know." She waved a hand.

"Believe me, I do know." And the thought wasn't far from his mind at the moment.

"But now that we've agreed to keep everything strictly businesslike between us, I'm okay with you being the trail boss. I'm thrilled about it, in fact."

Businesslike. He carefully squelched his urge to kiss her. Something about leaving a woman at her gate cried out for a warm embrace. "Just don't go putting too much importance on my part in this. I'm a small cog in a big wheel."

"Not exactly. You're more of a—"

"Small cog in a big wheel. And a replaceable one, at that. I need you to think in those terms. We'll get along much better if you do."

She took a deep breath. "Okay. I'll give it my best shot."

"Thank you."

"Good night, Vince." She put her hand on the gate latch. "I'll see you in the morning."

"Good night, Georgie." He touched the brim of his hat and turned to start back down the street. "Just so you know, I'll be ambling away. No need to stand there and watch, because there'll be nothing cute to see."

Her soft laughter had him racking his brain for some excuse to turn around and go back. But going back would achieve nothing. He still wouldn't be allowed to kiss her, per their agreement. And he definitely wouldn't be allowed to pull her into his arms and feel the softness of her breasts against his beating heart.

And it was beating at a fairly brisk pace, too. When she'd taken that deep breath a moment ago, she'd expanded her rib cage and lifted those inviting breasts in a way that had made his mouth water. Those were off-limits, too, so he kept walking.

He'd love to know if she'd gone inside or if she was still standing there watching him. He'd never know, because he wasn't about to turn around and look. Instead he did his best to walk with a determined stride that wasn't even remotely cute.

Sure, he was a little bowlegged, as she'd noticed. Nearly every working cowboy he knew was that way from all the hours they spent with their legs wrapped around a horse's belly. Most also had broken a bone or two while on the job. Vince's left wrist and his left ankle had taken a beating when a horse had rolled on him. Those two spots tended to ache when a storm was coming in.

He considered that a minor inconvenience. His reward was the privilege of working with horses all day and interacting with people who were mostly interesting and polite. The occasional bad apple didn't bother him because if they were a ranch guest, they'd soon be gone. If they were the boss of the operation, then he'd be gone.

Four years ago he'd been thinking about quitting his job at the Double J because the owners weren't much fun to work for. He hadn't been able to make himself follow through, though. He'd thought Mac and Travis had been the reasons because they'd wanted to hang on, but now he suspected Georgie had been the one who'd kept him there until the bitter end.

Maybe working with her day in and day out would take care of his fascination. He'd heard the phrase *familiarity breeds contempt.* Contempt would be helpful. Then he could leave town without a single regret because he'd be over Georgie.

When he reached the hotel, he considered going straight up to his room, but the evening's activities had jacked him up in many ways. His brain was buzzing and his body was restless. He hoped that wouldn't be a permanent condition for the next few months, but he was afraid it might turn out that way.

The poker game might have a little life in it, yet. Even though the night had seemed long and packed with events, he doubted that it was much past ten. He'd play a few hands and drink a beer. That should help him sleep.

When he walked in, the usual suspects were gathered around the poker table. Because the tables in the bar were square, Steve had provided a round, felt-covered topper that was hauled out whenever poker was on the agenda. Steve sat at the table, along with Clyde, Frank, and Ed, who had the biggest pile of chips and was chewing on a toothpick. A fifth chair had been drawn up and a small stack of chips were at that vacant seat.

"Come on over and take Ike's place," Steve said. "He's in the back reading the manual that came with the new deep fat fryer. The other one died soon after you and Georgie left."

"Yeah, take my place!" Ike called out from the kitchen. "I need to make sure this thing works right. Otherwise it's back to Amarillo tomorrow morning."

"'Cause we gotta have our fries," Clyde said with a wink. "Or life as we know it will cease to exist."

"Then deal me in." Vince pulled out the empty chair, sat down, and shoved his hat back with his thumb. "If Ike's in the kitchen, mind if I go behind the bar and get my own beer?"

"Help yourself," Steve said. "You'll be like family before long, anyway."

"I will?" Vince left his chair and went behind the bar. "Why's that? You got another daughter I don't know about who's looking for a husband?"

"Nope, just have the one daughter. I meant now that you'll be the trail boss for Wild Horse Canyon Adventures, you're—"

"Hang on." Vince grabbed his beer and returned to the table. "Number one, how'd you know I accepted the job?"

Ed glanced up and took the toothpick out of his mouth. "Ever hear of eavesdropping?"

"Oh."

Frank laughed. "Georgie wasn't exactly quiet about it after you agreed to take the job."

"I guess she wasn't." Vince twisted off the cap on his beer.

"But even though we knew already," Clyde said, "she texted us the news just now and asked the council members to meet with both of you at the store tomorrow at ten thirty. So we would have known either way."

"Yeah." Frank chuckled. "And we haven't heard Ida blasting John Philip Sousa, so she must be asleep and didn't get the text."

Vince glanced at him. "John Philip Sousa?"

"Whenever she thinks we have something to celebrate, she puts on 'Stars and Stripes Forever,' opens all her windows, and cranks it up. You can hear it all over town. 'Course, it isn't a big town, but still. It's loud."

"I'll have to remember that." Vince took a swallow of beer. "Second question—where did the name Wild Horse Canyon Adventures come from?"

"You like it?" Steve beamed at him. "If you do, then it was my idea. If you hate it, then it was Frank's idea."

Vince thought it over. "I do like it, but that canyon where the horses like to hang out has an actual name. I forget what it is, but I guarantee it's not Wild Horse Canyon."

"Nope." Frank rearranged his poker chips. "It's Wild Turkey Canyon."

"That's it." Vince nodded. "I didn't see turkeys this time, but I have before."

Ed gazed at him from across the table. "Now tell me—would you rather sign up for Wild Turkey Canyon Adventures or Wild Horse Canyon Adventures?"

Vince grinned. "I see your point."

"We just used a little creative license," Steve said. "Maybe we'll see about getting an official name change at some point, but we don't have time for that now. We have to move on this."

"We certainly do," Clyde said. "And now that the man of the hour is here, I say let's drink a toast to Wild Horse Canyon Adventures."

Vince raised his bottle. "I'll drink to that."

"And the man in charge of it all," Steve added.

"Whoa, whoa." Vince put down his bottle. "I'm not in charge of it. Georgie's in charge. I've agreed to help her, but she's the one who'll make sure this happens, not me."

Steve gave him an assessing glance, and then he shrugged. "Guess it doesn't make much difference who's in charge, just so we have the personnel we need."

"Absolutely," Clyde said. "It's all semantics, anyway. To Wild Horse Canyon Adventures!"

Vince raised his bottle and drank, but he was glad he'd spoken up. And he'd continue to do that whenever necessary. He was not in charge and he could leave whenever he felt like it. Georgie had promised him that, and he'd hold her to it.

# CHAPTER 15

At seven the next morning, John Philip Sousa woke Georgie from a very erotic dream in which Vince . . . Better not to think about what Vince had been doing in that dream. She'd be face-to-face with the man in less than three hours, and if she spent too much time reliving the details, they might pop back into her mind when she was with him. Awkward.

"Stars and Stripes Forever" serenaded Georgie as she climbed out of bed. Obviously Ida had finally read her text message and was celebrating. Evelyn wouldn't hear the music. She slept with earplugs and a face mask.

But Georgie selfishly hoped it would wake Anastasia. She'd been humming again last night and had probably worked late. When she was on a roll, that was her pattern. She'd never been a morning person, and whenever she stayed up to draw or paint, she was *really* not a morning person.

Plus she slept like the dead. John Philip Sousa had no effect on her, apparently, because when Georgie walked past her room, she heard only silence behind the closed door. Too bad. She would have liked Anastasia to go to the store with her this morning, mostly as a chaperone, although she could have handled any customers while Georgie and Vince looked online for horses. Besides, Georgie was eager to discuss website design ideas with her sister and they could have talked about that before Vince arrived.

She could postpone the website discussion until Anastasia was available, but it looked as if she'd have to brave her meeting with Vince alone. She wasn't worried about him at all. In spite of his vagabond lifestyle, he was a cowboy with a code of honor. He'd said he wouldn't make a pass, and he wouldn't.

But she'd had that pesky dream, and despite her best efforts, the dream clung to her through her morning routine. She was still thinking about it as she walked to the store and opened for business. As luck would have it, no customers came in during the half hour before Vince's appointment. Customers would have taken her mind off that blasted dream.

Vince was prompt, which didn't surprise her. When he said he was planning to do something, he did it, including going after the Ghost.

She met him with a smile. "Good morning. Sleep well?" It was the first idiotic thing that came out of her mouth and she longed to take it back.

"Not especially." His crisp white Western shirt and worn jeans brought with them the scent of laundry soap. Or maybe that was Vince himself, who looked scrubbed, shaved, and ready for whatever she had in mind. After her dream, she had plenty in mind.

"Sorry to hear that."

He shrugged. "Comes with the territory."

She decided not to ask what territory he was referring to. She probably knew, anyway. He wanted to get horizontal with her, but they'd agreed that wouldn't be happening, so he might be a wee bit frustrated. So was she. That dream had left her wet and achy.

In preparation for his arrival, she'd set up her computer behind the counter and brought in a couple of folding chairs. Her printer in the back was turned on so she could print out the info on any promising horses. Because nobody had come in during the first half hour, she'd had time to search out a few likely candidates.

She didn't feel confident choosing good riding stock, though. Prince was the only horse she'd owned, and her dad had bought him. But she'd learn from Vince, and by the time he left, she'd know how to buy a horse. "Come on back here and let me show you what I've found so far."

"Okay." He walked around the counter, trailing a delicious aroma of soap and virile man. But he seemed nervous and on edge.

"Have a seat." She gestured toward one of the chairs.

"I played a little poker with the guys last night." He settled into the folding chair, making it look small and delicate. "They've come up with a name for the trail ride."

"And I suppose we need one. What do they want to call it?"

"Wild Horse Canyon Adventures."

"But that's not the name of the canyon where we'll be taking people." She sat next to him. Too bad the chairs had to be so close, but it was the only way they could both see the screen.

"They know that, but they thought wild horses had more marketing potential than wild turkeys." He said it with a perfectly straight face.

She, however, started laughing. "Gee, you think?"

His expression relaxed into a smile. "Turkeys aren't very sexy."

No, but he was. His smile nearly did her in. The most exciting man she'd ever met was sitting inches away from her. He smelled wonderful and looked even better. Her heart began to pound. Could she do this?

She had to. The future of the town depended on the success of this project and she couldn't take a chance on jeopardizing it by going to bed with the trail boss. She'd never forgive herself if she somehow caused him to leave.

Her hand shook a little, but she focused on the screen and used her mouse to bring up a picture of the first horse. "This is Sarge, a fifteen-year-old gelding. He's not the prettiest animal I've ever seen with that splotchy brown coat, but they describe him as gentle. And he's relatively cheap."

Vince leaned forward, putting him dangerously close, but he had to see the screen. "Fifteen is a nice age. He's mature, but not the least bit over the hill. He'll never win any beauty contests, but he has decent conformation. Worth driving out to take a look."

"I thought so, too." She was pleased that he'd approved her first try at this, but she wished her voice sounded less breathy and her jumpy nerves would settle down. "This next guy is the total opposite, but he's also cheap. Meet Storm Cloud."

"Damn." He grinned. "There's trouble." He pointed to the screen. "See the way he holds himself, like he owns the world? You imagine him saying *I'm big, I'm black, and*

*I'm beautiful.* And he's only four. If he's this cheap, I can almost guarantee he has behavior problems. Betcha whoever has him can't handle him."

"You're probably right. But the price is seductive." Damn it, another Freudian slip.

Vince cleared his throat. "Yes, it is."

"But he's not what we're looking for. Moving on."

"Wait." Vince put his hand over hers before she could click the mouse. He took it away immediately, but the heat stayed. "Let me look at him a little longer."

"Judging from what you said, he's all wrong for our program."

"Oh, he is. I wouldn't put a greenhorn on that animal for all the tea in China. But I might buy him myself to use on the trail rides. Now that I have a job for the next few months, I could use my savings."

"I thought you'd ride Cinder."

He continued to study the gleaming black horse. "I can do that. In fact, I should do that. I was just thinking that if I'll be out on the trail all the time instead of working on a ranch, maybe it's finally time to get a horse. I've never had one of my own." He sounded a little wistful.

"Why not?"

He shrugged and his tone became brisk. "Just being practical. A horse is expensive and complicates things. I'd have to buy a trailer and hope that I could stable him wherever I landed my next job." He waved a hand. "Never mind. Buying that horse would be stupid on my part. I won't be here forever, and then I'd have him to drag around, unless I sold him."

"You could do that."

He shook his head. "I don't believe in buying a horse

unless you intend to keep him for a while. That's another reason to make sure this project flies. If it doesn't, you'll have to sell the horses we get, which means within a few months they'll be off to a new owner. They get disoriented when they're moved from pillar to post like that, and you can't blame them."

"No." She couldn't be sure, but he might have just given her a clue to his personality. She wanted to know if he'd moved a lot as a kid, although she didn't dare ask it now. Too pointed.

But she'd been touched by his initial eagerness to buy the horse and hated to see that disappear. "It wouldn't hurt to go look at him."

"Waste of time."

"What if he's not a behavior problem? Maybe he's a sweetheart and the owners are going bankrupt. In that case, he could be a good horse for more experienced riders and we'll probably get some of those, too."

"Maybe."

"I'll print out the page and we can decide later." She sent the command to the printer.

"Whatever."

"Next horse. Another gelding, named Skeeter. I was pretty sure geldings were what you'd want to focus on."

"I do. Obviously stallions wouldn't work, and I'd rather not take mares out there, either. The Ghost might get ideas."

"Ideas? About our trail horses? Oh, he's too shy. He'd never—"

"That's what you think. He stole one of the Double J mares right out of the corral."

"He actually did? I thought that was a rumor."

"Nope. He did it." He turned to look at her, his blue

eyes alight with laughter and a touch of admiration. "Came onto the ranch property one night, bold as brass, and talked her into jumping the fence and running off with him."

"I had no idea. That paints a slightly different picture of him. Did you ever get her back?"

"We tried, but we couldn't find her. Anyway, once she'd been with the herd for a while, there was no point. She'd had a taste of freedom and wouldn't make a good trail horse anymore, especially because of her foal that obviously had been sired by the Ghost."

"I see." She shouldn't be looking into his eyes when they discussed such a topic. They shouldn't be discussing the topic in the first place, but somehow they'd strayed into it. Heat flashed in his blue gaze. If he leaned forward a few inches, he could kiss her and she wouldn't stop him. For an electric moment, she thought he would do it.

Then he shoved back his chair and stood. "You have good instincts." His voice was husky. "I trust you to find us horses to look at. You don't need me to supervise. Make up a list and we'll head out this afternoon after you close the store."

She wasn't an idiot. He was fighting the restrictions they'd placed on themselves and finding the struggle difficult. God knows she was, too. "I'll check with Ed and see if he's available to go along."

Vince took off his Stetson and ran his fingers through his hair. "Good idea."

"He knows horses, and another opinion is always—"

He faced her. "That's not why we need him, and you know it."

The erotic details of her dream taunted her. "I do."

"I gave my word, Georgie, and I'll keep my word. But let's make sure we're never alone like this again, okay?"

She nodded. "I wanted to bring Anastasia this morning, but she was sound asleep and I hated to wake her up just because I . . . because I was afraid that we—"

"And we damned near did." Moving around to the other side of the counter, he began to pace. "You may not know how close we came, but I was figuring how much time I had before the council arrived and whether I could haul you into the back room and get you naked before that meeting."

She gasped.

"Oh, yeah. Never doubt it, Georgie. I don't have a condom in my pocket and never plan to have one on hand when I'm scheduled to meet with you. That's one way I can keep myself in line, but I was imagining all the fun we could have without that little raincoat."

As she watched him pace, her body grew hotter by the second. "I had a dream about you right before I woke up. Before John Philip Sousa woke me up. The dream was—"

"Don't tell me about it. That's only going to make things worse. I'm beginning to wonder if what we're attempting is impossible."

She panicked. "No, it can't be. We can make this work. I know we can."

"Then we'll have to plan better. This town is full of people eager to help, people who will be thrilled to be part of whatever you and I have to accomplish." He speared her with a sharp glance. "We need chaperones, Georgie."

"Obviously." Her heart thundered in her ears. He'd been ready to haul her into the storeroom. And she would have let him.

"I didn't think so. In my arrogance I figured an hour

in your store would be no problem." He glanced around. "I did figure on customers being here, though. Where are they?"

She tried to speak normally. "They hardly ever show up before ten." Speaking normally wasn't working. She sucked in more air. "That's why I can shorten the hours and nobody will even notice." Okay, she was a little better now, a little more in control. "I actually set the time for our meeting based on the fact that I wouldn't be busy with customers. I thought we needed time to concentrate on the horse selection."

"Except I can't concentrate on the horse selection because all I can think about is how delicious you smell, and how your eyes have that special light when you're happy that makes them almost golden, and when you're excited your breasts quiver."

Her heart shifted back into high gear. Instinctively she crossed her arms over her breasts, which were quivering again.

"Sorry." He took a deep breath. "According to our agreement I'm not even supposed to be aware of your breasts."

But knowing he was would be difficult to forget. She swallowed. "You're only . . . only being honest. I've put us in this difficult situation. I told myself it would be fine."

"I think it can be. Just get more people involved."

"I will."

"Oh, and I asked you to teach me how to use a whip, but we won't be doing that."

"No." She was sad because he'd been excited about learning, but under the circumstances, she was the wrong teacher.

"I'm going for a walk. I'll be back at ten thirty for the meeting."

"See you then." She hoped she sounded chipper and in control. She was anything but. Wow. She'd seriously underestimated the chemistry between them and how fast the combination of proximity and privacy would escalate the situation from simmer to boiling. She wouldn't be making that mistake again.

Taking several deep breaths so she wouldn't sound manic on the phone, she called Ed, who was available to go look at horses at three. Ed was their logical chaperone because he was knowledgeable about horses and tack. Anastasia could be pressed into service, too, especially if she understood why. Maybe it was time to confide in her.

Not now, though. With Ed scheduled for this afternoon, Georgie went back to searching for cheap saddle horses. She used her instincts as Vince had suggested, and soon had several more possibilities. Once she'd shortened the store hours, they could go out looking first thing in the morning, too.

Vince hadn't returned by the time Ida arrived. She sailed in with the exuberance of a hormonal teenager. If Georgie didn't know better, she'd think Ida was at least twenty years younger than she'd admitted to.

"You did it!" Ida rushed around the counter and gave Georgie an enthusiastic hug. "And my sources tell me you didn't even have to seduce him!"

"Ida! I would never—"

"Of course you wouldn't, sweetheart. I was just teasing you. But I wouldn't blame you for having a private celebration with that cowboy last night. In your boots, I would have."

Georgie took Ida by her thin shoulders and looked into her eyes. They were magnified by the thick lenses of her tortoiseshell glasses, but they were sharp and aware. "Let's get something straight once and for all. I'm not sleeping with Vince, and I won't be sleeping with Vince."

"Why the hell not? He's the best thing to hit this town in ages, and I know for a fact you haven't had that kind of fun in quite a while."

"Come on, Ida. You know how dicey a situation can get when coworkers get involved with each other. This project is too important to take that chance."

"Well, shoot. You're both mature adults. I think you can handle a little mattress bingo and still do the job."

"And I think it's too risky."

Ida sighed. "If you say so. I think you're passing up a golden opportunity, but it's your call."

"And his. We talked about it and agreed this was for the best. No matter how successful this trail ride becomes, Vince will eventually move on. By his own admission, he's not in it for the long-term."

"Oh, men love to say that because it makes them seem so romantic and mysterious, a rebel who can't stay in one place because they're so damned restless and sexy. This gun for hire and all that crap. Personally I think he's ripe for a change, but that's just me."

Georgie smiled. "Time will tell, but I'm not getting my hopes up." If he bought a horse, that might be a sign, but not a huge one, especially if he bought a trailer to go with it.

"I'm just glad he's here now. When I heard three of the Double J wranglers were back, I did a happy dance. I would have played Sousa, but I didn't want to startle the poor boys. I wasn't playing Sousa when they were here before."

"That's right, you weren't! I'd forgotten that. When did you start?"

"Must've been about two years ago. Everybody was moping around, and I thought it would perk 'em up." Her grin was mischievous. "And wake 'em up. Bet you popped right out of bed at seven this morning."

"I'll bet everybody did, except for the ones who sleep without their hearing aids. Well, and my sister Anastasia. I've never seen a person sleep as soundly as she does."

"That's because she puts her heart and soul into her work. Wrings herself out. Some folks get their beauty sleep, but Anastasia gets her creativity sleep."

Georgie was startled. "I never thought of it that way! You could be onto something. When she's working, she's oblivious to the rest of the world. Her ability to concentrate is amazing. It makes sense that she rejuvenates with deep sleep. Thanks for the insight."

"You're welcome. A person lucky enough to live as long as I have tends to pick up a few nuggets of information."

"More than a few, I'm sure."

"Nah, just a few. I'm not one of those wise women you read about. I'm just your garden-variety old fart. Anyway, I'm glad I didn't wake her up. She's our resident genius, you know."

"I do know, and I want the world to know."

"They will, honey. Your cowboy is going to be a big draw for this trail ride, and before you know it, Bickford will be back in the game. That will be a good thing for all of us, but a great thing for Anastasia."

"And that's why I won't sleep with him."

"Suit yourself. But you're leaving the door open for

some other gal to hop in his bed. Seems a shame when you're the front-runner."

"I'm not in the running at all." And if the idea of some other woman in Vince's bed bothered her, then she'd just get over it. Her priorities were clear, and having sex with Vince was not one of them.

# CHAPTER 16

The next two weeks fell into a pattern that guaranteed Vince would never be alone with Georgie. He could see how hard she was working to make sure of it and he was grateful . . . mostly. He knew about the concept of forbidden fruit and she was a perfect example. The more inaccessible she was, the more he wanted her.

Wanting a woman and not having her was an unusual circumstance for him. He hadn't encountered that problem since the last time he'd been in this town. Same town, same untouchable woman. If he'd hoped to rewrite history by coming back here, he'd been delusional.

Ed had ridden along on every horse-buying trip. They hadn't struck gold every time they'd gone out, but Vince had become a fan of the online method of tracking down good possibilities. Georgie was extremely good at that. Soon she could tell from the way a horse was described whether he'd work out for them. Once Vince left, she and Ed would make a great horse-buying team.

At this point, though, they had the animals they needed, along with some used tack. Selling a horse often meant people didn't want the extra saddle and bridle, either. They were usually in the mood to let those things go for a decent price.

Late Wednesday afternoon, Vince was at the wheel of his truck with Georgie in the passenger seat and Ed crammed in behind them in the backseat of the king cab. They'd kept that arrangement for two weeks. Georgie had tried to get Ed to switch with her countless times, but he was an old-fashioned cowboy who treated women with elaborate courtesy.

Ed would bite his tongue before he'd swear in front of a lady. Consequently, Vince had monitored his language to fit Ed's standards. That was good for him. He'd let himself get lax about that, and once he was leading trail rides, he couldn't swear at will. It wasn't classy, and this was shaping up to be a very classy enterprise.

Georgie had reined herself in, too, which was cute to watch. Not that she swore a lot, but he had to smile whenever she said *da-ang* with a little hitch in the middle. He'd bet money she'd started out to say something else before remembering they had Ed on board.

Today they were heading back to the stable with their last purchase in Ed's horse trailer. Georgie had found the big bay named Skeeter the first morning she'd started searching, but some personal business had kept Skeeter's owner from being available to close the deal until now. Counting Skeeter, they had seven mature geldings to work with. Added to the four horses Ed boarded, that was enough for the inaugural trail ride scheduled in a little over two weeks from now.

Vince remembered Skeeter. The bay gelding had been the last horse Vince had looked at before turning the online part of the operation over to Georgie. Huddled with her as they'd consulted her computer screen, he'd been on the verge of seducing her.

He was good at seducing women, and he very well might have succeeded that morning with Georgie. Somehow he'd pulled himself back from the edge. He'd learned the limits of his control that morning in her store, and he'd been humbled by that knowledge. Since then his frustration level had hovered in the red zone, but he hadn't cracked.

He blamed that nagging lack of satisfaction for his next move, though. Something had to change, and he'd finally settled on what it could be. Earlier today he'd tucked a blank check in his wallet, just in case he took a notion.

As they approached the road leading to the ranch where the four-year-old gelding named Storm Cloud had been for sale, he put on his turn signal, which got him a lift of the eyebrows from Georgie.

Someone could have bought the horse by now, and if so, then he'd look for another distraction. He'd already figured out that booze wasn't the answer. Drinking too much made him feel lousy in the morning and he needed to be sharp for the work he'd agreed to do.

He'd been using his midday hours to school the horses, and so far they'd turned out to be well-behaved animals. He could already tell that Skeeter would need very little training, which meant Vince was about to have some free time on his hands.

The website was live and a couple of reservations had come in for the first ride and a few more people had signed up for the following two weekends. Georgie had mailed out brochures to her contacts and they were responding. She'd also placed ads in the online editions of magazines that catered to travelers. Charmaine was supposedly talking up Wild Horse Canyon Adventures among her friends in Dallas, although nothing had come of that, yet.

The poker players had put together a chuck wagon with various parts they'd scrounged around town, and Henry was mulling over ideas for the cookout portion. Steve had already started interviewing for a temporary cook to take over in the hotel kitchen so that Henry could go out with the chuck wagon. The sleeping bags and tents Georgie had ordered should arrive any day.

Other than continuing to work with the horses, all Vince had left to do was map the trails and pick out some prospective campsites. Georgie had to go along for that, so they'd settled on this Sunday as the logical time. Ed had agreed to go, too, although he kept saying they didn't need him. Both Georgie and Vince had hesitated to tell Ed why they desperately did.

In short, Vince was running out of things to do, which was why he'd chosen to turn onto the dirt road leading to the Silver Saddle Ranch. "I hope y'all don't mind a little detour."

Georgie glanced at him. "Is this about what I think it is?"

"I've decided to take a look. He might not be there anymore. It's been two weeks."

Ed's voice came from the backseat. "Who might not be there? I thought we got all the ones on the list."

"We did." Vince met Ed's gaze in the rearview mirror. "But Georgie saw this four-year-old black gelding online. He caught my eye, but I doubt he'd be any good for the project, at least not without a lot of seasoning."

Ed chuckled. "Vince, are you fixin' to buy yourself a horse?"

"Probably not." Now that he was heading toward the ranch, he wondered if he'd gone crazy, after all. There were several reasons why he'd never bought a horse of his own. He shouldn't let sexual frustration make him forget those reasons. "He might not appeal to me once I see him. He might not even be there."

"He's still there," Georgie said. "I checked yesterday."

That surprised him. "You did? Why?"

"I . . . I remembered how much you'd liked the looks of him. I wondered if anybody had bought him, so I . . . I was just curious, I guess."

"Um, thanks. Thanks for checking it out." He didn't know what to think. She wouldn't have kept tabs on the horse unless she cared about him a little bit. It didn't matter to her whether the horse had been sold. But she'd sensed that it might matter to him.

That was touching and warmed him in a way that had nothing to do with sexual attraction. Even though she was resisting their mutual case of lust for all she was worth, she'd remembered how he'd responded to the picture of Storm Cloud. Apparently she hadn't wanted him to be disappointed if he changed his mind about buying the horse.

He'd assumed all along that although she valued him for his wrangler skills, she wasn't drawn to him as a person. He figured she'd be delighted if she could eliminate her pesky physical response to him. The thought that she might actually like him and want him to be happy was a whole new idea. It would take some getting used to.

The ranch was less than a mile down the dirt road. At the end the road forked. The left side went off toward the ranch house, while the right led to the barn, a couple of corrals, and various outbuildings.

Vince put on the brakes. "I should have taken down the phone number so somebody could meet us at the barn. Didn't think of it."

"I can probably find it." Georgie pulled her phone out of the little backpack she always brought along.

"Georgie to the rescue." Ed chuckled again. "I can't get over how folks can use their phones to find out nearly anything."

"It comes in handy." Georgie studied the screen. "Here it is." She handed the phone to Vince. "I'll let you do the talking."

"Thanks." His hand brushed hers as he took the phone. He should have been used to the sensation because they'd had to hand each other various items for a couple of weeks. But he felt a zing every time. He felt it more just now, because he was processing the information that she kind of liked him.

A man with a deep Texas drawl answered the phone and seemed delighted to know he had a prospect for Storm Cloud. "Drive on down to the barn, son. I'll have one of the hands bring that gelding right out. He's a beauty."

"We'll meet you down there." Vince disconnected and handed the phone back to Georgie. If a brief touch could make his pulse rate climb, he'd probably have a heart attack if he ever got her into bed.

Georgie tucked her phone away. "This is exciting."

"He sounded way too eager to sell that horse." Vince put the truck in gear and drove down to the barn. "So don't get your hopes up." Then he realized that was an odd thing to say. Technically Georgie shouldn't be hoping for anything, yet he knew that wasn't true. For whatever reason, she wanted him to have this horse.

But he wasn't willing to take on someone else's problems. He'd get this guy to level with him about Storm Cloud's faults. At the price quoted, the gelding was a steal. There had to be a reason for that.

He picked out a parking spot that would allow him to turn around so he wouldn't have to back the horse trailer out of there. As he shut off the engine, Georgie sucked in a breath.

"Vince, he's stunning."

Leaning down, he peered through the passenger window so he could see what she was seeing, and his chest tightened. Storm Cloud pranced behind the cowboy leading him over to a hitching post. Every movement allowed the late-afternoon sunlight to play over his gleaming coat.

The gelding was coal black. Not a bit of white softened the impression of restrained power radiating from him. Vince had never thought much about what sort of horse he'd want if he ever bought one. The possibility that he would buy one had been so remote he hadn't bothered to form an image in his mind.

He had an image now.

"He's a dandy, all right." Ed scooted closer to the small backseat window. "Probably full of the devil, but that's not all bad."

"No." Vince watched the horse toss his head and paw the ground. It was a wonder he wasn't breathing fire, too.

"You wouldn't want a boring horse," Georgie said.

"No."

Finally Ed cleared his throat. "Uh, Vince? You gonna go out there or sit in here and stare at him some more?"

Vince snapped out of his daze and straightened. "Just planning my strategy."

Georgie turned toward him with a knowing smile. She'd

obviously caught on that he'd been blindsided by this horse. "What's your strategy?"

"Ask a bunch of questions. Maybe even ride him." The thought made his gut curl with excitement. Then he remembered that he was here with two other people and Skeeter was in the trailer. "That's if y'all don't mind." He glanced at Georgie and turned around to gauge Ed's expression. "It would be a short ride, but I know it's getting late, and—"

"Take your time." Ed waved a hand. "It's not every day a man buys his first horse."

"I didn't say I was buying him."

Ed smiled. "If you don't plan on buying him, then you'd better wipe that look off your face."

"How am I looking?"

"Like you just fell in love."

Vince came close to muttering a swearword, but he caught himself just in time. "I'm not in love. I intend to ask the owner some tough questions and he'd better have some good answers. I think that's him driving down here, so we might as well see what he has to say for himself."

But just for good measure as the three of them walked toward the barn, he focused on the pewter truck with the silver logo on the door instead of the gelding tethered to the hitching post. He'd been awestruck by that horse. Ed and Georgie already knew that, but the rancher didn't, and that's how he wanted to keep it.

The rancher looked to be around fifty. He had a slight paunch and an air of authority. Smiling, he walked toward his visitors. "I'm John Caruthers. You must be Vince." He had a firm handshake, which was a good beginning.

Vince made introductions, and then John immediately herded them all over toward the horse. Vince did his best to keep his expression neutral, but it wasn't easy. That was one damned fine animal.

Storm Cloud eyed them, tossed his head, and snorted.

Vince struggled not to laugh. He had Storm Cloud's number. The gelding didn't want anybody telling him what to do or how to do it. They had a lot in common in that.

"Craig, lead him around a little for the folks," John said. "He shows off best when he's moving."

The ranch hand untied the lead rope and began walking the gelding in a circle, although Storm Cloud didn't seem capable of simply walking. He danced his way around, instead. Nimble-footed, just like the guy who was going to take him home.

"As you can tell, he's got some Thoroughbred in him," John said. "Spirited, but I personally like that in a horse, don't you, Vince?"

"Depends."

"He's a showy son-of-a-gun. He may be a gelding, but he acts more like a stallion. I tell you, he's exciting to ride."

Vince forced his attention away from the horse. "Then why are you selling him, John?"

There was a long silence in which the rancher seemed to struggle with what he was going to say. Finally he blew out a breath. "Well, hell. I've tried gilding the lily with other folks and that hasn't worked, so I'll just level with you. Storm Cloud is a pain in the butt."

Vince had been called that himself a time or two. Or fifty. He ducked his head so John wouldn't see him smile. The rancher probably thought he was about to get in his truck and head out. Lifting his head, he saw the resignation in the man's expression. "If we take him over to the trailer, will he load?"

"Maybe, maybe not. I can't guarantee a thing about his behavior. Doesn't matter, anyway. You don't want him."

"Let's see if he'll load."

"I predict he won't. He's gorgeous, but his previous owners let him get away with bloody murder. I thought I had the patience to overcome that, but it would take a damned saint to retrain that horse. And I'm no saint. Ask my wife."

"If we can load him, I'll buy him." He couldn't see Georgie's face from this angle, but he figured she was trying not to laugh. She had a right. She'd called it from the beginning.

"You do understand what I just told you?" John looked at him as if doubting his intelligence. "You're going to have trouble with this animal from the get-go. He has a mind of his own, and he'll inspire you to curse like you've never cursed before."

"I believe you. Let's see if we can get him in the trailer. If we can't, there's no more discussion. I move around quite a bit, so if he won't load, then he's not the horse for me."

Vince had no basis for thinking Storm Cloud would get in that trailer, but he had a hunch that he would. The gelding didn't belong on this ranch. He belonged with him, wherever he might choose to go. Illogical though it was, he thought Storm Cloud might know that.

"Okay. Just so you don't come crying to me later about what a hard time you're having."

"I wouldn't do that. How about I lead him over there?"

"Go ahead, but he's tricky. Watch yourself."

"I'll be on guard." He glanced at Ed. "You with me?"

"All the way." Ed had a big old grin on his face, too.

Vince accepted the lead rope from Craig, but he took

hold of Storm Cloud's halter as well so the horse couldn't toss his head. The gelding tried to pull away, but Vince held tight.

He hadn't expected the connection to feel so right so quickly. But from the moment he got a grip on the halter, he felt the horse's energy flowing around him. Oh, Storm Cloud would test him at first, probably quite a bit. But in the end, they would be bonded.

Connecting with the Ghost had been a fantasy that he'd nurtured because he hadn't allowed himself to imagine owning his own horse. Now that he was about to make that a reality, he wondered why he'd waited so long. Sure, he'd have to make some adjustments, but having Storm Cloud as a permanent part of his life was worth it.

"It's you and me, buddy," he murmured as he started toward the trailer. "And you'd better get used to it, because we're gonna be together for a long time."

# CHAPTER 17

By Saturday evening, Georgie was beginning to worry about the inaugural ride, and the other ones, too, truth be told. Although she'd had reservations trickling in, she hadn't been inundated the way she'd hoped, and the total number for the first ride continued to stand at two. She wanted to fill it with eight so they'd start off with a bang, and the lack of reservations had affected her mood.

But that wasn't the only thing making her grouchy. She'd wanted Vince to buy Storm Cloud and she'd thought it was a step in the right direction for a man who seemed unwilling to form close attachments to people or places. Apparently he'd formed a close attachment to Storm Cloud because he spent every free minute working with the gelding.

She was embarrassed to admit that she missed him. Even more embarrassing, she was jealous of a horse. She considered going to Sadie's for dinner tonight because she knew Vince would be there and Storm Cloud would not.

But at Sadie's she'd have to share Vince with the poker

players. They'd adopted him as if he were their long lost son, which was also a good thing. And she was messed up for resenting the old guys who claimed his attention every night.

After all, she was the one who'd insisted they couldn't get too chummy. She was the one who'd laid down a bunch of rules so the project wouldn't be jeopardized. But the man she'd pushed away three weeks ago wasn't the same man walking around Bickford today.

Sure, he'd probably leave town after a few months, or sooner if the trail rides took off as she wanted them to and she became confident enough to lead them. That part hadn't changed. He'd bought a trailer for his horse, which pretty much advertised his intention to move on at some point.

But his obvious affection for the troublesome horse he'd bought and his genuine pleasure in hanging out with his poker buddies at Sadie's was . . . endearing. She'd never thought of him in those terms before.

Yes, he was still drop-dead gorgeous. Ida wouldn't let her forget that. But he was so much more, now. She even nurtured a small hope that he might change his mind about moving on, the horse trailer notwithstanding.

Because she'd spent so little time with him recently, she was looking forward to their trail ride to map out a route for the first few events. Ed would go along because she'd set it up days ago. The way things had developed, she wondered if Ed was necessary, after all. Vince seemed totally over her.

And that was understandable. She'd put the poor guy through hell because she wouldn't go to bed with him, so his attempt to fill his time with other things was admirable. That was part of it, too. He'd accepted her restrictions and found a way to work within them. He was turning into the perfect man.

Around six that night, Evelyn was in the parlor with her pitcher of martinis and Georgie stood in the kitchen staring into the refrigerator. As she debated whether she should actually cook dinner or have crackers and cheese, Anastasia thundered down the stairs and dashed into the kitchen.

She gulped for air. "Have you checked the website recently?"

"Early this morning. What's the matter? Is it down?"

Anastasia's hazel eyes practically gave off sparks. "Two more people signed up for the inaugural ride!"

"Yay! That's awesome! I want to see." Georgie closed the refrigerator door and hurried upstairs behind her sister, who had her computer on in her bedroom. Sure enough, two singles with names she didn't recognize had brought the grand total to four. They still weren't full, but four was much better than two.

Georgie slapped Anastasia's outstretched palm and they grinned at each other. "I think this is going to work, after all," Georgie said.

"Me, too." Anastasia refreshed the screen. "There's another one! Now we have five!" No sooner had she said that, than her cell phone played Charmaine's jazzy little tune. She snatched it up from her desk. "Charmaine, we have five reservations for the first ride! Three more and we'll be full!" Then she was quiet for a minute. "Wow. That's impressive. You did? Okay, good to know. Talk to you soon."

Georgie sensed something significant going on. "What? What's impressive?"

Anastasia took a long, slow breath. "We wouldn't know

the difference because we don't move in those circles, but that last reservation is from a rich guy."

*"What?"*

"I know." Anastasia swallowed. "Charmaine's been working her connections, and this is a friend of a friend. But the other thing is, after calling to tell me, she was planning to call our—"

"Georgie! Anastasia!" Evelyn's screech was distinctive. "Get down here right now! We have plans to make!"

Georgie grabbed Anastasia's arm. "We'll go down there, and we'll see what she has in mind. But when we've placated her, we should—" She stopped, horrified. "That was extremely patronizing. I didn't mean it like that. We're going to discuss things, not—"

Anastasia smiled. "No, we're going to placate her. And what did you want to do after that?"

"Head down to Sadie's. They need to hear about this."

"You've got it. Now let's go placate my mother."

Fortunately all Evelyn really wanted was a guaranteed spot for Charmaine on the ride so she'd have the inside track to snag the man who'd made a reservation. With only five spots reserved out of eight, Georgie could grant that request, and Evelyn went back to her pitcher of martinis.

Georgie and Anastasia grabbed jackets and practically ran down to Sadie's. When they burst through the door, several of the men jumped, which sent the poker chips flying everywhere. But once Georgie announced their news, six for the inaugural ride including one rich dude, all was forgiven.

Ike went in the back and unearthed an old boom box that brought in an Amarillo station. He cranked up the volume as it belted out a country favorite. Before Georgie quite knew what had happened, she found herself dancing a two-step with Vince.

He twirled her under his arm. "Like old times, huh?"

"Better than old times." In the past they'd danced like this, but he'd been a cardboard character to her, a sexy cowboy with no substance. She didn't think of him that way anymore, which made the interaction a hundred times more exciting.

The oldsters danced with Anastasia, and when Georgie glanced over there, her sister seemed to be having a good time. But Georgie couldn't help wishing that Mac and Travis could have been here.

She was breathing hard by the time the song ended and she dropped into the nearest chair. "Whew. I'm out of shape."

"I thought you did a decent job for an old lady of twenty-eight."

"Speak for yourself, gramps." She thanked Ike for the celebratory glass of wine he brought over and lifted it in Vince's direction. "To Wild Horse Canyon Adventures."

"To Wild Horse Canyon Adventures." He raised his beer bottle in salute.

She couldn't remember when she'd felt happier. "Incidentally, if we have a rich guy from Dallas coming to this rodeo, we might have to step it up."

Holding his beer in one hand, Vince spun a chair around and straddled it. "Are you thinking caviar? Designer linens in the sleeping bags?"

"I don't know." She wondered if he had any idea how sexy he looked when he did that chair-straddling thing. "I don't speak rich guy."

"I had dealings with wealthy people at the Double J." His blue eyes were warm as he gazed at her. "I'm thinking this dude is looking for the opposite of all that crap if he signed up for our event. I'll bet he wants an old-fashioned trail ride and a chuck-wagon dinner by the campfire like he's seen in the movies. If we pamper him the way guests were at the Double J, he's liable to feel cheated."

"You're very smart." She took a long swallow of her wine. "Good thing you're in charge of this shindig."

His smile faded. "I thought we got that straight once before. I'm not in charge. You are. Well, you, Ida, Steve, Clyde, Ed, and whoever else is in on that limited partnership thing Frank drew up."

She was high on success and wasn't paying as much attention as she should have. Laughing, she shook her head. "Semantics. Everyone knows you're the guy. We're just along for the ride. Literally."

"Not true." His tone was mild but his expression was extremely focused. "This is important, Georgie. I told you from day one that I didn't want to be the leader of this deal. Don't think you can slide me into that role and I won't notice."

She gazed at him. "But you bought a horse." Maybe that wasn't the wisest thing to say, either. He might not recognize his action as significant, but she thought it spoke volumes.

"So?"

"You told me you didn't want a horse because that would complicate your life. But you bought one last Wednesday. What's that all about?"

He sighed. "I decided I could deal with that kind of complication. My truck's powerful enough to haul a trailer, and having my own horse could prove useful from time to time, like now, for instance. In this situation, where we're establishing a business of guided trail rides, I like the idea that I'll be on a horse I own."

"I actually like it, too. You've spent a lot of time with him, and I'm sure you'll spend a lot more before we take out the first group. You and Storm Cloud will be a solid team on the trail ride."

"That's the plan."

"But it's the long-range implications I'm talking about. You have a responsibility for an animal that possibly could live another forty years."

His jaw tightened. "I'm aware of how long horses can live. What's your point?"

Her point was that he was straying into commitment territory. Some marriages didn't last forty years. By taking on the care of this horse, he'd created a bond that could continue into his golden years. The man she'd met three weeks ago would never have considered such a drastic step.

He studied her as he sipped his beer. "You know what?"

"What?"

"I'm trying to figure out how we got from having fun dancing the two-step to sitting here debating this depressing topic."

"It's just that a horse is a major—"

"I know. But don't make too much of it, okay? I wanted a flashy horse the way some guys want a sports car. Getting Storm Cloud was no more significant than that."

She didn't agree, but he was in an argumentative mood so she decided to let it go. "Where's Ed, by the way? Doesn't he usually come down and play poker with you guys?"

"He does, and that's something we need to talk about."

"That he plays poker?"

"No, that he's not here. His arthritis is acting up really bad right now. He called me an hour ago and said he didn't feel up to making the ride with us tomorrow."

"Oh."

"Yeah."

She couldn't very well admit that she was thrilled at the idea that she would have a few hours alone with him. He might be so used to avoiding her that he wouldn't think of doing anything improper. He'd also ride Storm Cloud, because he wanted to get the horse acclimated to the trail. His attention would be firmly on that horse.

Besides that, they'd just had tense words about whether Vince was mellowing toward the concept of long-term commitment. That discussion had not gone well. All things considered, they wouldn't need a chaperone tomorrow. They'd moved too far apart and the temptation wouldn't be there the way it had been three weeks ago.

She studied him. "I guess it doesn't really matter whether Ed goes or not."

His gaze intensified, but then the heat was gone as he relaxed and took another sip of his beer. "No, I suppose it doesn't."

"Speaking of that, we're leaving pretty early in the morning, so I should head on home."

"Suit yourself."

She left most of her wine. Anastasia decided to stay awhile longer, so Georgie left by herself. She flashed back to when she'd made this short trek with Vince the night he'd agreed to take the trail-boss job.

He'd been wild for her then, but it looked as if she'd effectively put out that fire. That had been the wise course of action. Reservations were coming in for the first trail ride and she knew in her bones the project would take off. They had a wealthy Dallas businessman on board, for God's sake.

Once the operation was successful, she'd start looking for Vince's replacement and he'd be free to load Storm Cloud into that trailer and leave town. He wouldn't be back again. She knew that in her bones, too. When it came to Vince, she'd dodged a bullet. She wished she felt happier about it.

After Georgie left, Vince nursed his beer and considered his situation. If she thought taking a trail ride alone with him in the morning was no problem, maybe she'd become immune to him. She was a strong-willed woman who might have that kind of control over her impulses.

God, how he wished he did. But knowing that she'd apparently squashed her attraction to him should help. Even so, the thought of spending several hours on a private trail ride with her made his blood pump faster. If he allowed himself to think about it in any great detail, his overheated blood collected south of the Mason-Dixon Line.

Tomorrow would be a challenge. But he'd be damned if he'd tip his hand and let her find out that he wanted her more than ever. He'd trained horses until he was saddle sore and played poker until he was bleary-eyed. He slept pretty well because of all the activity, but his dreams . . .

She'd mentioned a dream she'd had about him once, but from the way she'd acted tonight, she didn't dream about him anymore. Well, if she could push him out of her thoughts that fast, then he didn't need to be fixated on her. He ought to take a page out of her book and learn how to turn off this inconvenient longing.

They were never meant to be, anyway. They were too

different. She'd underlined that a few minutes ago when she'd tried to get him to say that buying Storm Cloud was some kind of sign that he was becoming domesticated.

He'd bought the gelding because it was time he had a horse of his own. A cowboy shouldn't go his whole life without ever owning a horse. Pulling a horse trailer wasn't that big a deal, and he'd always lived below his means so he could afford the expense of a horse.

Storm Cloud had been a great distraction the past few days, but he was also fun to have around. Outthinking him had become a game, and the horse's behavior had improved enormously in only a few days of constant attention and training. In a year or two he'd be amazing.

Vince hadn't expected the sense of satisfaction that training Storm Cloud had given him. He'd always enjoyed working with horses and figuring out their personality quirks, but inevitably he'd leave those horses behind when he quit the job. This time the horse would go with him. He'd reap the benefits of all the training in the years ahead.

True, he hadn't figured out the forty-year thing. He knew intellectually that horses could live that long but he hadn't thought about the actuality. It was fine, though. The thought of spending that many years with Storm Cloud made him smile. They'd have a good time.

"You look happy." Cheeks flushed, Anastasia sat in the seat Georgie had recently vacated. She'd brought a glass of water with her and she fanned herself with a napkin.

"I usually am happy." The music had continued but the guys were back at the poker table picking up the scattered chips. "No more dancing?"

"They wore me out." She chugged half the water. "I tried to get them to dance with each other but they claimed it would take several more beers before they'd be ready for that."

"I'm tempted to buy them a few rounds. It would be well worth the outlay."

"I know, right?" She folded the napkin and looked at him. "I was surprised Georgie went home. She was super excited about those reservations. I thought she'd stay and party."

"We have an early trail ride in the morning."

"Nah, that's not it. I think you two got into a little spat. That's what I think."

"Not really."

"Spin it how you want, but I know my sister. If she left when we had so much to celebrate, then she has her undies in a bunch over something."

Vince wished she hadn't phrased it quite that way. He'd already spent many long nights imagining Georgie's undies, only they were never in a bunch. Mostly they were on her for a second or two and then they were gone.

"Looks like you'll get a chance to see Charmaine again. Did Georgie tell you about that?"

"Nope. Is she coming home for a visit?"

"Not to see us. For the first trail ride. When my mother found out a rich man had made a reservation, she told Georgie that Charmaine had to go on that ride or else."

Vince stared at her. "You're kidding."

"I wish."

"She's really trying to marry Charmaine off to someone with money?"

"It's all she talks about. She's desperate to get out of

Bickford, so she wants both of us to find wealthy husbands. I told her no way, Jose. Ugh City. But Charmaine's gone along with it. That's why she's in Dallas where all the money is. It would be ironic if she landed her sugar daddy right here in Bickford."

"I'm speechless."

"So Georgie didn't mention any of that before?"

"No. I would have remembered. I don't think I've ever met your mother." And now he hoped he wouldn't have to. He hated to think that Georgie put up with such a woman living in the house she cherished.

"Georgie thinks the whole idea is outrageous, but she'd probably love to have my mother move out of that house. Unfortunately, Mom told me if she could ever leave, she'll sell it."

"Your mother owns it?" Now he felt even worse for Georgie.

"She inherited everything, even the store. Georgie's dad was devoted to her and she always pretended like she loved Bickford, but she doesn't. Anyway, I haven't told Georgie that she might sell, and don't you, either. She has enough to worry about."

"But if— What's your mother's name?"

"Evelyn."

"If Evelyn owns the store, she could sell that, too, right?"

"Yes, and I think she would once she doesn't need the income from it anymore. She thinks Georgie's devotion to the store and the town is silly, and if she took it all away she could force Georgie to do something better with her life."

Vince had a few choice things to say about that, but they were talking about Anastasia's mother, after all.

Anastasia was in a tough position, too. She might not like her mother's behavior, but she didn't want to be disloyal, either. She walked a fine line between two women with totally opposite views. And she loved them both.

"Thanks for telling me about that," he said. "I won't discuss it with Georgie, but it helps me understand her a little better." No wonder she didn't want to risk having an affair that could potentially interfere with this project. Wild Horse Canyon Adventures could turn out to be the lifeline she could grab if her stepmother left her dangling.

"Georgie's great. I don't know what I'd do without her."

"She is great." He was only beginning to appreciate how great. "And she's no dummy. She's probably aware that your mother could sell everything, but worrying about it in advance isn't sensible."

"And Georgie's nothing if not sensible."

"I've discovered that." Vince thought about their ride tomorrow, which by all indications would be very sensible, indeed. Now that he knew what was at stake for her, he understood why that was important.

# CHAPTER 18

Georgie woke long before dawn, a good two hours before she was scheduled to saddle Prince and ride over to Ed's stable. Her stomach was in knots, which was stupid. She was going on a trail ride. No big deal.

Except it was a big deal because it was the closest thing to a date she'd had in a very long time. And the furthest thing from a date, too, because nothing the least bit romantic would go on today. That concept was complicated in itself without the addition of her growing feelings, both physical and emotional, for Vince.

She'd tried to convince herself that he was nothing more than a friend, but her body wasn't buying that. As she lay in the darkness staring up at the ceiling, she could feel every nerve sparking at the thought of being alone with him for several hours.

They'd only chanced being alone once, that morning in her store, and it had been electric. She'd never forget his little speech about not bringing condoms yet still imagining all the things they could do without one. That was when they'd agreed to make sure they were never alone again. Yet they would be today.

And it would be *fine*. He seemed to have lost interest and she would control herself. Yes, he was sexy, and he'd be even more appealing in cowboy mode riding Storm Cloud. She'd only seen him on a horse one time—the day he and his friends had gone after the Ghost, and he'd looked damn good mounted on Cinder. He'd look even better today.

Impatient with the way her body mocked her by growing hot and achy, she flung back the covers and climbed out of bed. Lying there thinking about Vince astride a powerful black horse wasn't helping. She'd get dressed and then make their lunch. She'd agreed to pack one because they weren't sure how long they'd be gone.

After making turkey sandwiches, a subtle hat-tip to Wild Turkey Canyon, she put them in a zippered nylon pouch along with a few chocolate chip cookies and two water bottles. When she saddled Prince she'd tuck everything in a saddlebag. She'd done this hundreds of times. Theoretically the routine should calm her nerves.

It didn't. She should eat breakfast, but that didn't sound like a good idea considering her jumpy stomach. Instead she checked the website on her phone and was startled to see two more reservations for the inaugural ride. She recognized the couple, Beth and Drew Hightower. They'd stayed at the Double J almost every April for as long as she could remember.

Eight people. They were officially full for the ride taking place in less than two weeks. Anyone who wanted to go now would have to settle for another weekend. She wondered what impact a wealthy Dallas businessman might have on future reservations. Maybe none, or maybe . . . no, she wouldn't project how this man, Randolph Jamison Steele III, would affect their fledgling project. She'd just wait and see. But she liked being able to tell Vince this morning that the first ride was full.

She wouldn't be going on the first couple of rides. Ed would be the other trail guide until Georgie hired someone to take over the store while she was gone. She'd intended to have someone lined up by now, but finding the right person was turning out to be a challenge. Anastasia could probably do it, but that wasn't a permanent solution. If all went well, Anastasia would be too busy with her art to fill in at the store.

By now the sky was light enough for her to go out and saddle Prince. The poor horse hadn't been ridden since the incident with the Ghost. He'd performed admirably that day, however, thanks to intensive training years ago. Her father had helped her teach the big bay to stay calm even when she cracked a whip in his immediate vicinity. Prince was steady as a rock.

"I don't want him spooking at anything," her father had said. "He's carrying precious cargo."

"I miss my dad so much, Prince." She buckled his bridle in place. "Why'd he have to go off and leave us with that woman, anyway?"

Affectionate as always, Prince nudged her shoulder.

"At least I have you, and I promise to spend more time with you in the future. I've been distracted by a certain cowboy."

By the time Prince was saddled and the lunch was stowed, she had another thirty minutes before she was supposed to meet Vince at the stable. Shoving her phone in the pocket of her denim jacket, she wondered what the heck she could do for thirty minutes. Then her phone chimed.

Pulling it out, she saw a text from Vince. *I'm ready. How about U?*

Her heart began to race. One silly text telling her he was early, and she was imagining all sorts of things that probably weren't true—that he was eager to see her, that he was as nervous about this ride as she was, that he'd also been awake for hours.

She calmed down enough to send him a return text. *B right there.* Then she put away her phone and mounted up. The steady motion of Prince's gait as they walked over to the stable was comforting.

The sun wasn't up yet when she arrived at the stable, but she had enough of the pearly predawn light to see Vince mounted on Storm Cloud. The horse was beautiful, but the man . . . She was in so much trouble it wasn't even funny.

There was nothing remarkable about his outfit. Instead of the chaps, spurs, and vest routine he'd brought out for the Ghost incident, he'd worn regular jeans and boots, a blue plaid Western shirt, and a denim jacket not much different from hers. His hat was the same one she'd seen on him countless times, a black Stetson that had seen better days.

None of that should have caused her to tremble. But regardless, looking at him inspired a shiver of anticipation. She doubted that he would have noticed, and even if he had, she'd pass it off as a response to the cool breeze.

"Good morning," he called out.

"Same to you. I checked the website before I came over, and we have another couple, which brings us to our max of eight." She walked Prince over to where Vince waited by the side of the stable wall.

"Excellent." His grin flashed, a smile guaranteed to turn a girl's head.

She wouldn't let hers be turned. She drew up alongside him. "I was worried, but now the next inquiries will be told the first ride is sold out. I like the sound of that."

"It's the sound of success, Georgie." His voice was warm. "Congratulations."

She was close enough now to get a whiff of his aftershave. She'd developed a fondness for its pine scent. "I'm not counting my chickens, yet, but I have to say the future looks promising for Wild Horse Canyon Adventures."

"And you've worked hard for that."

"So have you."

He shrugged. "Like I said, I'm just a small cog in the wheel. But I'm happy for you. You deserve for this to work out."

"Thanks." There was something in his tone that hadn't been there before, a cheerleader quality that told her he'd found out a few things about her circumstances. Her money was on Anastasia, who'd stayed at Sadie's after Georgie had left.

She decided not to question him about it. No sense in getting into a personal discussion when they had a job to accomplish. Personal discussion would only lower the barriers between them, and they certainly didn't want to do that.

He gestured toward the path leading to the trail. "After you."

"You want me to lead?"

"Absolutely. You know this territory better than I do. I'm here to make notes and learn. Some of it came back to me when I rode out here with Mac and Travis, but I don't pretend to be as up on this as you are."

"You're going to make notes?"

"I am." He reached inside his jacket and pulled out a small pad of paper. "After we've taken this preliminary ride, I'll come back out here with my notes and retrace the route until I have it down. I don't want any of us fumbling around come the big day."

She gazed at him. "You're not quite who I thought you were."

"If you mean I'm not a total screw-up, I'll take that as a compliment."

"I never thought you were a total screw-up. You've spent plenty of time doing this kind of work, and I've never heard anyone say you were careless about it. But I didn't expect . . . well, the notes and the plan to practice the route."

He laughed. "Maybe I just have a bad memory and I'm trying to compensate."

"Or maybe you've accepted this job and you intend to do it to the best of your ability. I think you have standards and you intend to live up to them."

"I do, but you make me sound like some kind of exception to the rule. Mac or Travis would have done the same. We may act goofy sometimes, but we all realize that when you put greenhorns together with a string of two-thousand-pound animals, you'd better be paying attention, and you'd better not leave anything to chance."

She drew in a breath of the sweet morning air and let it out, buying herself time as a sudden onslaught of emotion ebbed away. She was falling for him. Too bad for her. "I appreciate hearing you say that. You just made me really glad that I asked you to take part in this venture." There. That sounded businesslike.

He met her gaze. "I'm glad you did, too, Georgie."

For one heady moment, she let herself look into those eyes and pretend that he meant that as something more than a simple statement of gratitude. She allowed herself to imagine that he was still crazy about her and wished that life could be different so that they could indulge in what would be an amazing love affair.

But she didn't dare prolong that moment or he might suspect that in spite of all she'd said about not wanting to get involved, she longed for him with an intensity that scared the devil out of her. He couldn't ever know that. She'd be humiliated beyond belief.

She straightened in the saddle. "We need to go."

"Like I said, you're the leader."

"Then we're off." She nudged Prince into a fast walk. The first part of the trail was common knowledge and didn't require any narration from her, but she was super aware of Vince behind her.

The soft creak of his saddle reminded her of the parts of him currently in contact with that leather. She'd never fully appreciated the erotic image of a well-endowed man on a horse until now. Conversation wasn't necessary at this stage of the ride, but if she didn't start talking, she was liable to indulge in fantasies about the man riding behind her.

Talking about his new horse seemed like a safe topic. "Storm Cloud seems pretty steady."

"He's coming along. He's going to be a good mount for me."

"I'm glad, especially since you didn't get to ride him before you made the decision."

Vince chuckled. "That would have embarrassed both him and me, with him feeling honor-bound to try all his tricks, and me demonstrating what a good rider I am. Like a mother whose kid throws a tantrum in the grocery store, neither of us would have come out of it looking good."

"But we're always advised to ride a horse before buying him."

"I know, which is why I had that in my head, but the minute I tuned in to Storm Cloud, I could tell that riding him in front of an audience wasn't a good way to start our relationship. We've had our disagreements, but it's been in private, where we could both save face if necessary."

She hadn't given him credit for being that sensitive, but she should have. Ed had mentioned that Vince was good with horses and Ed didn't hand out praise often. She took a chance on a slightly more personal question. "Did you grow up with horses?"

"No."

When he didn't elaborate, she let it go. The birds were waking up and she picked out a mockingbird going through its repertoire, along with the distinct caw of a raven interspersed with the twitter of smaller birds. She loved this time of day when the canyon came alive. Maybe if she immersed herself in her surroundings she wouldn't obsess about her sexy trail partner.

Then, surprisingly, he offered some information. "My dad worked in the oil fields."

She noticed he'd said *worked*. "He doesn't now?"

"He's on disability. He and my mom live in Fort Worth."

Little by little, she was adding pieces to the puzzle that was Vince Durant. "So you must have had a chance to see them before you came here."

"I did."

"And they're doing okay?" She wondered if she'd get another short answer.

"Yeah, but the job took its toll on my dad. It's not an easy life. Hard work, moving a lot."

Ah. She'd wondered about that when he'd been so concerned about relocating the horses if Wild Horse Canyon Adventures didn't make it. "So you moved a lot, too."

"We did, but that didn't bother me. The oil rigs aren't my thing, though. Once I figured out that cowboys weren't extinct, espccially in Texas, I set out to work on ranches, which were mostly dude ranches. That's okay. I don't have to herd cattle to feel like a real man."

Georgie listened in fascination. It was the most he'd ever revealed about himself, and she doubted he would have told her any of that if they'd been sitting face-to-face. But out here on the trail he might have decided it was a safe thing to do.

Or maybe he was trying to keep from thinking about sex, too. Either way, she wanted to keep the conversation rolling. "Except for when I went away to school, I've never lived anywhere besides here."

"I figured as much."

"Does that seem boring to you?" She thought it must. When her father was alive the family had traveled a little, mostly around Texas and a couple of trips to New Mexico. But taking a vacation somewhere didn't count the same as living in a different place.

"Not boring as much as really foreign to me. You grew up in that house. It's the only place you've called home. I've had so many places that were temporarily my home that they blur together."

"And that seems foreign to me. I can't imagine it."

"It was what I knew. My folks' town house in Fort Worth is the first place they've owned. But I don't have any memories stored there, either. It's just a place I go to see my parents."

He was becoming more real to her with each passing moment, but that had its dangers, too. Riding in silence invited her to fantasize about him sexually, but getting to know him through easy conversation invited a different fantasy—that they'd create a relationship that wouldn't end with him leaving Bickford and never looking back.

Apparently she couldn't win unless she wanted to chat about the weather. That didn't appeal to her, so she chose the lesser of two evils. "With all that moving as a kid, I'll bet you're more resilient than I am."

"I don't know about that."

"You must be. If you're forced to move, like when the Double J closed down, you can do it. If I'm forced to leave that house . . ." She hadn't meant to say that. She didn't like to put the thought out into the universe.

"I hope you don't ever have to, but if you did, you'd make it. You're tough, Georgie."

That made her laugh. "No, I'm not."

"Any woman who rides full tilt into a clearing cracking a whip over her head is— "

"Oh, for heaven's sake. That's a parlor trick. If you had a few hours of training and the right horse, you could do it, too."

"I'll bet it would take more than a few hours."

"Probably not in your case. You already know how to rope and ride, plus you have a sense of rhythm and good coordination. That pretty much guarantees sex . . . I mean *success.* Sorry. Got a little tongue-tied there." She forced a laugh, but inside she was dying of embarrassment.

He didn't join in her laughter, which was troubling. The chatter of small birds and the whistle of a hawk in flight filled the silence as she struggled to think of something, anything, to say.

Then he spoke. "Ever hear of a Freudian slip?"

Not a change of topic. Too bad. "Um, I think so." Oh, yes, and her previous comment had *Freudian slip* flashing all around it in colored neon lights.

"This psychologist who was a guest at the Double J told me about it. You mean to say one thing but what comes out is what your subconscious is dwelling on."

"And sometimes you just get tongue-tied."

"Sometimes."

She didn't have to look at him to know he was smiling. He might even be trying not to laugh. Nothing she said now would help the situation, either. The more she insisted that sex wasn't the main thing on her mind, the more he'd think that it was. And he'd be right. Busted.

# CHAPTER 19

Vince didn't know whether to laugh or cuss. He'd thought he was riding into this canyon with a woman who'd written him off. Sure, he couldn't help the tug of lust whenever he looked at her, but he'd had that under control until her Freudian slip.

He'd been intrigued by the concept when he'd found out about it and had noticed that it happened a lot. Most of the time it was just funny, but this time it was both funny and arousing as hell. Now what?

Now nothing, that's what. Just because she still wanted him didn't mean he should do anything about it. Their conversation had made him even more aware of how different they were. He wouldn't know how to live in one place for the rest of his life, and that was all she could imagine.

But the differences went deeper than that. She was the kind of woman who got attached — to people, places, and animals. He was the kind of man who had no practice in forming attachments. She'd implied that buying Storm Cloud was significant, but he rejected that concept. One small choice didn't mean he'd had a personality transplant.

They left the open range with its thickets of mesquite and wound their way into the shadows of the canyon. She hadn't tried to initiate conversation, probably because she was afraid of revealing more secret thoughts. But she'd closed the barn door after the horse got out.

Besides, they needed to discuss the trail ride. So he broke the silence. "I was thinking I'd get a bird guide to take along. I can identify the wildlife, but I'm not up on all the birds."

"Good idea, but don't buy one. I have a small book that would be perfect. You can borrow that while you're here."

That was pointed. No sense paying for something he'd only need a short while. She was right, but it irked him that she was already envisioning his departure. "That's okay. I'll get my own." Maybe he'd get into bird watching. It could happen.

"Suit yourself." She shifted her weight in the saddle.

He shouldn't watch her do that. He really shouldn't. He shouldn't imagine what it would feel like to cup her firm little bottom and align her hips with his. And he especially shouldn't be thinking about what would happen after that.

"We're coming up on a trail that goes off to the left," she said. "It's a good way to extend the length of the ride. You don't want to go straight to the meadow."

"Not if we're going to use it for the overnight camp, which I think we should." Now he was imagining what could happen in that meadow today. The grass was still new and soft.

"I agree. It's perfect for that."

Perfect for other things, too. Things that shouldn't be on his mind. Except here he was, riding behind her while her body moved in time with her horse. She was so delicious.

Thinking of how *he* wanted to move in time with Georgie must have caused him to unconsciously tighten his thighs. Storm Cloud snorted and leaped forward, nearly bumping into her horse. Vince pulled back on the reins. "Easy, boy. Sorry about that, Georgie."

Prince danced a little but Georgie soon had him settled down. She turned around in the saddle. "Everything okay back there?"

"Yep. Something must have startled him."

"To tell the truth, I thought he'd be harder to handle. So far this has been a piece of cake."

Yeah, except for the extreme sexual frustration of the rider. "The day's not over." Vince had counted on his horse acting up some. Working with a misbehaving mount would have helped keep his mind off Georgie and the constant temptation she presented. Storm Cloud wasn't cooperating.

"So do you want to make a note about this trail?"

"Um, yes, yes, I do. Pull up for a bit." He needed to get his mind back on business and fast. Just now he'd been staring at her mouth. After both horses halted, he found his pad of paper and a pen, both of which advertised the Bickford Hotel.

Georgie turned Prince back to face him. "I recognize that paper and pen. Steve and Myra were thinking of not ordering any more of them, but now they're stocking up. Anastasia's designing Wild Horse Canyon Adventures bumper stickers. Did I tell you that?"

"No, but I want one for my truck." He finished making his notes and tucked the pad and pen back inside his jacket.

"Hey, that would be good if you had a bumper sticker. When you travel around you can be our ambassador."

"Right." There it was again, a reminder that he was only temporary. He should be glad that she accepted it so readily. Hell, he *was* glad, but she didn't have to keep mentioning it.

"So here's what I think about the trail ride. We'll take this part fast to save time, but you can meander during the actual event. Let them stop to take pictures. Point out the flora and fauna. A little history about Coronado, the Apaches, stuff like that."

"Ed gave me a couple of books on the history. I've read both of them." When he couldn't sleep from thinking about Georgie, he'd pull out a history book until he dozed off.

"Okay, good. The terrain along this trail is fairly wide and level, so we can canter if you want. Let our guys stretch their legs, get some aerobic exercise."

"Works for me." He couldn't speak for Storm Cloud, but he wouldn't mind blowing off a little steam.

"There's a potential lunch spot at the point where we turn back toward the meadow and the creek. We can stop there or just go on to the meadow."

"Let's go on to the meadow." He was playing with fire to suggest it, considering his state of mind. But he also wanted to change her perception of him in connection with that meadow. Last time they'd been there together had been confrontational. He didn't want to leave her with that memory.

He had another memory he'd love to leave her with. Would that be so terrible? Some gentle pleasure, a moment out of time, his one chance to hold her when nobody was around to judge or condemn. And that would be it. Once they rode back to town, he'd leave her strictly alone.

Probably a really, really bad idea. Unless . . . well, he'd wait and see how things turned out.

She fastened the string on her hat under her chin. "Ready?"

He pulled his hat a little lower. He had a string but hated using it. She looked cute with a string under her chin. He wasn't so fond of that look on him. He'd grab the hat if necessary. "Ready."

Georgie was ready for something, either for this ride to be over or . . . something. Vince might be doing fine, but she was swamped with X-rated images every time she looked at him. Or even when she didn't. His sexy self was burned into her retina.

Facing Prince forward again, she nudged him into a trot and then quickly into a canter. That was better. Wind in her face, her horse moving under her, and the scenery sliding past at a much faster pace.

If they continued moseying along the trail as they had been, she couldn't be responsible for her actions. At least twice she'd considered leaping off Prince, pulling Vince down from Storm Cloud, and kissing him until she ran out of breath. She'd been having wild thoughts, such as *what would be so bad about doing that?*

Probably plenty, so she'd decided to get them moving and shorten the time she had to be alone with a man who pushed all her buttons. He'd always had that effect on her, but now that she saw him as a nice guy in addition to being hotter than hell, the urge to jump him had become almost irresistible. Fortunately she couldn't do that from a fast-moving horse.

They paused briefly at the little grove of oak and juniper she thought would make a good lunch stop for the trail ride. Vince made some quick notes, and they were off again, cantering when they could and trotting when the trail was less forgiving.

About a quarter-mile from the meadow, she slowed Prince to a walk and pointed to a rocky outcropping. "That's the marker I use to know I'm getting close to the meadow. You can't see the cottonwoods yet but you'll be able to when we round this bend. Let's walk them in so they can cool down."

"Good idea."

He had the sexiest voice of any man she'd known, too. Two words spoken in that husky baritone and the value of the fast ride began to drain away. Her erotic fantasies came back with a vengeance.

Maybe the Ghost and his herd would be in the meadow. That would provide a good distraction. He probably wasn't there, though. The noise they'd made cantering down the trail would have alerted him. If he had been there, he was probably guiding his charges to some other part of the canyon.

"I hope you weren't counting on seeing the Ghost," she said. "He probably heard us coming."

"He wasn't on my agenda. I hope to be seeing a lot of him in the next few weeks."

"You will. You'll need to caution everybody to keep it down when you approach any of the areas where he might be. Sometimes he hides the herd in that grove of aspen and oak by your lunch stop. Not often, but you could get lucky."

"I'd like that."

She heard the smile in his voice and resisted the urge

to turn around and glare at him for teasing her. That might backfire. Vince wearing a killer smile was dynamite, and she had a very short fuse.

The gurgle of Sing-Song Creek, which she could hear before the meadow came into view, always gave her a lift. She loved this place and felt a moment of doubt. Would bringing trail rides here every weekend ruin it?

But she had to take that chance. Everyone who wanted Bickford to continue as a community had to take that chance. She'd monitor the situation as best she could and hope for the best.

Even though she didn't expect the wild horses to be grazing in the meadow, she guided Prince carefully out into the open. The clearing was empty of horses, but she could see the spots where they'd helped themselves to the new spring grass. They hadn't eaten all the wildflowers, though. Splashes of yellow and purple dotted the edges of the meadow.

Vince rode up beside her. "Seems a shame to dig a fire pit in the middle of this place."

"I know, but that's part of the image, sleeping under the stars around a campfire."

"I know, but this . . . belongs to the wild horses. I think it should be preserved if at all possible."

"Vince, I don't know if it is possible. This is the obvious spot to pitch the tents, and camping beside a stream is always appealing to people."

He scanned the area. "Where does that little path go?" He pointed to a faint trail that paralleled the creek.

"Back up into the canyon, I guess. It's too narrow for Prince so I've never followed it."

"Let's leave the horses here and see where it leads. We might find an alternative."

"You want to *hike*?"

He grinned at her. "You say that like it's the equivalent of hugging a porcupine."

"You're wearing boots."

"I know. So are you. It'll be fine." He dismounted. "Let's go explore alternatives to digging up this meadow."

"I'll go, but I don't hold out much hope." She climbed down and led Prince over to a tree so she could tie him. "Even if we find something, we'd have to create a wider trail to get the horses over there. And what about the chuck wagon?"

"I haven't figured that out, not even if we park it here." Vince tied Storm Cloud to a different tree. "I think we'll have to take it apart, haul it here in pieces, and reassemble it on-site. The guys did an excellent job, but the thing's ginormous. Trundling it back and forth every weekend won't be good for it."

"I guess setting it up permanently might work." She walked with him over to the trail he'd spotted. "So you'd store the tents and sleeping bags there, too?"

"Yeah, in weatherproof containers of some kind. Then all Henry has to bring in is the food. Less transporting things back and forth would be better." He started up the narrow path, which made a gradual ascent.

"Good point." The trail was barely wide enough for one person, so she followed behind. "I think we're literally on a bunny trail, Vince. Are you sure you want to follow it?"

"Trust me."

She decided to do that. He operated in a more creative way than she did and followed his instincts far more readily. She didn't want to dig up this pristine meadow, either. If he could figure out a way not to, so much the better.

They dodged around bushes and stepped over rocks as they climbed. Georgie had to watch the trail to make sure she didn't trip, so when he stopped in front of her, she ran into him. It was like hitting a solid wall. His back was all muscle.

"Sorry! Should have signaled!" He turned around and grabbed her arm to keep her from stumbling. His grip was firm, yet incredibly gentle. "Sorry," he murmured again.

"No worries." She felt the warmth of his touch travel with the speed of light through every nerve in her body. He wasn't holding on very tightly, and she'd regained her balance. She should pull away. Instead she lifted her gaze to his.

He drew in a sharp breath. "Damn, Georgie."

As she watched the clear blue of his eyes slowly darken, anticipation thrummed in her veins.

"Before this day is over, I'm going to kiss you." His husky promise hung in the air between them. "But this is not the time or the place." He loosened his grip on her arm. "I hear the sound of a waterfall. Let's keep going."

She nodded, not trusting herself to open her mouth in case a whimper escaped. When he reached a mass of heavy foliage, she figured he'd want to turn around, although she could hear the waterfall now, too.

He wrestled with the branches and created an opening. "You go on through and I'll hold these back. You can let me know if it's worth me coming through there."

After taking off her hat, she hung it by the string from a bush. Then she crawled on her hands and knees through the space he'd given her. She kept her head down so the branches wouldn't scratch her face, and her jacket protected her arms.

Once she was free of the bushes, she stood. "Oh, my goodness!" She gasped in wonder.

"That good, huh? I'm coming through."

She spun around to help, but he'd already pushed himself through the opening. He'd left his hat behind, too, and bits of leaves and twigs were in his hair and stuck to his clothes.

He didn't seem to mind as he stared at the box canyon that lay before them. "Perfect!"

She turned back to the view. "I know. It's like something out of a movie."

The canyon walls had a reddish tinge and a delicate waterfall cascaded in a single thin stream from the highest cliff to a small pool below. The pool fed the creek that undulated gracefully through the clearing before rushing down to the meadow below. The grass wasn't as lush here as in the meadow, no doubt because the box canyon got less sun. But the area was the right size for a chuck wagon, a few tents, and a fire pit.

"Guaranteed not many people know about this place," Vince said.

"And the horses wouldn't come here because there's no exit."

"That's true." Vince glanced back at the hole he'd made in the bushes. "There's barely an entrance. I can clear it, though, and widen the trail. I think there's time before we have to bring in the chuck wagon parts."

She had a pretty good idea of how much work would go into clearing the brush and widening the trail. Working alone, he'd need a chunk of time, and he should continue to work with the horses. "If we started early in the morning, I could help."

He smiled and shook his head. "I know you could, but it's really not practical when you have to open the store at ten."

"Then see if Ike can do it, and maybe even Henry. They're the two youngest men in Bickford, and I think they'd get a kick out of helping."

"I'll do that." He brushed leaves and twigs from his jacket. "Good idea."

She glanced at him. Several leaves and a couple of twigs were tangled in his dark hair. "Lean down here. You have stuff in your curly locks."

"It's not curly. It's wavy."

"Whatever, you look like you're trying to camouflage yourself." She motioned with her hand. "Tilt your head down so I can get it out."

"Yes, ma'am." He leaned over and she plucked the first twig and tossed it to the ground. Then she pulled out the second one. "You have leaves everywhere." She combed her fingers through his thick hair. She told herself it was the only way she'd find them all, but oh, did that feel good.

"Got 'em all?"

"I don't know. Let me double-check." Closing her eyes, she worked her fingers though the silken strands one more time, slowly.

"Georgie." His voice had a rough edge to it.

"Hmm?"

"Don't play games with me, lady."

She opened her eyes. "I don't know what you—"

"I think you do." He captured her wrist and drew her hand away. He kept a hold on her as he straightened and looked down at her. "You know exactly what you do to me, how your touch gets me hot."

She lifted her chin. "It's a two-way street. You know what you do to me when you look at me like that."

His voice softened. "Do I get you hot, Georgie?"

She began to quiver. "Yes."

"Want to get even hotter?"

She forgot to breathe.

"I'm going to kiss you," he murmured, drawing her closer. "It seems we've come to the time and the place."

# CHAPTER 20

Vince savored the heat in her brown eyes for a brief moment. Oh, yes, she wanted him. He couldn't believe she craved him with the same intensity he felt for her, but that fire burning in her gaze was more than enough to tell him she did.

Three long weeks he'd suffered, watching her smile, watching her laugh, and remembering the velvet feel of her mouth. As he closed his eyes and touched his lips to hers, the sensation was everything he'd remembered. This time she met him halfway, her arms already around his neck, her breasts snug against his chest.

He didn't have to wonder if she wanted the thrust of his tongue. She parted her lips and invited him in. He accepted that invitation without hesitation, sliding deep as she moaned in pleasure.

The last time he'd held her this way they'd been standing in the middle of town under a lighted sign. Not so today. He'd found a hidden paradise away from prying eyes. The birds wouldn't gossip about what he and Georgie did here. The rabbits wouldn't care if he peeled off her jacket and unsnapped her shirt. The squirrels wouldn't give a damn if he reached behind her back and unhooked her bra.

. She trembled in his arms and whimpered when he cupped one full breast and stroked his thumb over her tight nipple. Her satin skin was so warm, so supple beneath his fingers. But he had the hands of a working cowboy, rough and callused.

He interrupted the kiss to ask if she minded that roughness, but she pulled his head down again, her mouth hot and demanding. So he stroked and massaged her breast because she seemed to want that, and God knows he did. She groaned and pushed her hips against his.

He wanted to accept that invitation, too, but he wouldn't. Couldn't, in fact. True to his word, he hadn't brought a condom. And that was as it should be. Foregoing that ultimate connection meant he could live with himself. He would give, but he wouldn't take.

Yet he needed a little something for himself—the chance to see her breasts rosy from his touch and soon wet from his seeking mouth. Continuing to kiss her, he drew off her shirt and let it fall to the ground. Her bra was next, and when that was gone, he lifted his head to gaze down at her flushed face. "I want to look at you."

Her lashes fluttered upward to reveal a gaze that spoke of total surrender. His chest tightened as he realized how vulnerable she was at this moment. He'd guessed that she hadn't been with someone in a long time, and he was glad that she'd chosen to let down her guard with him instead of some idiot who would take advantage of her.

Resting his hands on her slender shoulders, he held her away from him and let the morning sunlight caress her pale skin. "So beautiful," he murmured. "So sweet."

She greeted his praise with a heartfelt sigh. "And so lonely."

"I know."

"No, you don't."

She was right, he thought. As a man, and one on the move, he'd had opportunities, whereas she'd had virtually none. He traced her collarbone with his forefinger. "No tan lines."

"I'm inside a lot."

Her full breasts bore the signs of his eager touch, though. He touched the red marks gently before looking into her eyes. "My hands are too rough. I've hurt you."

"Not at all." Her slow smile convinced him she meant that.

"I can make it better." Leaning down, he kissed each reddened place on her delicate skin. Then he began to lap at those chafed spots with slow sweeps of his tongue.

Her breathing quickened and her lashes drifted downward again. "That's very . . . nice."

"There's more." Balancing the weight of her breast in his palm, he closed his mouth over her nipple and drew it in deep.

She whimpered and clutched his head with both hands as he sucked in and out, in and out. Her fingertips tightened against his scalp as she arched into his caress.

Following his instincts, he freed the metal button on her jeans and drew the zipper down. As he continued to cradle her breast with one hand, he slid the other hand inside her panties. His blood thundered in his ears as he tunneled his fingers through damp curls and found her slick, hot, and ready for . . . But they wouldn't be doing that. No matter how his cock ached. No matter how desperate he was to sink into her body and find paradise there.

Instead he thrust his fingers deep. She clutched his shoulders and gasped. One stroke, two, three, and she was there, pulsing around his fingers, whimpering and shaking in the grip of her climax.

Yet he felt tension still buried deep within her. He suspected this had been only a preview of the passion she kept locked away. He wanted to free that passion, to unleash the bold woman who had charged toward him wielding a whip.

Releasing her breast, he sank to his knees and wrenched down her jeans, taking her panties with them. He shoved everything to the tops of her boots, which didn't give him a lot of maneuverability, but enough.

"Vince . . ." She moaned in protest but didn't try to stop him.

"Shh. I'm only kissing you." He settled in. He'd always thought she looked delicious, and now he knew that she tasted that way, too.

"That's . . . some . . . kiss . . ." She kept her balance by clutching the back of his head. "Oh, my." She began to pant. "You're pretty good . . . at this."

If he was, it was only because he'd been practicing for this special moment when he could make Georgie come apart in his arms. Kneading her firm bottom, he nibbled and licked, sucked and nuzzled until her groans became low and throaty. When she gasped out a soft curse, he had a feeling he was getting somewhere.

So he zeroed in, pushing her a little harder, a little faster, guiding her relentlessly toward an orgasm that would strip away her civilized veneer and expose her primitive instincts.

Her fingers tightened on his scalp and her breathing roughened.

Then she began to participate, tilting her hips and guiding his movements. "Yes, *there.*" She gasped. "Oh, Vince . . . oh, like that, just like that. Don't stop."

He wasn't about to. He had her now, the gutsy, passionate woman of his dreams.

"*Now!* Oh, please, *now!*"

He sucked hard, and with a shout of pure triumph that echoed off the canyon walls, she erupted in a spectacular climax. She almost knocked them both to the ground.

He took a quick look and decided they weren't beside any jagged rocks. Maybe the ground would be a good place to recover. After easing her jeans back up, even if they weren't buttoned and zipped, he managed to guide her down so that her head and shoulders were on her jacket.

Then he settled down beside her. Miraculously, nothing jabbed into his side. The ground was lumpy, but they happened to be in an area without any serious hazards. He would have endured that if necessary, but he didn't want rocks bruising her tender skin.

She lay there looking at him, her expression dazed.

"You okay?" He combed her hair back from her cheek.

She swallowed. "Yeah." Her voice was husky. "I haven't been this okay in . . . a while."

"Good. I mean not that it's been a while, but that you're feeling better."

Her mouth tilted in a smile. "You make it sound like I was sick."

"No, I— You know what I mean."

Her smile widened. "I do. You helped a frustrated lady out, and I appreciate it."

Irritation pricked him. "Hey, I wasn't simply doing my good deed for the day."

"But there wasn't much in it for you."

"That's where you're wrong. You let me kiss you, hold you, touch you." He hesitated. Oh, what the hell. "I've wanted to do that for a long time."

Her gaze searched his. "Surely you haven't been thinking about me ever since you left."

"Not constantly, but I did think about you." He traced her cheekbone with his finger. "It wasn't only the Ghost I wanted to see when I came back. I honestly didn't realize you were part of the reason I set up the reunion, but Mac and Travis helped me figure out that you were a big part of it."

"And then I gave you hell."

"Yeah, you did." He grinned. "Which was no more than I deserved."

She took a deep breath. "I like you, Vince. I like you a lot more than I thought I would."

"Nice to hear."

"I confess I've been wondering if . . . well, if the trail rides are a big success and everything, if you'd maybe stick around."

"You mean for a year or so?"

Her gaze was steady. "No, longer than that."

He wanted to tell her he would. No doubt she'd be happy about that because she was a long-term kind of woman. If he told her he'd be around for the foreseeable future, the barriers would come down and they'd become lovers. After today, he could imagine how wonderful that would be.

"But you won't stay, will you?" Disappointment and sadness edged her words.

"Georgie, I don't know how. Moving around and making new connections is what I'm good at. That's why guest ranches are such a great fit for me. The guests come and they go. Just like me."

"Maybe you could learn how to stay in one place."

He cupped her cheek. "Maybe I could, but I don't have a lot of confidence in that. I've been this way all my life."

"But you could at least try it out!"

"That wouldn't be fair to you. You deserve more than some cowboy who doesn't know whether he could cut it. Even though promising I'd give it my best shot would probably get me into your bed."

"It *would*."

"Or you into my bed." He tried to lighten the mood. "I'm past the age where I'll climb up drainpipes and crawl through windows to have sex."

A mixture of sadness and defiance shone in her eyes. "I could get you to do it. And the drainpipe on that Victorian would hold because I'm the one who bolted it on there."

"If anyone could get me to climb a drainpipe, it would be you. And I'm sure you have it bolted down tight." He brushed the pad of his thumb over her cheek.

"Then say you'll stick around. I dare you. Take a chance."

"I'm not taking that kind of chance with your heart, Georgie." He leaned forward and kissed her softly.

She bit his lip.

"Ouch!" He drew back and swiped his tongue over his bottom lip. He tasted blood. "Hey!"

"That's for being a damned coward, Vince." She scrambled to her feet and began pulling on her clothes. "And for your information, it was a different part of me I was thinking would benefit if I convinced you to stay. Don't worry about my heart, okay? What happens to it is none of your business."

"Obviously." He got to his feet and dusted himself off. So much for trying to be sensitive and caring. Now his lip was bleeding.

She finished dressing and stalked over to the overgrown bushes. "Meet you in the meadow."

"Hang on. I'll help you through the—"

"Never mind." She crawled through the opening.

He winced at the sound of branches scraping her clothes, but she clearly wanted nothing to do with his help. Too bad he couldn't have lied to her. All he had to do was make some vague promise about staying and she'd take it without asking questions.

But he wasn't made that way. She'd asked an honest question, one that had probably required some courage on her part. He couldn't shine her on just so he'd be allowed to make sweet love to her. And it would have been sweet, damn it. He'd thought so before and now he knew it for sure.

By the time he got to the meadow, she was there digging out their lunch from her saddlebag. She threw his sandwich at him. Good thing he was fairly coordinated. The water bottle sailed in his direction next. He managed to catch that, too, although he could swear she'd aimed for his head.

He thought that was it, which was plenty good enough, but then a cookie came at him like a tiny Frisbee. He plucked it out of the air, but a piece broke off and hit the ground. Reaching down, he picked up the broken piece. He was a sucker for chocolate chip cookies. That's how he missed the launch of a second cookie and it fell at his feet.

He picked that up, too, and blew on it. A little dirt and grass wouldn't hurt anything, especially when talking about a chocolate chip cookie. That seemed to be the end of the flying food, so he looked to see where Georgie had gone.

Not surprisingly, she'd retreated to a boulder over by Sing-Song Creek and sat with her back to him while she ate her lunch. Okay, he could take a hint. He found another flat rock at the edge of the meadow, which was about as far away as he could get without riding down the trail.

He wouldn't leave her, but he wasn't convinced that she wouldn't leave him. She could have hopped on Prince and ridden away with their lunch, but that wasn't Georgie. She might be royally pissed, but denying someone food would have been petty. She didn't have it in her to be like that.

As he ate the sandwich she'd made, he thought about her putting it together this morning and felt a pang of remorse. If he'd kept his hands to himself, they might still be friends. They'd had a good morning, a nice morning, and then he'd allowed his libido to take over.

Oh, and he couldn't forget that he'd admitted to her that she was the main reason he'd come back here. He *never* should have said that. Apparently the combination of her obvious satisfaction and his aching cock had made him temporarily stupid.

Or maybe, and this was depressing, he'd hoped she'd take pity on him and come to his hotel room tonight. He hoped he wasn't that pathetic. In any case, he'd officially ruined their relationship, and it was totally his fault that she'd brought up the issue of him staying.

She'd naturally viewed his admission as one more piece of evidence that he was becoming attached to her and to this place. First he'd bought a horse and stabled him at Ed's. Then he'd pushed past the boundaries of friendship during this trail ride. Then he'd capped that off by revealing his ongoing crush.

Eating made his lip sting, but that was okay, because he deserved a sore lip. He'd given her mixed messages, and when she'd tried to sort through the bullshit, he'd piled on more of it with his idiotic remark about not wanting to take a chance with her heart. Yeah, like she might fall in love with him. *That* was never gonna happen.

There she sat on that rock, her back straight as a lodgepole pine, probably cussing him out as she ate her lunch, and he wanted her more than ever. He tried to take comfort in the knowledge that she was less sexually frustrated than she'd been when they'd ridden out this morning.

She'd mentioned that she'd appreciated what he'd done for her. Okay, that's why he'd told her about his longstanding crush. Now he remembered. Her comment had struck him wrong, like he'd done her some kind of favor out of the goodness of his heart because he felt sorry for her lack of good sex.

He hadn't liked that image at all, so he'd wanted to let her know that he didn't go around satisfying every deprived woman he ran across. This had been a special circumstance. How had he thought of it when they'd been on the trail? *A moment out of time.* A moment out of his effing mind was more like it.

She wasn't eating her lunch anymore. Instead she just sat there staring off into space, probably thinking of how much fun it would be to bury him next to an anthill and pour honey on his head. Then she sighed so loudly that he could hear it clear across the meadow. Hell, the Ghost could probably hear it from wherever he was hiding out.

As if Vince's thought had conjured him up, the gray horse appeared through the cottonwoods on the far side of the creek. Georgie went completely still. Vince glanced over to where they'd tied Storm Cloud and Prince. They stood motionless and alert, their attention fixed on the stallion.

The Ghost sniffed the air and surveyed the scene. Then he walked cautiously over to the creek, dipped his nose into it, and took a drink. He was less than ten yards away from Georgie.

Vince wondered if she'd ever been this near to the stallion before. Even if she had, it couldn't be that often that she got up close and personal. Vince held his breath. Even the birds stopped chirping as silence descended over the meadow.

Suddenly the Ghost lifted his head, water dripping from his mouth. He looked straight at Georgie, snorted, and spun on his back hooves like a Lipizzaner. Then he bolted into the trees and was gone.

What a magical moment, and if he hadn't driven a wedge between them, they could have shared it. They had sort of shared it, but from a distance. He was glad for her that she'd been the one down by the creek, the one with the best view. She must be thrilled.

She sat on the boulder a little longer and finally climbed down. As she walked back over to him, she kept looking over her shoulder, as if hoping the stallion would return. He didn't, and so she continued toward Vince.

Fortunately her angry frown had been replaced with an expression of wonder. "That was *amazing*. I've never been that close. I could see a little notch on his ear.

There's a small crescent-shaped scar on his right foreleg. And he had a burr tangled in his mane. In fact, his mane and tail both need to be combed out. My fingers itched to do it."

He smiled at the excitement in her voice. "I'm glad he showed up." He also didn't miss the contrast between her reaction to the stallion and his. He'd wanted to rope him. She wanted to groom him. But he must be making progress, because he'd had no desire to throw a rope at that horse today. None.

"Listen, I want to thank you."

"For being a pain in the ass?"

She pressed her lips together as if working hard not to laugh at that. "Well, you are, but you're also the one who said we shouldn't dig up this meadow, and you're absolutely right. If the trail rides camped here every weekend, it would be so stressful for the Ghost. He'd be afraid to come down to the creek. Besides that, you found an alternative. So thank you."

"You're welcome." He wished they could be a little less formal with each other, but at least she wasn't throwing things at him anymore.

"We should be getting back. We'll take a different trail from the one you used to get here three weeks ago. You can see if you like it any better or if you want to use the one you already know."

"Great. Choices are good." He wadded up the paper she'd used to wrap his sandwich. "Thanks for the lunch. It was delicious." He wondered if she'd apologize for throwing it at him.

She didn't. "I'll take that back in my saddlebag." She held out her hand.

When he gave her the crumpled paper, their hands

touched. He longed to draw her into his arms and apologize for being a jerk, but that would be the wrong way to go about it. "Georgie, I'm sorry for . . . everything."

She met his gaze and hers was sad. "Me, too." Then she broke eye contact and walked over to Prince.

At that point he made a decision. The minute Wild Horse Canyon Adventures was a guaranteed success, he'd call Mac and Travis. Surely one of them would take over for him if they knew the money would be steady and the work fun.

It would be fun, too. Under different circumstances he might have stayed on the job longer. But he now realized he hadn't been the only one with an ongoing crush. She might not want him to worry about her heart, but he couldn't seem to help it.

# CHAPTER 21

After Georgie arrived home, she gave Prince a thorough brushing and rubdown, a small ration of oats, and a hug. Then she went into the house through the kitchen door, which would allow her to head upstairs without passing the parlor. It was nearly five, so the TV would be on and happy hour would be in progress.

She'd started upstairs when Evelyn called to her. As she walked over to the doorway, she hoped that whatever her stepmother wanted would only take a minute or two. A long, hot shower sounded like heaven right now. Talking to Evelyn sounded like hell.

Evelyn beckoned to her. "Come on in. Want a martini? I can get another glass."

"No, thanks." She edged into the room. "I shouldn't sit down. I've been out riding all day and I have horsehair all over me."

Evelyn waved a hand dismissively. "Don't worry about it."

Georgie did, though, because she was usually the one on cleanup duty. Anastasia helped when she thought of it, but her cleaning standards weren't very high. Georgie was no neat freak, but the house was beautiful and she didn't like to see clutter and dust coating the furniture. Sitting on the upholstery would leave a layer of trail dust and horsehair, so she remained standing.

That meant her stepmother had to look up at her, which wasn't all bad, either. Evelyn was a handsome woman who was well aware of that fact. She had a hairdresser in Amarillo who made sure her gray roots never showed themselves, and she had excellent bone structure. At fifty, she had almost no wrinkles, but she'd talked often about getting a face-lift when her ship came in.

Georgie figured the ship was Charmaine, or else the rich guy Charmaine was supposed to lure onto the rocks of unholy matrimony. Charmaine had said once that it was as easy to love a rich man as a poor man. Georgie hoped for her sister's sake that was true.

"So I wanted to talk to you about this trail ride." Evelyn picked up her martini glass and took a delicate sip.

"Okay."

"Charmaine isn't an accomplished horsewoman."

"I know, but it doesn't matter. The horses will all be walking. Anybody could do it."

"Yes, but I've decided she needs to look good out there. At first I thought maybe her inexperience would work in her favor, and Randolph would find himself coming to her aid, but I've reconsidered that approach. I think she needs to know what she's doing, at least somewhat. I don't know if she's ever been on a horse, come to think of it."

So Evelyn considered herself already on a first-name basis with the rich guy. Not surprising. "Charmaine hasn't ridden as far as I know, but it won't matter. Those horses are extremely docile. She'll be riding in a line with other horses so she won't have to do anything but sit there. She'd have to work at falling off."

"Be that as it may, I've told her to come home a couple of days early so you can give her riding lessons."

Georgie stared at her. Talk about the last thing in the world she wanted to do. "I don't have time."

"Of course you do, now that you're opening the store later and closing it earlier."

"But I'm in charge of making sure everything's organized. There could be last-minute issues that I'll be responsible for. I can't be giving Charmaine riding lessons when I should be available in case I have to put out fires."

"Nonsense. There won't be any fires to put out. You're too efficient." She gazed at Georgie, her expression confident. "When I told Charmaine that you'd love to give her lessons, the poor girl practically burst into tears of gratitude. Randolph's a good rider and she doesn't want to make a fool of herself. She told me to tell you that she owes you, big-time."

And that, Georgie thought, was a classic example of how Evelyn operated. "All right. I'll find the time somehow."

"I knew you would." Evelyn smiled. Then she wrinkled her nose. "Now go take a shower. You smell like horse."

Georgie waited until she was in the shower with the bathroom door closed before she let loose with a few choice swearwords. And then a few more. She thought nobody could hear her.

But apparently Anastasia had, because she knocked on the door. "Are you okay?"

"Yes! Just . . . I'm fine!"

"When you're done, come down to my room. I want to make sure you're fine."

"Okay." Georgie didn't like lying to the one person in the family who sincerely cared about her. And she wasn't really fine. She was in turmoil over Vince. She should forget him, but instead all she could remember were his kisses. All his kisses. Everywhere he'd kissed her.

Someday soon he'd leave town, and when he did, he'd take that clever mouth with him, along with the rest of the goodies she hadn't sampled yet. If he was that accomplished at oral sex, she could only imagine what the main event would be like. The prospect made her stand in the shower thinking about it until the hot water ran out. She really should install a bigger tank and just not tell Evelyn she was doing it.

Anastasia knocked on the door again. "What are you doing in there? You should be out by now."

"Almost done."

"Georgie, you don't usually swear in the shower. Come out and let me see that you're okay."

With a sigh, Georgie switched off the tepid water and reached for the towel hanging near the combination tub and shower. "Be right there."

Moments later, her body encircled by her favorite bath sheet and her hair wrapped in a regular towel, she opened the door. "See? Fine."

"Your mouth is red. You've been kissing somebody. Vince, right?"

"No, Ed."

Anastasia's eyes widened.

"Yes, of course Vince! He's the only kissing candidate in this whole damned town!" Evelyn hadn't noticed her red mouth, but that was typical. Evelyn didn't notice anything that wasn't linked to herself and her ambitions. Georgie's love life wouldn't concern her at all.

"Come down to my room. I think you need to talk."

"No, I don't." But she padded barefoot down the hall to her sister's room, because she probably did need to talk. She sat on the bed and Anastasia took the desk chair.

"So you've been kissing Vince."

"Yes."

"In front of Ed?"

"Ed didn't go. I guess you didn't catch that last night."

"No. I was dancing with the guys while you and Vince had your argument, but that must be settled."

"It wasn't an argument, and how did you know about it?"

Anastasia folded her arms over her chest. "I've watched *Sherlock*. I know how to make deductions."

"Oh, really?"

"You left early after talking to him. That's all the evidence I need. But if you were out in the boonies kissing each other, I guess all is well. Except that doesn't explain the swearing in the shower."

Georgie gave her a quick update on Charmaine and the riding lessons.

"I'm sorry. If I knew how to ride, I'd do it."

"That's okay. I'll do it."

"But that will cut into your time with Vince. I can see why you were swearing. He's hot."

Her sister had no idea how hot. "That's not a problem. I won't be spending time alone with Vince anymore."

"What?" Anastasia gave her the googlie eye, which was a whole other thing from her hairy eyeball. "Why not?"

"Because he won't be staying on any longer than necessary to get Wild Horse Canyon Adventures launched. There's no future with Vince, so it's better if I—"

"Stop right there. Have you had sex with him yet?"

"Um, sort of. Not totally."

Anastasia gazed at her. "Would you like to?"

"God, yes."

"Then do it, Georgie. Go to his hotel room and say *here I am*."

"Oh, Anastasia, I don't know. It feels sort of—"

"Illicit?"

"Yeah."

"What's wrong with that? You're an adult and so is he. Besides, we can't know how soon a cowboy as sexy as Vince will come along again. You deserve a romp in the hay. And I can tell you really like him."

"I really do, but I can't just march into the lobby of that hotel and walk upstairs to his room. I don't relish being the talk of the town."

"Let me think." Anastasia tapped her chin with her finger. "I know! Remember when you kept tabs on things when Steve and Myra went to their daughter's wedding? Didn't they give you a key?"

"Yes. One for the front and one for the back." She stared at her sister. "I still have them. Steve told me to hang on to them in case they needed me to watch the place again."

"Bingo. Wait until the place is quiet and go in the back way so nobody sees you. Vince is the only guest. Do you know his room number?"

Georgie's shoulders slumped. This had started to sound like an excellent plan. "No, damn it."

"Take a little flashlight and look him up on that big register Steve leaves on the desk because he thinks it's so old-fashioned and cool. It's a security nightmare, but in this case, it'll serve your purposes nicely. The alternative is to go up and down the hall knocking on doors."

"I'd rather not."

"Don't blame you. So we're good? You're going over there tonight?"

"Tonight?" Butterflies started doing maneuvers in her stomach. "Maybe I should wait."

"For what? You have a week and a half before my sister hits town, and trust me—there will be no sneaking off to the hotel once she's in residence. If she's not getting any, she won't want you to be getting any, either."

"How do you know she's not getting any?"

"She sends me texts every once in a while. She's met some cute guys in Dallas, but they don't have bucks, and she can't take a chance on having a fling with them and falling in love. She does have *some* moral fiber."

"I'm sure she does." Georgie wasn't all that sure, but she was willing to give Charmaine the benefit of the doubt for Anastasia's sake.

"Anyway, competition for the men with money is fierce. Consequently she's as celibate as we are. And not happy about it."

"Who would be?"

"Exactly. Which is why you need to temporarily put aside your happily-ever-after dreams and climb on that cowboy, girlfriend."

Georgie laughed. "I've been taking this situation way too seriously, haven't I?"

"Yes, but that's how you are. And it's the reason I love you."

"Aw." Georgie left the bed to give her sister a hug. "Thanks for talking me down."

"Are you going to give me details so I can live vicariously?"

"No."

"Didn't think so, but it was worth a try."

"You'll get a turn. This trail-ride thing will bring people into town, and logically some of them have to be eligible single guys, right?"

Anastasia smiled. "Logically they'll be prosperous middle-aged tourists and we both know it."

"When Vince bails, and he will, I'll ask Mac and Travis if they're interested. If they can be promised a steady job, they might agree to work for Wild Horse Canyon Adventures." She watched Anastasia's reaction to that possibility.

Her sister shrugged and glanced away. "That would be cool."

"Come on, tell me the truth. I've bared my soul. Which of those two guys does it for you?"

Anastasia glanced up. "Truthfully? I'm not sure. They were only here for a weekend. I liked them both. At first I thought I was all about Mac, but after spending more time with Travis, I can't say." She laughed. "It would be nice to have the choice, you know? More than one possibility in town would be awesome."

"I hear you. This has turned into an impossible situation for a couple of twentysomething women. Vince is a short-term fix. A Band-Aid."

"But a mighty good-looking one."

"Yes." Anticipation fizzed in her veins. "Yes, he is."

"If you want to play it safe, you probably shouldn't go over there until around midnight."

"What if he's asleep?"

Anastasia began to laugh. "Are you worried about waking him up?"

Georgie thought of what had taken place in the canyon today and felt her cheeks grow warm. "Guess not."

"He will be so glad to see you standing at his door that he won't care if he never sleeps again. You're going to make Vince a very happy man tonight. What are you going to wear?"

"I don't know. Jeans, a nice shirt, boots, a jacket."

"Wrong. Let's think about this. You want something that's easy off and easy on again. You'll have to set your phone alarm so you leave before it gets light out. You don't want to do the walk of shame down Main Street."

"The walk of shame?"

Anastasia sighed. "I keep forgetting that you only got a couple of years of college before you had to come home. I may be younger than you, but those last two years in school were quite educational, and I'm not talking about the classwork."

"Did you ever have to take the walk of shame?"

"Oh, no. I was careful. But one of my friends stayed at her boyfriend's apartment after a wild night in which she somehow misplaced her clothes. He was dead to the world the next morning, but she had an early class, so she had to walk back home wrapped in a pink-and-yellow beach towel."

"Yikes. If that's what I missed, I'm glad I didn't go all four years."

"You probably didn't miss very much, come to think of it. But let me suggest a different outfit from what you have in mind, okay?"

Georgie smiled. "I'll bow to your superior knowledge."

"Cool! And once we get that figured out, what are you going to do between now and then?"

"Hyperventilate?"

"Wrong again. We'll bring food up here and play gin."

"Anastasia, what would I do without you?"

"You wouldn't be heading over to the Bickford Hotel for a hot night of sex—that's for sure."

"No, I wouldn't." She pulled her into another hug. "Thank you."

"Sure you won't give me a postmortem tomorrow?"

"Absolutely not."

"Then let's go to your room and organize your outfit."

Georgie left the house on the stroke of midnight. It appealed to her sense of drama to walk through the front door as the grandfather clock in the entryway began counting down the hour. Dressed the way she was, she didn't feel like the woman who managed the Bickford General Store and took care of electrical and plumbing issues at home. She felt like a princess.

Anastasia had unearthed a white off-the-shoulder blouse trimmed with blue ribbon and a flowered skirt that swirled around her ankles. She hadn't worn either of them in years. Ditto the sandals with a three-inch heel and the white lace shawl. It didn't provide much warmth, but adrenaline had stoked up her inner furnace.

She barely noticed the cool night air as she walked down Main Street, lit only by its historic streetlamps. Even the signs for the hotel and Sadie's had been switched off. She glanced up at the crescent moon and glittering stars above her and realized she hadn't really looked at them in a long time. She'd been too busy and too worried about the town and Evelyn's control over her future.

Tonight she would forget all that and give herself the gift of pleasure. If Vince was willing, and she thought he would be, she'd continue her stealth visits until Charmaine arrived. This had been a brilliant idea and Anastasia was indeed a genius.

A small silk bag dangling from her wrist held the hotel keys and a small flashlight. But she wouldn't need the flashlight. The moment she'd started down the street she'd noticed a rectangle of light shining down from the second floor onto the pavement.

If she'd been thinking more clearly, she would have guessed he'd be in that street-view room. He'd made the original reservations, and he would have requested the hotel's finest. The room across the hall also looked out on the street, but it had two doubles instead of a king and wasn't furnished quite as nicely. Maybe Mac and Travis, who seemed to be more strapped for cash, had shared that one.

Her heart beat faster the closer she came to the hotel, and it had already been pumping hard. In her mental rehearsals, he'd answer the door groggy and a little disoriented from sleep. Sure, he'd probably switch on the bedside lamp before answering her knock, but it would give off a mellow glow. From the looks of the light spilling from his window, he was wide awake and had every fixture in the room blazing.

She gulped. When she'd first set out on this adventure, she'd felt powerful and sexy, capable of seducing this gorgeous cowboy. Now, seeing all that bright light made her feel suddenly exposed. She'd never done anything like this in her life.

Fear of the unknown made her hesitate. She could turn around now, walk back home, and nobody except Anastasia would ever know. But she'd give up the chance, probably forever, of feeling Vince's strong arms around her, his hot kisses searing her body, and his hard . . . yeah, *that*. Okay, she was going through with it.

# CHAPTER 22

When Vince heard a knock at the door, he put down his book. Could he have imagined it? Steve and Myra should be sound asleep in their apartment downstairs, and they were the only ones in the building besides him.

The Bickford Hotel was more than a hundred years old and built of wood, so it creaked and groaned whenever the wind blew especially hard. But there was no wind tonight. His new poker friends had spun a few yarns about supposed hauntings, but Vince didn't believe in that stuff. Yet a shiver went down his spine.

Until now, he'd kind of liked being the only guest. He didn't have to worry about disturbing anybody or having anybody disturb him. But that knock, if it really had been a knock, made him suddenly aware of how alone he was up here on the second floor. And how flimsy that old door was.

Ah, he was probably hearing things. Sometimes the ancient pipes rattled in the walls. But they didn't rattle unless someone was running water somewhere in the hotel. And everything was shut down for the night.

He'd seen *A Christmas Carol*, both the regular version and the Muppet one. The first ghosts had shown up after midnight. But he didn't consider himself particularly Scrooge-like, and it wasn't Christmas. Aw, hell, he was letting his imagination run away with him because it was late and he was tired. He should just go to bed.

The second knock sent him bolting from the chair, adrenaline pumping through his system. Then he heard a voice.

"Vince? It's me."

The breath whooshed out of his lungs. "Georgie?" He crossed the room in two strides, unlocked the door, and yanked it open. "What's wrong?" And how the hell did she get in here?

"Nothing's wrong. Did I scare you?"

He tried to calm his breathing. "Uh, no. Well, maybe a little." As he adjusted to the fact that Georgie was standing there and that she wasn't some apparition from the spirit world, he finally noticed how she was dressed.

Maybe he was dreaming this. He'd never seen her in a skirt and blouse before. And sexy heels. He scrubbed a hand over his face. That felt real enough. Same bristle that he usually developed by this time.

But technically she shouldn't be here unless she could walk through walls. "How did you get in?"

"I have a key." She spoke fast, and she sounded breathless. "Steve gave me one to both the front and back when he and Myra went to their daughter's wedding, and I checked on things here while they were gone."

"She wasn't married in Bickford? No, forget that. I don't give a damn where she was married. Now I know how you got here. But I don't know why."

She opened her mouth as if to say something and then closed it again. Her cheeks turned pink.

He stared at her. "Georgie?" Gradually it dawned on him why she might be standing at his door in the middle of the night, but he couldn't quite believe it. They'd been over all that. He'd told her where he stood. And she'd bitten him.

Yet here she was, dressed like a woman who might have certain things on her mind. His brain went on tilt and he had trouble organizing his thoughts. He could be on the brink of something incredible, but he didn't trust that concept. He'd wanted her too much for too long.

She cleared her throat. "Could I please come in?"

"Oh, sure! Absolutely!" He stepped back and watched her walk into his room. His *bed*room. Her hips swayed a little as she maneuvered on those heels. He could tell she wasn't used to them, and he found that touching.

She wandered over to the easy chair and glanced down at the book he'd left on the end table. "Is this one of the history books Ed loaned you?" With her back to him, she took off the lace shawl and tossed it over the back of the chair.

"Yeah, I'm rereading it so I can be sure to remember the important facts. Listen, Georgie, if you . . ." He lost his train of thought as she turned around and he saw what the shawl had concealed. The material of her blouse was thin. And she wasn't wearing a bra.

He swallowed. "You'd better be here for what I think you are, because—"

"I am."

Excitement surged through him and he was almost instantly hard. "Thank God."

"But I just thought of a potential problem."

He groaned. "What now?"

"Do you have condoms?"

*"Yes."* Somewhere in his suitcase, which was tucked away on the top shelf of the tiny closet.

She took a deep breath. "Then I guess you should get them while I shut the door."

He spun around and sure enough, the door stood open, exactly the way he'd left it. She made him crazy, but tonight he would return the favor.

While she closed and locked the door, he grabbed his suitcase out of the closet and threw it on the floor. Crouching was tough on his family jewels, but he had to accomplish this before he could do anything about that. He unzipped the little roller bag with shaky fingers.

Traveling with condoms had become an unconscious habit, but he didn't know how many he had. Or how many he'd need. The way he felt right now, he'd need a lot. He found them lying loose in a side pocket and grabbed out as many as he could hold.

She was here. She was really here. Soon they'd be naked and rolling around on his bed. He should probably ask some questions about what had changed her mind, but he didn't want to look too closely at this miracle and risk screwing up what appeared to be an incredible gift from the universe.

His breath hissed out between his teeth as he stood. His cock was in misery being squeezed inside the unforgiving denim of his jeans. It was fair to say he'd never wanted anyone as much as he wanted Georgie. That could be trouble. He might go off like a rocket with one thrust.

He turned to find her sitting in his easy chair unbuckling the straps on her shoes. Her blouse gaped open as she leaned down. If she'd been anyone besides Georgie, he would think she'd done that on purpose, but he figured she didn't know.

The view of her creamy breasts overloaded his already supercharged libido. Stuffing one condom in his pocket, he let the others fall to the floor as he walked over to the chair. He hauled her out of it without asking.

She gasped, which meant when he kissed her, he had easy access. He thrust his tongue into her mouth as he pushed her blouse down over her shoulders and cupped those warm, quivering breasts. Somebody moaned. It could've been her. It could've been him.

It could've been both of them, because apparently he'd lit her fuse, too. She tore at his shirt, popping the snaps as it came open. Then she flattened her palms against his chest and curled her fingertips into his pecs. God, it felt great to have her hands on him, to have his hands on her.

Still kissing her for all he was worth, he grabbed her around the waist and lifted her off her feet. Her shoes clattered to the floor as she wrapped her legs around his hips. Her heat seemed to seek his through the material separating them as he carried her to the bed.

When he laid her across the mattress, he followed her down, unwilling to stop kissing her for even a second as he rolled slightly to one side and pushed up her skirt. Then he went very still. Lifting his head to gaze into her flushed face, he slipped his hand between her satin thighs and encountered nothing but warm, moist woman. "No panties, Georgie?"

Her brown eyes darkened as he caressed her there. "Less to take off."

"True." His fingers slid easily back and forth. He didn't need to make her ready for him. She was already drenched. He pictured her taking off her panties before knocking on his door. "Are they stuffed in your little satchel?"

"No."

"Then where —"

"At home."

That surprised a laugh out of him. "You walked down Main Street without panties?"

Her breath caught as he circled her clit with his thumb. "Y-yes."

"I underestimated you."

"I hope I didn't . . . *over*estimate . . . you."

He smiled at that. "Me, too." Curving his fingers, he found her G-spot and watched her pupils dilate as he stroked.

His balls ached as if he'd taken a hit to the groin, but she'd walked down here without underwear. After a gutsy move like that, the least he could do was make sure he gave her an orgasm before he plunged into her and lost his mind.

"Let's start with this and see how it goes." He teased her clit as he massaged with his fingertips. Yeah, this was a good place to start. Her thighs began to quiver. "Good?"

"Mm." She closed her eyes and lifted her hips, participating again. "Faster."

He loved it when she forgot to be shy and started giving directions. Apparently she had to reach a certain point of arousal before that happened. She was there, now. "I'll go faster if you'll open your eyes."

Her lashes fluttered upward.

He locked his gaze with hers as he increased the pace. "Tell me how that feels, Georgie."

Her lips parted as her breathing grew shallow and quick. "Like . . . like I'm a jet flying down the runway."

"Nice." He watched the pleasure build in her eyes as she tightened around his fingers. "Takeoff will be any second."

She gasped and clutched handfuls of the bedspread. "Uh-huh." She started to close her eyes again.

"Let me watch," he murmured, coaxing her higher with firm pressure on her clit. "Let me share."

She opened her eyes again.

He absorbed the hot passion reflected there and the anticipated thrill of release. He saw the shift in her expression, felt the first spasm roll over his fingers, and right before she arched upward in surrender, he glimpsed something deeper in her eyes. For a brief moment he felt as if she'd allowed him to see her essence, the truest part of Georgie Bickford.

That rocked him. Caressing her gently now, he helped bring her back to earth with soft kisses and murmured words. A tender emotion settled in his chest, a feeling so new that it almost hurt. It reminded him of growing pains when he was a kid.

He'd been to bed with women on many occasions, women he'd liked and admired. Yet he'd never experienced anything quite like this reaction. He had a sneaking suspicion of what might be happening, and it would be a first for him.

If he was right, then spending this time with Georgie might not be the wisest move he could make. Apparently he wasn't particularly wise. Easing from the bed, he helped her out of her clothes, what there was of them.

A blouse, a skirt, shoes, and a shawl. She'd obviously made the decision to have sex with him and she'd chosen an outfit that would present no challenges. He still didn't know why she'd made the decision to become his lover, but the question could wait.

After maneuvering her under the covers, he turned off all the lights except the one beside the bed, stripped off his clothes, and rolled on the condom. She'd watched him through the whole operation, and when he was finished, she folded back the covers and held out her arms.

He went into them with a sense of wonder and gratitude. He'd never expected to be with her like this, and whatever the personal cost, he'd pay it. But as he moved between her thighs, he thought a disclaimer was in order. "This might be over way too fast. I've dreamed about it for a long time."

"So have I, but I never admitted it to myself."

He sighed. "No pressure, right?"

"None at all." Sliding her hands down his back, she gripped his butt. "I have *always* wanted to fondle you like this."

"Too bad you didn't do it sooner. Then maybe I wouldn't feel like I'm going to explode right now."

She wrapped her legs around his and pulled him forward. "Go for it. There's always round two."

And three and four, he thought. Then he nudged her damp entrance with the head of his cock, found his place there, and pushed deep. All thought disappeared. Nothing mattered but this.

He never lost control with a woman. It was a point of honor with him, but he lost control with Georgie. He pumped into her with a wild joy that stole his breath, his words, his sense of where he left off and she began.

Dimly he heard her voice urging him on, and a jubilant cry that must have been when she came. He felt the tremors massage his cock, and some primitive instinct took over. He pounded into her with greater purpose then, and when he climaxed, he felt as if the top of his head was coming off. He shouted and cursed, and only later wondered if he'd been loud enough to wake Myra and Steve.

When it was over he staggered from the bed with the little strength he had left, because he wanted to cuddle with Georgie, and a guy couldn't cuddle when he had to dispose of a damned condom. He appreciated the reason for the little raincoats, but they sure could bust up a mood.

Turned out it didn't destroy this one, though. When he climbed back into bed, she was lying on her side, smiling at him.

She combed his hair back from his forehead. "Feeling better?"

"You have no idea." Her touch was like rain on parched earth.

"I might." She ran her fingers along his stubble. "I'm familiar with sexual frustration."

"I guess so." The scratchy sound of her fingertips on his beard made him study her face in the lamplight. "Damn it, I gave you razor burn."

"I don't care."

He leaned toward her and placed tiny kisses where he'd reddened her skin. "You will in the morning when you open the store. I doubt you want to advertise where you were tonight."

"That's what makeup is for." Stroking his shoulder, she gazed at him. "Besides, I have to admit that while at first I thought we should keep this a secret, now it doesn't matter to me."

Instinctively he wanted to protect her from gossip, but it wasn't all up to him. "That's your choice."

She caressed the nape of his neck in a slow, mesmerizing massage. "It doesn't matter to me, but it might make things unpleasant for you."

If he were a tomcat, he'd start to purr. "I can deal with it." He'd walk through fire to have this chance. A little gossip was nothing.

"People around here are protective of me. They were supportive after I lost my mom, and they doubled down after my dad died. They might blame this on you, thinking you'd seduced me."

His conscience pricked him. He'd made the first move this morning. "Did I?"

She smiled. "You've been seducing me from the first day we met."

"No fair. I meant recently. Like today in the canyon."

"That had an impact, but—"

"Damn it. I was afraid of that. I should never have kissed you . . . everywhere. My fault. All my fault."

"Shh." She laid a finger against his mouth. "Yes, you should have. I was dying for you to do something. You would have had to be blind and deaf not to notice."

"I suppose you're right. I was picking up on all of that." He had to say it. "But you wanted—may still want—more than I have to give. By all rights I should have sent you away tonight, but I'm not that noble."

"If you'd sent me away you probably would have scarred me for life. Halfway here I was ready to turn back."

He thought of her blush when he'd asked why she'd shown up at his door. She had been nervous and tentative. Seen from her perspective, a rejection would have been a crushing blow. Thank God he hadn't been noble, after all.

Yet he wondered if he'd saved her ego only to cause greater damage in the long run. "But you haven't told me what changed between this afternoon and now." He looked into those soft brown eyes and knew he didn't want to hurt her if he could help it, but she might have put him in an impossible situation.

"I talked to my sister."

"Anastasia?" He hadn't expected that answer. "I didn't think she was a fan of mine."

"She wasn't when she thought you were going to harass the wild horses, but now that you've given that up, she's mellowing toward you. Her argument was more logical than emotional, though, which is interesting, coming from her."

Vince folded the pillow and propped it under his head so he could get a better view of her expression as she explained this. He thought it was important and he didn't want to miss any of the subtle parts. "What did she say?"

"She pointed out that the town isn't exactly crawling with sexy guys and might never be. The people who sign up for the rides are more likely to be couples with discretionary income, not hot single guys."

He couldn't help chuckling, but Anastasia was right. "So she thought you should take advantage of what recently blew into town?"

"That sounds opportunistic, and I don't feel that way about you, but, in a way, yes."

He let that sink in. "So you're not hoping that eventually I'll—"

"No, Vince." Her gaze was earnest. "I'm here because I decided Anastasia is right. Guys aren't coming out of the woodwork these days, and frankly, I miss sex. Depriving myself of this chance to have it with a man I like a lot smacks of martyrdom, and I'm not into that."

It was perfect, absolutely perfect. He couldn't have set it up better if he'd tried. If something about her statement didn't sit right with him, it probably had to do with those tender feelings he'd experienced earlier.

He'd been worried about those feelings, but he didn't have to be, now. She was here for fun and games, not an everlasting love. She'd accepted his limitations and was willing to work within them.

"Great." He gave her a quick kiss. "Relax for a few minutes while I shave. Then I'll gather up the condoms I dropped. The night is young."

# CHAPTER 23

In the next few days, Georgie developed a love-hate relationship with time. She yearned for midnight when she could hurry down the street to the hotel and cherish every second spent with Vince. But once she was with him, she wanted time to stop and she highly resented the arrival of dawn. The next day she'd go through it all again.

Each night brought them closer to the last one they'd have together, and she dreaded that moment. Yet each day also brought them closer to the first trail ride and her hope that Wild Horse Canyon Adventures would save the town she loved. It seemed cruel that she had to give up this pleasure with Vince in order to realize her dream for the town, but that was the way things had worked out.

Because the future brought such conflicting emotions, she did her best to live in the present, where she'd never had so much sex or so little sleep. Vince proved to be a creative and enthusiastic lover, and Georgie learned not to take sex so seriously. They laughed a lot, before, during, and after. But no matter how lightly they treated the act, at least once each night Vince would make the ultimate connection with a heartfelt sigh and utter some version of *this is the best*.

And her breath would catch, because in those moments she knew that she was in love with him and she would have to give him up. It was because she loved him that she would wave good-bye with a smile. If he wasn't comfortable with the idea of settling down, she wouldn't try to change that or wish he were different.

He'd transformed her world during their magic nights together, and she would always be grateful that life had brought her Vince Durant, if only for a short time. Charmaine's arrival would rob them of two precious nights, but once the first riders checked into the hotel, the interlude would be permanently altered, anyway.

If all went as planned, those guests would be the beginning of a turnaround for the hotel and Bickford. Years ago Ida had bought up all the shops that had gone out of business and had insisted the town would rebound eventually. That day might come, but in the meantime, Georgie had talked her into letting people open a couple of them rent-free for a month.

Frank's wife, Sue, had volunteered to run a small crafts shop in one of the locations. Once again the retirees would have a place to market what they made. Anastasia didn't feel ready to take an entire storefront for her artwork, but she'd agreed to set up a table at Sadie's where she could sell her watercolors and create charcoal portraits.

The ice-cream shop would reopen under the supervision of the mayor and his wife, who'd decided to dip into their savings in order to stock it. Clyde and Inez didn't want to have to operate it for long, but if it was successful, they could more easily find employees to run it, or a buyer.

As for the rest of the shops on Main Street, exterior painting was in progress. The boards over the windows were being replaced with posters hand-lettered by Anastasia that read WATCH THIS SPACE! NEW SHOPS COMING SOON!

Meanwhile Vince, Ike, and Henry spent their mornings clearing a trail to the box canyon. They'd convinced the poker players to disassemble the chuck wagon so it could be hauled out to the canyon and permanently reassembled there. Georgie had faith it would be completed by the weekend.

Most of her faith was based on her new understanding of Vince's work ethic. He wasn't getting any more sleep than she was, but that didn't stop him from putting in hours on the trail construction and spending his afternoons schooling the horses they'd purchased. Those seven horses, eight counting Storm Cloud, would be as well-mannered as Vince could make them.

Georgie's last night with Vince arrived way too soon. Within five minutes of the time she walked into his room, she lay on his bed gasping from the climax he'd just given her. Damn, this was good, but soon it would be over and she'd miss this man for the rest of her life. She did her best to focus on the rebirth of the town, yet every nerve in her body hummed in delight whenever he touched her, and how could she do without that feeling?

Slowly he kissed his way from his position between her thighs up to her mouth. "I love how you taste," he murmured. "Yummy." Then he proceeded to stroke his sex-flavored tongue over hers. "Good, isn't it?"

She was no longer hesitant about showing him exactly

how she felt about his erotic teasing. She grabbed his head and gave him an open-mouthed kiss that soon had her blood pumping again. With a new burst of energy, she rolled him to his back and climbed on top of him.

Perched on his taut abs, his rigid cock nestled against her backside, she braced her hands on his chest while she gazed down at him. He was beautiful. And clean-shaven. After that first night, he'd made sure of that.

"Feeling feisty, are you?" His blue eyes glittered as he reached up to play with her breasts.

"Guess so." She was restless, not wanting this to be the end, yet knowing it had to be, and wanting to wring every last bit of satisfaction out of the time left.

"I could come just looking at you."

"Go ahead." She wiggled against him.

He sucked in a breath and squeezed her breasts. "No. I want to make it count."

"And how do you intend to do that?" She eased back just enough so he was more firmly wedged between her cheeks. Then she moved up and down, taunting him.

He grabbed her hips. "Stop it."

"Make me."

Heat flashed in his eyes. "I believe I will."

In a split second she was on her back again with both hands pinned over her head and his body pressing her to the mattress. His cock was an iron rod against her thigh. They'd played this game before, and she found it exciting because she trusted him not to hurt her. She knew him, now, and he would die before he'd physically mistreat her.

He was strong enough to manacle both her wrists with one hand, leaving his other free to inflict whatever sweet torture he chose. But tonight he didn't seem to have teasing on his mind. He reached for a condom on the nightstand, tore the package open with his teeth, and shifted his position just enough to roll it on.

She smiled. "Impressive."

"You inspire me." Still holding her wrists so her arms were stretched over her head, he gripped her thigh and positioned it over his hip, opening her to his first thrust. It was swift and sure, lifting her off the mattress.

She sank back with a low moan of pleasure. Yes, this was the best, when he was locked in deep and they were as close as a man and woman could be.

Looking into her eyes, he let go of her wrists and braced himself above her. "Please touch me," he murmured. A familiar yearning flickered in his gaze, one that often appeared when they were face-to-face with his cock buried up to the hilt.

She cupped his face in both hands. "Where?"

"Anywhere." As if he realized the vulnerability he'd revealed, he turned his head and kissed her open palm. "I just need . . . your touch."

She started with his face, stroking her thumbs over his dark eyebrows. So expressive, those eyebrows. They lifted when he was surprised, drew together when he was puzzled, and arched fiercely downward when he was angry, although she hadn't seen that happen much. When she'd described Evelyn's manipulations he'd looked angry for a moment, but then he'd mentioned something about having no right to judge and had let it go.

Next she ran her forefinger down his straight nose. It was a strong nose, prominent. Ida had once told her his nose indicated he was well-endowed. Lately Ida had been dropping hints that she thought Georgie might know whether that was true or not. Georgie had ignored her.

He stayed perfectly still, his gaze intent, as she explored the high ridge of his cheekbones and the firm line of his jaw. She wondered if he might be memorizing the sensation of her fingers roaming at will over his face.

When she touched his mouth, he caught her finger between his teeth. Then he drew it slowly into his mouth. Sucking gently, he began moving his hips in an easy rhythm.

Her body's reaction caught her off guard. With no warning, her womb contracted. He kept pumping and she came effortlessly, sliding into her climax as if immersing herself in a warm Jacuzzi. A small whimper of surprise was the only noise she made as the delicious sensation rolled through her.

Releasing her finger, he pushed home one more time and stayed there as he smiled down at her. "That was fun."

She sighed happily. "Yeah. Did you know that would happen?"

"Nope. Just went with my instincts. You felt ready, and sucking on your finger made me want to move."

"It was all so . . . easy."

"Maybe because you weren't thinking about it. You were busy memorizing my face."

She laughed. "Egotist." But he'd nailed it. She'd wondered if he'd been memorizing her touch, but all the while she'd been mapping him with the tips of her fingers. She didn't want to forget.

"I've already memorized yours."

Suddenly her throat hurt. The onset of sadness was as quick and without warning as her climax had been. "Stick around and you could save yourself the trouble."

Pain flashed in his eyes. "Don't, Georgie."

"Sorry. I promised myself I wouldn't make remarks

like that." But it was their last night, and she was feeling a little reckless. "But seriously, why did you memorize my face? Do you do that with all your women?"

"No."

"Then why me?"

He didn't answer.

"Why me, Vince?" She was pushing him, but she couldn't seem to help it. "What's so special about me?"

"Everything. If I ever thought I could commit to someone, it would be—"

"Don't you dare, Vince Durant. Don't you dare tell me that I'm close, but not quite close enough to change your mind." Her throat really hurt now. She swallowed and hoped she wouldn't embarrass herself by starting to cry.

"Just the opposite. You're perfect. You deserve somebody better than me."

"Shut up." She swallowed again. "Just shut up."

"Do you want to go home?"

"Not yet." She took hold of his hips and glared up at him. "First I want you to finish what you started. You said you wanted to make this one count, so go for it. If you can't give me what I need, then give me what you've got."

He looked as if she'd slapped him. "Georgie . . ."

Instantly she regretted her outburst. She didn't want their last memories to be filled with pain. "I'm sorry. That was uncalled for. You've been the best, most considerate lover I've ever had."

"But I'm hurting you."

"Ah, what the hell. You're worth it. Now make love to me, Vince. Please just . . . make love to me."

His mouth firmed. Holding her gaze, he began to thrust. At first his movements were abrupt and angry, but gradually his expression changed. Tenderness glowed in his eyes as he began to love her with long, gentle strokes.

She smiled and wrapped her arms around his strong back, holding him tight as his big muscles flexed. He knew exactly how to take her to the top with no detours. She'd thought at first he would do that, but as her climax hovered near, he changed his pace and angle and the urge to come receded.

Moments later, he bore down again, coaxing her back up. She rose to meet each rapid stroke as her body tightened in anticipation. Watching her intently, he eased off again.

"I know what you're doing."

His mouth curved. "I should hope so."

"I mean drawing it out so it'll last longer."

"I want to make this one count."

She didn't have to ask why. Although she didn't have to leave yet, she would. Their lighthearted approach to sex wouldn't work for them anymore, so it would be for the best if she took off for home before the mood deteriorated any further.

Considering that, she wouldn't mind if she didn't come for a while. Feeling the easy glide of his cock and listening to the sweet music it made as he pumped in and out was plenty good enough for now.

She'd just enjoy that and not worry about . . . oh, no. So much for that plan. It seemed when she focused her senses on Vince's gentle invasion, her body responded whether that was her goal or not. She clenched her jaw and tried to hold back, but it was no use. With a wail of surrender, she came.

"Didn't want to give in, did you?"

She gulped in air. "No, but it's okay. Your turn."

"Not yet." He paused and took a shaky breath. His blue eyes were dark with passion and a muscle twitched in his jaw. "Not yet."

Reaching up, she cupped his face. "Let go. I'm fine. Don't torture yourself so that I can have another orgasm."

His laugh was choked. "Torture myself? You think this is torture?"

"You look very fierce, almost like you're in pain."

"That isn't pain you're seeing, it's intense pleasure, but I don't want it to end . . . yet."

The *yet* had been tacked on as an afterthought. That warmed her heart. "I know, but—"

"Don't worry about me. When I finally come, it'll be the climax of the century. You should probably stuff a pillow in my mouth so I don't wake the whole damn town."

"You'll be as loud as Sousa?"

"Louder." He started to move. "And just to reassure you, it won't be because I'm in pain."

"Good to know." And they were joking with each other again. Much better.

She'd always known he was a talented lover, but she might not have thoroughly appreciated his gift until now. Knowing he was fighting off his own climax every time he pushed deep, she thought he'd be intent on not coming. Instead he was all about pleasing her.

By sliding his arm under her hips and tilting her slightly, he created a different kind of friction that sizzled along her nerve endings. She moaned softly.

"Good?"

"Oh, yeah. More of that."

"You bet." He drove in faster. "Torture." His chuckle was strained. "Yeah, right. This is . . . pure torture."

She moaned again, louder this time, as the tension

built. This would be no gentle climax like the ones she'd just had. Oh, no. This one would come stampeding through her like a herd of wild horses.

Vince was right with her. She could tell by the sound of his breathing and the fire in his eyes that he wouldn't be slowing down this time. He pounded into her with enough force to shake the bed.

"Georgie . . . I'm . . ."

"Me, too." She gasped as the first tremor hit. "Me, too." And she came, and came hard, which meant she yelled pretty loud.

Vince, however, was louder. His big body shook and his deep groan seemed to fill the tiny room. "God, Georgie." His eyes were glazed and he struggled to breathe as he stared down at her.

She stared right back. She'd just had the most incredible sexual experience of her life and now she'd have to walk away. Judging from his shell-shocked expression, he was in the same shape, and he planned to let her go. She didn't get it, but she wasn't going to say one more word on the subject.

He, however, looked as if he might want to say something. What he wanted to say was there in his eyes. She waited, heart trembling, to see if he'd own up to what was hovering in the air between them.

But instead he gave his head a little shake. The moment was gone. He started to lean down as if to give her a tender kiss.

"I wouldn't do that if I were you."

He paused. "Because you might bite me?"

"It's a distinct possibility."

# CHAPTER 24

After Vince let Georgie leave without telling her he loved her, he waited until she'd had time to get all the way home. Then he quickly dressed, put on his hat, grabbed his key for the front door of the hotel, and went for a walk. He would have preferred to go for a ride, but it was two in the morning and he couldn't get to his horse without potentially alarming Ed and his wife.

The fresh air helped, and he liked not having a jacket on. Being cold suited his mood, as did the dark and deserted street. He could no more have stayed in that room with its memories of Georgie than fly to the moon on gossamer wings.

Telling her he loved her — which he did, damn it — would have been selfish. What was she supposed to do with that information? She might interpret it to mean he wanted to stay and live happily ever after. In reality, he loved her enough to get the hell out of town before things became any more complicated.

Striding rapidly down the street away from her house, he quickly was out of street to stride down. This place really was small. He didn't feel like walking out in the middle of nowhere, so he turned around and went the other way. He'd stop before he got close to her house.

Although he hadn't figured this out before, he knew he wouldn't be able to keep that same room now. Tomorrow he'd give the excuse that it should be available for the trail riders, since a front room had to be a premium spot. Myra and Steve might believe him.

They also might know exactly why he wanted to switch rooms. He and Georgie might kid themselves that they'd pulled the wool over everyone's eyes, but Vince wasn't so sure. He'd been getting some assessing looks from his poker buddies recently.

So long as Georgie seemed happy with the situation, they'd likely pretend not to know what was going on. In their shoes he would have done the same. But let Georgie show any signs of distress, and they'd be all over him like stink on shit. He wouldn't blame them.

She would probably begin showing signs of distress soon, so he hoped to hell the trail rides took off like a rocket. He'd call Mac and Travis in the morning and put them on standby. They might enjoy the security of their jobs, but this would be a hell of a lot more fun, provided it could keep them afloat financially.

Vince figured the rich dude was the one to impress, and he planned to do his best in that regard. He hoped Charmaine wouldn't be a pain in the butt and hang all over the guy. If she did, Vince was prepared to step in, whether Georgie's stepmother liked it or not.

He'd already decided he didn't like the woman, but he'd kept his mouth shut. He wouldn't be sticking around and therefore wasn't in a position to voice an opinion. Still, when he realized the power she held over Georgie's life, he got pretty steamed.

And here he was, right in front of her house. He'd been thinking so hard that he hadn't paid attention to how close he'd come. He turned around.

"Vince?"

He glanced over his shoulder and discovered Georgie coming down the steps of her front porch. She must have been sitting on the old porch swing all this time, which meant she'd seen him approaching. Maybe she thought he'd had second thoughts. This was going to be awkward.

"Hey, Georgie."

"Why are you walking around at two thirty in the morning?"

He chose to play offense instead of defense. "Why aren't you inside?"

"I asked you first."

He sighed, took off his hat, and ran his fingers through his hair. Then he repositioned the hat. Wouldn't want to get moonlight in his eyes. "I didn't want to stay in that room."

"Neither did I." She kept the little garden gate closed, which was probably a good thing.

"I noticed. You took off out of there like your tail was on fire."

She was mostly in shadows, so he couldn't tell if she'd smiled at that. "Interesting description. But you haven't answered my question about why you're standing in front of my house."

He liked that she called it *her* house even though technically she didn't own it. But it was hers in any way that counted, at least in his opinion. "I decided to take a walk and ended up here by accident."

"I've heard people say there are no accidents."

"That's not true, because when I started this walk I

specifically told myself that I wouldn't come this far. Then I got to thinking and ended up here."

"I think you're here because we're not done with our conversation and we couldn't have it in a room with a bed."

"That's not logical, Georgie." He hated not being able to see her face and read her expression. "I had no idea you'd be sitting on the porch."

"You might have if you thought about it. I'm as upset as you, so I wouldn't want to go back to my room, either. I needed to sit out here and think. And unlike you, I have a jacket to keep me warm."

So now he felt sort of stupid for going out in only his shirtsleeves, although it had made sense at the time. She had on a jacket, though. After that first night, she'd agreed that a warmer outfit was required, so she'd worn her usual clothes except that she always left off her bra.

Knowing she was standing on the other side of the gate without her bra on got him hot. He didn't like admitting he was so susceptible, but with her, he was. "The cold air felt good." That was especially true now, when a breeze brought the scent of her perfume and sex.

She gripped the top of the gate but didn't make a move to open it. "Do you have anything you'd like to say to me, now that we're not surrounded by memories of hot sex?"

"Speak for yourself. All I have to do is be within a few feet of you and I'm surrounded by memories of hot sex."

"Let me rephrase that. Now that we're not in a position to actually *have* hot sex."

"That's not true, either. The porch steps would work, or the porch floor. The swing is dicey because—"

"Vince, for God's sake."

He noticed a quiver in her voice. She was thinking

about it. That put them on a more level playing field. "Do you have anything to say to me, Georgie? I have a feeling you might, since you think our conversation isn't finished."

"Yes, I do have something to say, now that you mention it."

He prepared himself. She was about to rip him a new one, and he probably deserved it. Well, that was okay. Let her get it out of her system.

"I love you."

He gasped. He needed something to hold on to, but she'd already claimed the garden gate so he was left sort of standing there shaking, torn between wanting to shout for joy and swear in frustration.

"I know you weren't expecting that."

"No." His voice was a feeble whisper.

"But I doubt I'll get another chance to tell you. I've been sitting on the porch swing thinking that I should have said it while I was in your room, even if you weren't man enough to."

His throat closed up, but he managed to choke out one word. *"What?"*

"You heard me. I've seen the look in your eyes, especially when we're having sex. You love me at least as much as I love you, but you don't have the cojones to admit it. That doesn't mean I shouldn't, so I just have. I love you. I know that makes no difference to anything, but it feels good to get it off my chest."

He opened his mouth, but nothing came out. He tried again. Nada. He was very afraid he was giving a great imitation of a fish out of water.

"Don't feel obligated to follow my lead. I don't need you to say the words to know they're true. Nobody displays that much tenderness during sex unless they're in love. You'd probably rather not be, but we can't always control these things." Her face continued to be in shadow, but she obviously was looking at him. "Good night, Vince." She turned and started back down the walk.

"Wait."

She kept walking.

He could have tried to figure out the gate, but he didn't want to take the time. Putting a hand on the post, he vaulted it, caught up with her, and grabbed her arm.

She turned back to him, and in this light, he could see the soft smile. "That was heroic."

"Damn the heroics, Georgie. Yes, I love you! I've tried hard not to because we're not right for each other. I had everything under control, sort of, and then you showed up at my door."

"Don't tell me you regret that."

"Hell, no. It's been the best ten days of my life. But it ended up with us being in love with each other, and that's bad."

She reached up and touched his cheek. "When I left your room tonight I thought so, too. I was feeling sorry for myself and angry that you wouldn't say what was in your heart. But you have your reasons."

"I did. I do." He captured her hand and held it against his cheek. So soft. "You don't need a guy like me being in love with you."

"Yes, I do." She slipped her other arm around his neck. "Even if you won't stay, I need to know that you've loved me, that this wasn't some interlude that you'll forget as soon as you leave town."

He pulled her close. How he ached for her, even now, when he was trying to do the noble thing. "I'll never forget you, Georgie."

She gazed up at him, starlight in her eyes. "That's good enough for me. Now let me go inside. I have a long day ahead of me. Charmaine's arriving, and that's always a big deal."

"Georgie." He had to kiss her one more time. He poured his heart into that kiss and felt her give hers to him, too. When she eased out of his arms, he let her go.

She walked away without saying anything more. There was nothing more to say. They loved each other, but their lives were headed in different directions. He hoped she didn't hurt as much as he did, but he was afraid she might.

If he knew for certain that he wouldn't make her miserable, he'd consider taking a shot at staying and see how it worked out. But the road was all he knew and he could so easily fail at being a steady guy. He wasn't sure either of them would survive if he tried and failed. Better not to take that chance.

But God, the ache was almost more than he could bear.

Georgie climbed into bed with a clear conscience and slept like the dead until well past nine. She quickly showered, dressed, and walked down to open the store. Every step of the way she battled her sadness at not seeing Vince tonight. It was better this way, though. He needed to rest up before taking the group out on Saturday. And she had to deal with Charmaine.

Anastasia was picking her up at Amarillo International that afternoon. Georgie was supposed to give her a riding lesson on Prince after closing the store at three. After that, Charmaine had asked to go down to Sadie's for dinner.

It should be an interesting evening. Anastasia had agreed to bring her oil paints and touch up Sadie's nipple. Apparently it had become a topic of conversation among the poker buddies and Steve had contacted Anastasia about handling that little artistic chore tonight.

And Vince would be there. Whether he wanted to see her or not, he had to eat and Sadie's was the only game in town. She would have been more nervous about running into Vince if they hadn't had their last conversation.

But now they'd left nothing unsaid. There were no land mines that would explode in their faces. They might have secrets from the rest of the town, but she doubted even that was true. In a place the size of Bickford, no secret lasted long. People were simply being polite and choosing not to mention what they suspected.

That meant eventually everyone would figure out that the hot love affair had cooled. When that happened, Georgie was determined to protect Vince from censure. He was the outsider. Although he didn't deserve any blame, if people started choosing sides, no one would choose Vince.

At three she locked up the store and started home. But the view of Main Street brought her to an abrupt halt. For the first time in four years, her town looked almost normal. The changes had been happening for days, but until now the street had continued to look like a work in progress.

Not anymore. All the painting was finished and windows sparkled in the midafternoon sunshine. The posters Anastasia had made were mounted in vacant store windows, making them look less empty.

But the crafts store display windows were tastefully arranged with quilts, wood carvings, garden ornaments, and sun-catchers. The new sign was up. The Bickford Boutique was ready for customers, and if Georgie hadn't promised to give Charmaine a riding lesson, she'd have stopped in.

She walked past the movie theater and although it wouldn't be opening anytime soon, the poker buddies had spruced up the exterior. They'd also put up WATCH THIS SPACE! signs where the old movie posters used to be.

Next door to the theater, the Double Dip ice-cream shop looked nearly ready, too. Georgie saw Clyde and Inez behind the counter in deep discussion. Clyde glanced up and waved. Georgie smiled and waved back.

It was really happening. Her chest tightened with anticipation and anxiety. People had their hopes up again and Georgie desperately wanted those hopes to be realized. Wild Horse Canyon Adventures simply had to succeed. Failure was not an option.

Taking a deep breath and thinking positive thoughts, she walked on. Anastasia's little hybrid sedan was parked in the driveway beside the house, so that meant Charmaine was in residence. Georgie hadn't seen her stepsister since a brief visit at Christmas. Funny how with Charmaine she always thought in terms of *stepsister*, but Anastasia was her sister with no qualifier.

She hadn't stopped to think about that until now, but it was no mystery. Charmaine had challenged her from day one, whereas Anastasia had tried to fit into this new family and make friends. Georgie had found it easy to resent Charmaine because she was so haughty, but resenting Anastasia had been impossible. She'd always been sweet and accommodating.

When Georgie walked in the front door, she heard Evelyn and Charmaine having an animated conversation in the parlor.

"There's Georgie!" Charmaine rushed out of the parlor to give her a hug.

Startled though she was, she hugged Charmaine back.

She could only remember one hug from Charmaine in her life, and that had been right after her father died.

"It's so good to see you, Georgie!" Charmaine stepped back with a smile that was both open and real. The rest of her was about the way Georgie remembered. Her brown hair was still blond, her naturally rounded figure had been starved down to a size two, and her expertly applied makeup made her look airbrushed.

"It's good to see you, too, Charmaine. Ready for a riding lesson?"

"Oh, I can't risk it."

"Risk what? Prince is a sweetheart and I'll be right there. Nothing will happen."

Evelyn appeared in the doorway. "It's better if she waits until tomorrow. Tonight could be significant, and you never know what will happen with a horse. She could end up getting an ugly bruise somewhere, or a scratch, or twist her ankle."

Bewildered, Georgie looked from her stepmother to Charmaine. "I seriously doubt she'll end up getting damaged, but what's the big deal about tonight?"

"RJ's in town." Charmaine used the same tone she adopted when talking about British royalty, which she held in total awe.

Evelyn looked wise. "I'm sure he found out Charmaine was coming in early and decided he would, too. And you know what that means."

"Not a clue." Georgie felt as if she'd landed on Mars. "Who's RJ?"

"Randolph Jamison Steele to the uninitiated," Evelyn said. "But his close friends call him RJ."

Georgie grinned and started to make a smart remark. A week ago Evelyn had tossed out *Randolph* with a knowing smirk and Georgie was itching to call her on it. Then she composed herself.

She didn't want to fight about this. In fact, if this guy had the hots for Charmaine, so much the better. That could contribute to the success of the weekend and the potential success of Wild Horse Canyon Adventures.

A split second after she had that thought, she cringed. Now she was thinking like her stepmother, who was willing to use Charmaine to get what she wanted. That was a sobering revelation. She still thought Evelyn's manipulations were horrific, but she better understood the temptation presented when you had ammunition like Charmaine.

"Also," Charmaine said, "I don't want to smell like horse tonight when I see RJ. I know I'll be smelly on that trail ride, but we'll all be smelly, so it won't matter quite so much."

"We do have a shower," Georgie said gently.

"I know, and I plan to shower again, anyway. But if we practice riding, I might have to rush and not get completely clean. I want to make sure my hair's right, too, and that takes time. And what if I broke a nail?" Her eyes widened at the thought of such a tragedy.

Georgie glanced at Charmaine's perfect French manicure. She'd probably had it done yesterday at some expensive salon, and Georgie doubted it would last through an overnight trail ride. It might not even survive a riding lesson. "I see your point. We can put it off." Indefinitely.

Evelyn sighed. "Honestly, I wish Wild Horse Canyon Adventures involved helicopter rides instead of horses. Have you thought of that, Georgie? It would be far better, in my opinion."

"That wouldn't work, Mama," Charmaine said.

Georgie glanced at Charmaine in surprise. Maybe she

realized, even if Evelyn didn't, that a helicopter would scare the living daylights out of the wild horses and ruin the entire concept. "You're right, Charmaine. Helicopters wouldn't work at all."

"I know." She gave Georgie a look of sisterly solidarity.

"Why not?" Evelyn still didn't seem to get it.

"For a lot of reasons," Charmaine said, "but mostly because nobody in Bickford even *has* a helicopter, let alone knows how to fly the danged thing."

Georgie ducked her head because she didn't want to be caught laughing. Maybe it was Charmaine's enthusiastic hug when she'd first walked in, but she was feeling both affection and sympathy for her stepsister and didn't want to hurt her feelings.

The grandfather clock struck three thirty, and Charmaine jumped. "Yikes. That clock always catches me by surprise. Listen, y'all, I'd better go upstairs and start getting ready. I haven't even thought about what I'll wear. Come on up with me, Georgie. You can help me decide."

"I'll be glad to advise you, Charmaine," Evelyn said.

"Thanks, Mama, but Georgie's tuned in to what people wear around here." She headed up to the second floor.

It was a small triumph, but Georgie enjoyed it anyway. She followed Charmaine up the stairs. "Anastasia's way better at choosing clothes than I am." Especially for seductions.

"We'll haul her in there, too. It'll be like old times."

No, it wouldn't. The three of them had never hung out in each other's bedrooms talking about boys, clothes, and movies. Her father probably had been disappointed by their lack of sisterly bonding. But maybe it wasn't too late.

# CHAPTER 25

RJ Steele was a surprise. Maybe Georgie had expected some version of J. R. Ewing because of his initials and the Dallas connection. Instead she discovered an easygoing guy who was nice to look at but not strikingly handsome. Still, he had a presence about him, a quiet confidence that was very appealing.

He wore a white dress shirt unbuttoned at the neck, jeans, and loafers. She couldn't tell designer from discount, so they could have been wildly expensive and she'd never know. His dark-brown hair had been cut in a salon, but plenty of men who weren't rich had similar haircuts.

In short, if no one had told her he was fabulously wealthy, she never would have guessed. She thought he might want it that way. His gray eyes were friendly, not piercing as she would have expected from a wheeler-dealer. She liked him.

So did everyone else who came into the saloon. Sadie's was doing a good business this evening, obviously because the word was out that the rich dude was in town. Most of the residents had wandered in and out of Sadie's in the past hour, with the exception of Vince. Georgie hadn't seen him at all. It was the dinner hour, and she couldn't believe he'd eaten and left.

RJ sat at a table with Charmaine on his right and Georgie on his left. They had drinks and fries while they waited for their order. They tried to hold a spot across from RJ for Anastasia, who was working on the mural, but people kept dropping into her designated seat to chat with RJ.

"I apologize," Charmaine said during a break in the parade. "Bickford is a small town so of course everyone knows who you are and they want to meet you."

"Don't worry about it."

"I do, though. I don't want you to get a bad impression of the place." Charmaine was certainly holding up her end. She was easily the most beautiful woman in the room and maybe in the county.

She'd styled her hair so most of it was on top of her head but little curls hung artfully over her temples and dangled down her graceful neck. Her low-cut purple tee showed off her cleavage without being trashy, and her jeans were snug without looking painted on. Georgie tried to get a fix on whether RJ was dazzled by Charmaine. No telling what it took to impress someone like him. He might be pretty jaded by now.

If he was dazzled, he was playing his cards close to his vest. He seemed perfectly relaxed as he sipped his draft. He hadn't even requested an imported beer. "I like talking to everybody," he said. "I grew up in a small town, so I know how exciting a newcomer can be."

"Which small town?" Georgie liked the idea that he hadn't always been a big-city guy. That might explain why he fit into the atmosphere of Sadie's so easily. "Was it in Texas?"

"Yes, but you wouldn't have heard of it. It's gone, now. I was too late to save it."

Georgie turned in her chair. It was a subject dear to her heart. "Why too late?"

"By the time I had enough money to make a difference, it was too far gone. The most historic buildings had either burned down or been hopelessly trashed by vagrants." He glanced around Sadie's. "This hotel and saloon remind me of the one they had there. I was hoping it would."

"Hoping what would?" Ida plopped into Anastasia's vacant chair. "Pleased to meet you, by the way. Ida Harrington, at your service."

"RJ Steele." He shook her hand.

"I know who you are. We all do. So what were you hoping for when you came to Bickford, Mr. Steele?"

"Please call me RJ."

He'd told everybody that, which made Georgie smile. Apparently he considered everyone his friend until proven not to be. She liked that, too.

"RJ, then," Ida said.

"I was hoping to find exactly what is here," he said. "A town full of good people in bad financial circumstances through no fault of their own. But more than that, it's a town with a plan. That's important. You're not sitting around moaning about your lousy luck."

"Oh, but we used to," Ida said. "You should have been here before the cowboys showed up, specifically one certain cowboy." She winked at Georgie.

"Oh?" His eyebrows lifted. "Maybe I need to hear about these cowboys."

Ida related the story with far more drama than it required, in Georgie's opinion, although she was pleased that Ida gave Vince so much credit. He became the hero of Ida's tale, but she couldn't resist casting Georgie as the heroine. "Between the two of them, they kicked this plan into high gear," Ida said. "And furthermore, I look to see them get hitched one of these days."

Georgie panicked. "Ida, that's not—"

"Really?" Charmaine turned a startled glance on Georgie.

"No, not really. We're not even dating." Technically they never had. Meeting for sex every night wasn't her idea of dating.

"But he's here, right? I mean he has to be in town if he's the trail boss. But where is he? Except for RJ and Ike, all I've seen are old . . . I mean, *older* guys."

"I don't know," Georgie said. "Like I mentioned, we're not dating, so I don't keep track of his activities."

Ida gave her a hard stare. "You two had a fight, didn't you?"

"No! We're perfectly friendly . . . friends." Her cheeks felt hot, which wasn't helping.

Ida reached over and patted her hand. "It'll work itself out, honey. You're both under pressure because the first trail ride is this weekend. Once you get past that, you'll be fine."

"Ida . . . Never mind." She could see that she'd only make things worse if she kept protesting. Ida hadn't lived to be ninety-four without learning a bit about human nature. She knew that Georgie was more than *friends* with Vince, whether she had any real evidence or not.

Charmaine glanced toward the outside door of the saloon and drew in a sharp breath. "Is your cowboy tall, with broad shoulders and really blue eyes?"

"Um, yeah." She didn't bother to correct the *your cow-*

*boy* part of that. It seemed that Vince had just walked in. Her heart began to pound.

"Georgie, if you're not dating him, then you have rocks for brains. He's . . . perfect for you." She glanced quickly at RJ. "Not my type, but my sister likes rugged, and this guy is rugged."

"No, I don't." She wondered where Charmaine was getting this. She'd never discussed her preferences with her stepsister.

"Yes, you do. I distinctly remember you saying that you like rugged cowboy types when you frog-marched me home from Sadie's that night."

"I didn't, either." She was developing a headache.

"Yes, you did. I think it was because you'd had some wine and people say stuff they wouldn't normally say when they're a little sloshed, right, RJ?"

He smiled. "Right."

Georgie wanted to crawl under the table. "Listen, could we drop the subject, please? I'm sure RJ doesn't want to hear about any of this old history."

"On the contrary. I'm highly entertained."

"Me, too." Ida settled back with a wide grin. "Do go on."

Charmaine leaned toward RJ. "See, they used to have live music in Sadie's, and I was slightly underage but I sneaked in, hoping Georgie wouldn't notice me. She was dancing with someone, and on the way home she said that guy turned her on but she wished he didn't. And he was rugged, like the cowboy who just came in."

"Charmaine, I'm begging you. Stop."

"Okay, but that's what happened, which is why I know your type." She glanced over toward the bar where Vince had perched on a stool. "In fact, he looked a lot like . . . wait . . . that's *him*. It's the same darned guy you were dancing with that night!" She lowered her voice. "That's *Vince*."

Apparently she'd said it loud enough that he heard, because to Georgie's horror, he glanced over his shoulder.

The humiliation wasn't going to end, either, because Ida called out to him. "We're talking about you, Vince. Come on over and say hello to Charmaine and RJ."

Georgie sat like a rabbit trying to blend into its surroundings. She yearned to be invisible. She'd totally lost control of the situation, and she was going to *kill* her sister the minute they got home. She didn't remember spilling her secrets to Charmaine, but she'd been a little tipsy from wine and high on the thrill of dancing with Vince. She'd probably done it and now she was paying the price.

Vince slowly unfolded his long legs and stood. As he ambled over to the table, he adjusted the tilt of his Stetson. He must have just finished working with the horses, because he was sweaty and dusty. And unshaven. From the looks of him, he hadn't shaved since . . . since right before midnight.

Heat sluiced through her veins and warmed her skin. She tried to blame it on embarrassment, but it was more than that. Watching this sexy cowboy walk toward them, his blue eyes more brilliant than ever in contrast to his beard and a thin layer of dust, made her squirm in her seat.

Rugged didn't begin to describe Vince Durant. He was the hard, strong, yet vulnerable man of her dreams. She longed for him to throw her over his shoulder and carry her off into the sunset, then make love to her until dawn. She didn't give a damn about the stubble, either. Some men were worth a little razor burn.

RJ stood and offered his seat. "Won't you join us? I can get another chair."

"No, thanks. I came straight from the stable and I didn't expect to be socializing." His gaze flicked briefly to Georgie. "I'll just grab a quick beer at the bar and go upstairs to shower."

RJ took the rejection in stride. "Then I'll just introduce myself. I'm RJ Steele. And I guess you know Charmaine. And of course Ida and Georgie."

"Good to meet you, Steele." Vince clasped his hand. The men were about the same height, but Vince's hat gave him an advantage. He nodded at Ida and Georgie in turn. "Glad to see you both."

Georgie tried not to be irritated that he'd given exactly the same greeting to Ida that he had to her.

Then his gaze settled on Charmaine. "It's been a few years, Charmaine. I hear you're coming out with us on Saturday."

"I am. I didn't think you'd remember me. I was only a senior in high school that night I snuck into Sadie's."

Vince smiled. "A mighty pretty senior, as I recall."

"Thank you." Charmaine flushed with pleasure. "That's nice of you to say."

"You made an impression. But I think that's the only time I saw you."

"Mama had a hissy-fit over me coming down here, so I promised to keep away from Sadie's. Come August, she shipped me off to college." If Georgie hadn't spent so much time with Vince, she would have thought he was flirting with Charmaine. But she knew him well enough to see the automatic charm being turned on for the benefit of a woman who would appreciate it. It was a sweet gesture.

"A lot of guys were upset that Georgie dragged you out of Sadie's that night. My friend Mac, in particular."

"I'm sorry." Charmaine sounded genuinely distressed. "I'm afraid I don't remember which one he was."

"He remembered you. Wondered where you were now."

"That's very flattering. I'm working in Dallas as a personal shopper."

"Georgie told us. Mac was sorry he missed you when he was here a few weeks ago. Next time I see him, I'll tell him you're prettier than ever."

"Goodness!" Charmaine waved a hand in front of her face. "You're making me blush."

"Then my work here is done." Vince winked at her. "If y'all will excuse me, I'll go drink my beer and then get cleaned up."

"Look for me when you come back down," RJ said. "I'd like to discuss a few things with you about the trail ride."

"Absolutely." Vince tipped his hat. "Ladies." Then he turned and went back to his barstool.

The minute he was gone, Charmaine grabbed Georgie's arm. "Are you out of your mind? He's *gorgeous*. And so well-mannered. I think it's fate that he's back here after all these years."

Georgie had had about all she could stand. Her head was killing her, so she didn't have to fake her excuse. "Y'all, I hate to be a party pooper, but I've got a massive headache. I'm going to head on home and get some rest."

"Aw, Georgie, I'm sorry." Charmaine's green gaze was filled with sympathy. "I'll walk you home."

"No, please. Don't do that. Stay here and have fun. You and Anastasia can represent the family."

"Okay." Charmaine glanced at RJ and Ida. "If y'all don't mind, I'll step outside with Georgie. I have a couple of things I wanted to mention to her. I'll be right back."

"Don't hurry," Ida said. "I'll be happy to entertain our honored guest. Maybe he'll give me some stock tips."

Despite the pounding in her head, Georgie got a kick out of that. "I hope he does, Ida."

Charmaine wrapped an arm around Georgie's waist as they headed outside. "I'll bet your headache is my fault for revealing your deep dark secrets."

"It's okay. Things between Vince and me are . . . complicated."

"I can tell, and I should have kept my mouth shut. I'm not always good at that."

The cool air felt wonderful and Georgie took a deep breath once they were out the door.

"I won't keep you here because I know you're hurting," Charmaine said. "But I wanted to say something and I don't dare when we're at the house."

As Georgie faced her, she couldn't imagine what was coming next. Charmaine had turned out to be a series of surprises.

"First of all, I know how hard you're working to keep this family together, and I know a lot of money's being shoveled in my direction."

Georgie blinked. She hadn't expected that. "Well, your mother wants—"

"Not just her. So do I. You're good at running the store and fixing things around the house, but I'm not good at any of that. I am good at getting men to like me, though, and as I've said, I can love a rich man as well as a poor one."

"Are you absolutely sure about that?"

"I am." She said it with conviction. "It may take me a while, but I'll make this work. See, I have a plan. I'll find a rich husband like Mama wants me to do, but that's not the end of it."

"It's not?"

"No, because I know she's liable to sell the house and the store out from under you once she doesn't need that income. Any idiot could see that coming. She doesn't give two whoops about them, but you do. It's your heritage."

Georgie swallowed. "I try not to think about the fact she could do that."

"You don't have to, because I've got it all figured out. When I find Mr. Right, I'll make a deal with him that he'll buy the house and the store, which will delight her. Then we'll deed both of them over to you."

Georgie stood openmouthed.

"It's a good plan, right?"

Tears filled Georgie's eyes. "It's a great plan, but if you find the right guy, I can't ask you to just give me back the—"

"Of course you can. We're family, and family looks out for each other. You deserve to have those properties. God knows you've worked hard enough to earn that right. Now go home and take care of your headache."

Now it was Georgie's turn to give Charmaine a big hug. "I had you all wrong, Charmaine. You're amazing."

Her sister laughed. "You didn't have me all wrong. I was a brat when I lived here. But people grow up, you know."

"Guess so." Georgie sniffed. "Thank God."

"No kidding. The way I used to be, I would never have

caught a rich husband. I'd better get back in there. I don't know if RJ is the one, but he's a nice guy."

"Yes, he is. But I want you to be in love. Promise me you won't marry anybody just for the money. That's wrong."

"I *never* intended to do that. I'm not that noble. But I've seen Cinderella a million times. I honestly believe that someday my prince will come."

"Mine already did."

"You mean Vince. I totally agree with you there. He's a cutie."

"No, not Vince. My horse."

Charmaine started laughing. "That's so you, Georgie. I never thought of the fact you'd named him Prince."

"He's big, he's strong, and he never lets me down."

"Yes, but he can't warm your bed at night. Keep looking for a human prince, okay?"

"If you insist."

"I do. We both deserve to be happy. Shoot, we all do, including Anastasia." She gave her another quick hug. "'Night, sis."

Georgie smiled. "Same to you, sis." She didn't know what would happen with Vince, but this sister situation was working out better than she'd ever hoped it would.

As she walked home she gazed up at the night sky. "Thanks, Dad."

# CHAPTER 26

Vince had intended to talk with RJ Steele. He didn't want to piss him off when he might take an interest in the trail rides and spread the word to his other well-heeled buddies. Vince appreciated the significance of having someone like Steele on the ride and he would cater to him if necessary.

But the good people of Bickford had other ideas about how the evening would go, and Steele was surrounded by a crowd the entire night. Charmaine stuck close to him, but Vince didn't notice any romantic sparks flying. Steele had seemed far more interested in Georgie, and she in him.

When he'd come over to their table earlier, her color had been high and she'd looked embarrassed. He wasn't sure how he should take that, but she hadn't seemed overjoyed to see him. He certainly didn't want to get in her way if she found herself interested in Steele.

That's how it should be, in fact. A quality woman like Georgie should be drawn to a man who'd accomplished so much, and vice versa. Vince was glad to see it. He really was.

The hell he was. When he'd walked into Sadie's and noticed Georgie and Steele with their heads together, his first instinct had been to walk over there, haul the guy up by his shirtfront, and demand to know his intentions toward Georgie.

Good thing he hadn't. That would have screwed things up royally and Georgie might have decked him. He wouldn't have been surprised if she had a mean right hook to go with her whip-cracking skills.

But after she'd left and he'd made himself more presentable, he looked for an opportunity to have a conversation with Steele. The guy had sounded as if he had something on his mind. Whatever it was, Vince wasn't destined to hear it, because by ten he was fading. Lack of sleep combined with plenty of physical labor had caught up with him.

He managed to get Steele aside and explain that he was bushed and needed to hit the hay.

"No worries." Steele clapped him on the back. "We'll catch up later. And thanks for giving up your room. Myra told me it's the best one in the hotel. You didn't have to do that."

Vince dredged up a smile. "Yeah, I did. Enjoy." Then he went upstairs and got the first full night's sleep he'd had in more than a week. He didn't even dream, which was a blessing.

The following two days were a blur of last-minute preparations, so he didn't have time for that talk with Steele, after all. He and Ed rode the trail one more time to make sure Ed had the route down. Ed would lead and Vince would bring up the rear, a position that gave him the best view of how everyone was doing.

The chuck wagon was loaded with camping supplies and the tack cleaned and ready. The horses were as well-trained as he could get them, and he wasn't worried. They'd all be fine, including Storm Cloud.

He and Georgie had a couple of hurried conversations about little issues that had cropped up—a person with food allergies and another who wanted to use a cell phone during the ride. He and Georgie had agreed on that—no cell phone use except for emergencies. That would destroy the ambiance and scare the wild horses. Other than those two discussions, he didn't see much of her except in passing.

That was just as well. The way things were going, he wouldn't be around much longer. He'd called Mac and Travis to let them know the project seemed likely to succeed. Assuming it did, he knew Georgie would be thrilled if one or both of them would take over for him. They'd sounded excited about the idea.

On Saturday morning, even the weather cooperated—mostly blue skies with a few puffy clouds to make the view more picturesque. If the cool breeze continued, nobody should get overheated.

Georgie was there to see them off. No doubt she wanted to make sure Charmaine felt comfy on her horse. Vince had given her Skeeter, the calmest animal of the group, and planned to position her at the back where he could keep an eye on her. She broke a nail mounting up, but after a little wailing, she shrugged it off.

"Heading out!" Ed called from the lead position.

Georgie gave her sister's leg a squeeze. "Have fun!"

"I actually think I will." Skeeter started to move and Charmaine clutched the saddle horn. "At least this thing has a handle!"

"I'll see you tomorrow, sis." Georgie smiled. Then she turned to Vince as he approached, and her smile faded. "Well, this is it."

"It'll go well. Don't worry."

"I won't. After all, you're in charge."

He opened his mouth to contradict her, but then changed his mind. For the trail ride itself, that was mostly true. Besides, he liked the way she'd said it, as if she had complete faith that he'd carry this off. "I'll do my best."

"I know." She held his gaze for a moment. "Thank you."

"You're welcome." He touched the brim of his hat. "See you tomorrow." Then he nudged Storm Cloud into a trot so he could catch up with Skeeter and Charmaine.

It seemed weird that Georgie wasn't going, but he knew she'd had trouble finding the right person to cover the store. For now it would be a part-time job, but it could work into more hours later on. Once people started moving back to town, someone probably would show up who was perfect for that position, but that person wasn't here now.

Riding away from Georgie this morning gave Vince a little taste of what it would be like to leave her for good, whenever that turned out to be. It wasn't a pleasant feeling. He stuffed it down so he could concentrate on his duties as trail boss.

The ride went like clockwork. The lunch stop came right when everyone was starting to sag, but they perked up after that, and by late afternoon seemed excited about making camp for the night. Everyone exclaimed over the campsite and the beauty of the little box canyon.

Vince would consider the event a brilliant success except for one thing. They'd seen no trace of the wild horses.

But he had a scheme in mind that might increase their chances, and after their excellent chuck-wagon dinner, he got everyone's attention.

"I know we didn't guarantee that you'd see the Ghost and his wild herd, but I'm betting you're all hoping to get a glimpse."

Everyone nodded and murmured their agreement.

"Now that it's dark, I think we might find them down in that meadow we passed through, but we'll have to walk back there. If we take the horses, we'll make too much noise."

"I don't mind walking," Charmaine said. "How about the rest of y'all?"

"Fine with me," said Steele.

In the end, everyone agreed to go except Henry, who was busy putting away the food in critter-proof containers. Someone needed to keep tabs on the campfire, and Henry had seen the horses before, anyway.

"Everyone has flashlights," Vince said. "If you keep them on low beam and we're very quiet, maybe we won't startle them. That's assuming they're in the meadow. If not, we'll have a stroll in the moonlight before turning in. So follow me. Stay close. And don't talk."

Vince used his flashlight mostly so he could demonstrate the technique of keeping the beam pointed at the ground a little ahead of where they were walking. But he'd built this trail. He could walk it in his sleep. Mentally crossing his fingers, he led the group back to the meadow.

As they drew close, he heard them before he saw them. His pulse rate shot up at the distinctive sound of blunt teeth pulling at grass and the soft thud of hooves as the horses shifted their weight. He held up his hand.

Charmaine was right behind him. She sucked in a breath and her whispered *"They're here"* was carried on down the line.

Moonlight bathed the meadow, and Vince shut off his flashlight as he crept along the perimeter. When he'd gone far enough to allow everyone behind him to see, he stopped. The breeze blew toward them, which was lucky.

Everyone froze in place and the horses showed no sign that they were aware of the humans watching them. Vince counted eleven, including Jezebel, the mare taken from the Double J corral. But no gray stallion was among them. He had to have been nearby, though.

Then, as if he'd been waiting for his cue, the Ghost stepped out into the clearing. Head high, he surveyed the meadow as moonlight gilded his coat. Vince held his breath and didn't move a muscle.

Yet somehow, as if he'd communicated with the stallion, the Ghost looked straight at him. The horse trembled, snorted once, and with a shrill cry, issued a command. Galloping toward his herd, he sent them running toward the water. The ground vibrated with the pounding of their hooves. Then they leaped over the narrow creek and bolted into the trees beyond.

Everyone started talking at once with words like *amazing* and *thrilling* peppering the excited conversation.

"Hey, y'all!" Charmaine clapped her hands. "Listen up. We should go. We disturbed their dinner, but maybe if we leave, they'll come back and finish it."

Vince smiled. "I couldn't have said it better myself. Thanks, Charmaine." He hadn't thought he'd like her, but she was growing on him.

Once they were settled around the campfire again, Henry brought out drinks and snacks. He also mentioned that he had a ukulele if anybody played. Once again Vince was surprised when Charmaine volunteered.

During a break in the sing-along, Steele came over and sat on the ground next to Vince. "That stallion of yours is magnificent."

"He's not mine. He doesn't belong to anybody. That's what's so great about him."

"Oh, he belongs to somebody—his herd. We just saw how much responsibility he takes for them."

Vince hadn't thought of it that way. "I guess you're right."

"Anyway, I have a proposition for you."

"For me?" Vince put down his tin mug of coffee and stared at him.

"Yep. You have a great concept here, a chance to make the general public more aware of what a treasure we have in our wild horses, both these and others scattered around the West. That's the main thing, but it can be economically beneficial to the town, too. I want to be a part of it."

"You'll need to talk to Georgie, but I can tell you she's going to be really excited. She's devoted to those wild horses and she wants to see this town like it was, better than it was."

"It will be, although there are potential obstacles. Betting on a live animal, especially a wild horse, is chancy. Anything could happen. He could get sick or be injured, maybe even die, so this is far from a sure thing. But you're the one I want to talk to first, because I see you as the spokesperson for Wild Horse Canyon Adventures. You'd be a tremendous asset for a media campaign."

Vince gulped. "Uh, no, I'm afraid you're heading down

the wrong path there. Once this thing gets off the ground, I'm moving on."

"But it was your idea."

"That may be true, but I don't stay anywhere for very long. I'm like that stallion. I value my freedom."

Steele gazed at him for a few moments. "I see." He was clearly disappointed by that response.

"You could get somebody else to be the spokesperson, no problem. I'm really glad you're thinking this way, and I can see why you're so successful, but I'm not your guy."

"So let me get this straight. You're willing to give up the chance to watch this town prosper as a result of your efforts, the chance to travel the country promoting humane stewardship of wild horses, and the chance to be with a woman who's crazy about you, all in the name of preserving your precious freedom?"

Vince had to admit when he put it that way, it sounded pretty damned stupid. And Georgie was crazy about him, just like he was crazy about her. He took a deep breath. "Here's the problem. All that sounds wonderful, but I really am used to being able to pick up and go whenever I want. What if I agree to this thing you're suggesting, and months down the road, I want out? I'd get everyone's hopes up and then disappoint them." Mostly Georgie's hopes.

"How old are you?"

"Thirty."

Steele nodded. "That thirst for freedom makes sense when you're raising hell in your twenties. I was like that, too, but now that I'm thirty-five, things look different."

"I don't think we're much alike, you and me."

"You might be surprised. Listen, I'll give you some time to consider it. I'm staying on a few days."

"Good. I wasn't prepared for this."

"Vince, you've been preparing for this all your life. You're a natural with people and you're the real deal, a genuine cowboy."

"Nah, I'm not—"

"Don't sell yourself short. I'd like to invite a small news crew in here and get some buzz going, but I'll need to check with Georgie and the other folks first. It's the town's project, not mine."

"I appreciate that you said that. They might let you take over, but that wouldn't be a good thing. Everybody needs to have a stake in the project."

"I agree, and I won't take over. But I will make suggestions." He gave Vince another long look. "If they agree to the camera crew, I'd sure like to get some shots of you on that black horse of yours. Think about it."

Vince figured he wouldn't be doing much else *but* think about it. Steele was asking him to change his entire approach to life. But sometimes he wondered if falling in love with Georgie had already done that.

Later that night, as he lay in his sleeping bag looking up at the stars, he remembered something else about the conversation. Steele had pointed out that the Ghost wasn't as fancy-free as Vince liked to think. The stallion was responsible for the welfare of the herd.

The realization struck him like a blow, one that made him suck in a breath. Without his herd, the Ghost was just another horse. Watching over the herd gave him a purpose beyond just living for himself.

That's what RJ had been trying to say. Without Georgie

and this trail-riding project, Vince was just another guy. Until now, that had been fine with him. It wasn't fine anymore.

Georgie kept thinking that at some point Vince would seek her out to discuss this exciting new idea of RJ's. People in town could talk of nothing else. They were ecstatic that a news crew was coming at the end of the week and that RJ had asked Vince to take on the job of spokesperson for Wild Horse Canyon Adventures. But Vince himself was MIA.

When Monday came and went with no contact from Vince, and Tuesday looked as if it would turn out the same way, Georgie concluded that he didn't want to talk to her about the job offer or anything else. She would have loved to hear his version of how the trail ride had gone, but he hadn't briefed her on that, either.

Technically she could have called his cell and demanded that he do so because he was an employee. But she didn't actually need his recap. She knew the ride had been a huge success.

Vince's truck wasn't parked in front of the hotel as usual all day Monday, and Georgie had finally called Steve to make sure he hadn't checked out. Nope. But Steve didn't know where he was. His truck was gone again Tuesday when she walked to work. She'd considered hanging out at Sadie's because he had to eat sometime, but when she did talk to him, she didn't want it to be in front of a bunch of people.

Finally on Tuesday night she found herself in Anastasia's room pouring out her woes to both her sisters. Because Charmaine ran her own business, she'd been able to stretch out her visit a few more days.

"Well, I know what I'd do." Charmaine sat propped by pillows against the headboard of Anastasia's bed while her sister painted an exotic design on her toenails.

"What?" Georgie had commandeered the desk chair and she swiveled it back and forth, unable to be still.

"Stop that." Charmaine gave her a stern glance. "Tormenting that poor chair isn't going to help."

She stopped swiveling, but then she had to get up and pace. "It's driving me nuts, not knowing. I realize he'll have to give RJ his decision before the news crew arrives, but I really think he's going to turn it down and I want to be prepared."

Anastasia blew on Charmaine's toes. "If he's going to turn it down, wouldn't he have done it by now?"

"Yes. No. I don't know! That's the problem! I don't know, and after all we've been through, I just wish he'd talk to me."

"So go to him," Charmaine said. "Repeat your little trick from before and pay him a visit at midnight. Beard the lion in his den, as they say."

"You don't think I'll look too needy if I do that?"

Charmaine rolled her eyes. "You *are* needy! Look at you! If he doesn't know he's making you suffer, and guys can be dense about those things, then he needs to know. If I had to make a guess, I'd say he thinks he's sparing you by working this out on his own."

Georgie groaned. "He probably does, the idiot. That sounds just like him. Okay, I'll go."

She coincided leaving the house with the chiming of the grandfather clock at midnight because it seemed appropriate. This would probably mark the absolute end of their relationship. Travis and Mac were due to arrive sometime next week. Whether Vince accepted RJ's offer—not likely—or left town—more likely—his buddies would be needed.

She'd told herself that he'd leave. She'd rather do that than allow herself to hope that he might stay. Maybe by going tonight she'd push him out the door that much faster, but her sisters were right. He needed to know that his behavior was putting her through hell.

Her outfit was the opposite of the one she'd worn the first time she'd come to his room. She wore old jeans, tennis shoes, and a Dallas Cowboys sweatshirt that had seen better days. But her heart was pounding as wildly as it had that first night when she'd knocked on the door.

The sound of his footsteps made her hyperventilate. This had been a dumb idea. But she couldn't do anything about it now. She'd see it through. The door opened. She stared. RJ Steele stared back.

She clapped her hand to her mouth. Dear God, she should have thought of this. Of course Vince would have given up his premier room to RJ. Pulling her hand away, she launched into her apology.

He quickly interrupted. "It's okay," he said gently. "Were you looking for Vince?"

"Um, yeah." Heat flooded her cheeks. He had to know this wasn't her first midnight visit to Vince's hotel room.

"Two doors down on the left."

"Thanks. I'm so sorry."

"Don't be. I hope you knock some sense into his thick skull."

"RJ, if he really doesn't want to stay, then I'm not going to force him to."

"No?" He grinned. "I heard about that incident with the whip. I was hoping you'd brought it."

She held out her empty hands. "Nope."

"Too bad." And he closed the door.

She took her time going down to Vince's room. She wondered if he'd heard any of that. The doors were flimsy, so he very well might have. Then she thought about that day she'd charged toward him cracking a whip.

That woman wouldn't meekly accept his stubborn decision to leave town. That woman would give him a piece of her mind and tell him he was a complete idiot for even considering leaving this place, this job opportunity, and mostly her, the love of his life.

She'd worked up a good head of steam by the time she raised her hand to knock on his door. As she brought her fist down with a little more force than normal, he opened the door and she almost lost her balance as she pulled it back. RJ might have suggested knocking some sense into him, but she didn't want to take that too literally.

She recovered quickly and straightened. "You're a complete idiot, Vince Durant."

"I know."

"I'm the best thing that ever happened to you, and if you don't get that, then you don't deserve me."

"You're absolutely right."

"So what's with the disappearing act? What the *hell* have you been doing for two solid days? Because I want an explanation. I've been going crazy wondering—"

"Come in here." He grabbed her arm, pulled her through the door, and shoved it closed. "No point in keeping Steele awake."

She faced him. "Just so you know, he hopes I knock some sense into your thick skull."

"I heard."

"Well, what do you have to say for yourself?" She became aware of a nearly overpowering sweet smell and glanced around. The room was filled with flowers—roses, carnations, gerbera daisies, tulips, and several she couldn't identify. Eyes wide, she looked at Vince, who wore a sheepish expression. "What's all this?"

"It's sort of embarrassing."

"You've decided to open a florist shop in Bickford?"

"No, they're for you."

"Me? Why?"

"Because . . ." He sighed and ran his fingers through his hair. "I never expected to propose to anyone, and I had no idea how to do it, so I—"

"Hold it." Her throat tightened. "Back up the bus, cowboy. Propose?"

He nodded. "I only plan to do this once in my life, so I've spent the last two days in Amarillo at the library, reading up on the best way to—"

*"Propose?"* This didn't seem real, yet the scent of the flowers nearly knocked her over. "You want to marry me?"

"God, yes. And let me say up front that I'll probably disappoint you every damned day, but I'll love you every damned day, too, and I hope that makes up for all the times I'll be a complete jerk."

She flew at him, wrapping her arms around his neck and peppering his face with kisses. "I accept. I totally accept."

He gathered her close. "But this isn't the way it's supposed to go. You need a grand gesture. Lots of flowers, a flashy presentation, me down on one knee."

"Bull. I need you."

He captured her face in his big hands and gazed down at her. "But Georgie, you'll only do this once, too. Don't you want it to be special?"

"It is special, you big goof." Her smile trembled. Her

heart was so full that she wondered if she could hold all that joy without blubbering. "This will make a great story for the grandchildren. You tried to plan a grand gesture and I jumped the gun. They'll love it."

"I love you."

"And I love you." She gazed into his beloved face. "This is a terrific proposal, Vince. The best."

"Yeah?" His blue eyes sparkled. "Why?"

"Because it's from you."

Read on for a sneak peek at the next book in
Vicki Lewis Thompson's Sexy Texans series,

## *WILD ABOUT THE WRANGLER*

Available from Signet Eclipse in October 2015.

"Mac, you must be craving that cold beer." Travis hurried to keep up as they walked down Bickford's main street after another successful trail ride. "You haven't moved this fast since the time Vince snuck a tarantula into your shower."

"And let the record show I haven't forgiven him for that." But Mac modified his pace. Yeah, he was looking forward to sipping a cold one at Sadie's Saloon, but he was more focused on showing Anastasia the new pictures on his phone.

He'd snapped some beauties of the wild stallion and his herd while they were out this weekend and Anastasia would go nuts over them. But he didn't want Travis to know that was why he'd unconsciously lengthened his stride. Knowing Travis, he'd read too much into it.

Anastasia Bickford was just a friend and that's the way it would always stay. In the short time he'd lived here, they'd established the kind of relationship where they could talk about anything. Because Anastasia had such a creative mind, the topics were never dull.

"I like to savor my walk down Main Street after a trail ride," Travis said. "Makes me feel like a hero." He tipped his hat to a resident who walked by and called out a greeting. "People are grateful to us, Mac. I mean, just look at the difference we've made." He gestured toward the colorful storefronts and the bustling tourist trade.

"Just remember, Vince got the ball rolling, not us."

"Yeah, but we keep it rolling."

"True." Mac did take satisfaction in that as he gazed at the revitalized town. They were having a mild fall season, not much rain and not a hint of snow. Mac's denim jacket kept him plenty warm in the evenings, and during the day he was in his shirtsleeves. Perfect weather for trail rides.

Most shops had one of Anastasia's posters in the window advertising Wild Horse Canyon Adventures. It was a great image, but then Anastasia was a great artist. The poster featured a majestic gray stallion against a blue Texas Panhandle sky. That stallion, officially called the Ghost, had saved Bickford's ass.

Six months ago, Mac, Travis, and Vince had driven here, thinking they'd relive the fun times they'd had while working at a nearby guest ranch. They'd arrived to find stores boarded up and the town on the verge of collapse. After the guest ranch closed, the local economy had tanked, but Vince's brainstorm to offer trail rides into the canyon to see wild horses had saved the day.

"The way I look at it," Travis said, "we guide the trail rides, right?"

"Right."

"And according to those online surveys Anastasia sends out, customer satisfaction is high."

"So she says." He got a kick out of Anastasia's excitement over those surveys. He also suspected she deleted the negative ones.

"Which means we're doing a helluva job and I'm gonna claim some credit. Hello, ladies." He touched the brim of his hat as they passed a couple of tourists laden down with shopping bags. "You oughta come on the trail ride," he called after them. "I lead it!"

"Then we just might, cowboy!" one of them called back.

Mac shook his head. The actual trail boss was the one bringing up the rear, which would be Mac, but the women might not know that and Travis did love to flirt.

"See? I just drummed up more business by being my usual outgoing self. You and I are vital to the success of this venture."

"You certainly are. I think you need a sandwich board and a bullhorn."

"Nope. Doesn't fit my cool-dude image. But speaking of sandwiches, I'm hungry." Travis paused at the entrance to the Double Dip, Bickford's refurbished ice-cream shop with its red-and-white-striped decor. "I have a hankering for a hot fudge sundae with extra fudge and nuts. Let's do it."

"You go right ahead. I'd rather have a cold beer."

"We'll have both. We'll drink beer after we finish the sundaes."

Mac grimaced.

"You're such a finicky eater, Mac Foster. Go ahead to Sadie's. I'll catch up with you after I have my primo sundae."

"Suits me."

"But don't start the darts tournament until I get there."

"Wouldn't dream of it." They'd formed the habit of playing darts in the afternoons with Anastasia and anyone else who was interested. "I'll just drink until you get there."

"Perfect. I'll be sharp and you'll be sloshed."

"Keep thinking that, amigo." Mac grinned and continued on to Sadie's. He was just as glad Travis had decided to stop for ice cream. Talking to Anastasia about the pictures would be easier without Travis hanging over his shoulder, making comments and doing his usual flirting. Travis wouldn't ask her out, though, for the same reason he wouldn't.

Anastasia was Georgie Bickford's little sis, and Georgie was officially in charge of Wild Horse Canyon Adventures. Vince had dreamed up the idea but he'd never planned on running the thing. He hadn't planned on sticking around, either, but he'd fallen for Georgie.

So Georgie still ran the operation, but Vince had become the official spokesperson for the venture, the one who handled the media. Surprisingly, there was media. A wild stallion and his band had turned out to be a story that had captured national attention.

In fact, Vince was in Houston this weekend talking to an animal advocacy group, and a film crew from Dallas would arrive in three weeks to shoot a documentary. Bickford residents were busting their buttons with civic pride. Nothing this big had ever happened here. Dwarfed by Amarillo to the north and Lubbock to the south, the town had always been small potatoes, even when the guest ranch had been operating.

Mac was happy for everyone, especially Anastasia. She deserved recognition for her work, and the documentary would help give her that. Sure, she had some art in a local gallery in Amarillo, thanks to Georgie's prodding, but that wasn't nearly enough exposure. With her talent, she should have been famous.

Opening the street door to the saloon, Mac looked straight over to the corner where she'd set up shop. Georgie had urged her to rent a storefront and create an actual studio, but so far Anastasia hadn't made that happen. She seemed to prefer the familiar atmosphere of Sadie's.

Maybe that wasn't such a bad idea. Lots of people came in here and her work hung all over the walls with For Sale tags on them. Ever since the trail rides had taken off, she'd sold plenty of her watercolors depicting the town and, of course, the Ghost. Plus she did charcoal portraits, and she'd picked up a lot of business sitting in a corner of the saloon with her sketch pad at the ready.

She was sketching someone right now, in fact. Mac smiled when he saw Ida Harrington sitting at Anastasia's table having her portrait done. Some people might laugh at a ninetysomething woman who colored her hair bright red and wore jeans and vests decorated with bling.

Mac thought Ida was terrific. She'd moved to Bickford after her wealthy husband died and left her a pile of money. But rather than offering it to the town when the residents had no viable plan, she'd waited until Vince had suggested the trail rides. Then she'd underwritten the bulk of the expenses.

Because Mac didn't want to interrupt Ida's portrait sitting, he walked over to the bar and ordered a beer.

Ike Plunkett had been the bartender when Mac had been a wrangler at the guest ranch, and Ike had hung on through the economic downturn. He was probably only in his forties, but had started losing his hair early. That plus his wire-framed glasses made him look brainy.

But it was his welcoming smile that brought customers into Sadie's, and he flashed it now. "The conquering heroes return. Where's Travis?"

Mac slid onto a stool. "Eating ice cream. And don't tell Travis he's a conquering hero. He's already out of control on that subject. I keep trying to convince him that we're just regular working guys."

"Not to a lot of people around here." Ike set a foaming glass in front of him. "You're like knights in shining armor."

"More like tarnished armor." Mac reached for his wallet.

"Put that away. This one's on the house, like always."

Mac gazed at him in frustration. "I know the saloon's doing better, but you still have to make a living."

"I make a good one, thanks to Wild Horse Canyon Adventures. Steve and Myra are doing handsprings over the number of hotel reservations that came in this week."

Mac grinned at the image of Steve and Myra Jenson, both middle-aged and stocky, doing handsprings. They'd bought the Bickford Hotel and the attached saloon years ago when business was booming. They'd weathered the bad years, and now business was booming again. They deserved to reap the rewards.

"I'm glad everyone's happy," he said, "but I still think I should pay for my beer."

"Don't tell me." Ike swiped a bar rag over a polished mahogany surface that had been the resting place for drinks for more than a century. "Steve gave me my orders. You'll have to take it up with him."

"Maybe I will." Mac sipped his beer and licked the foam from his lip. He liked it here in Bickford. He liked it so well he'd bought a fixer-upper east of town and was gradually getting it the way he wanted. First house ever. That was probably a sign he was growing up.

"Hey, handsome." Ida appeared at his elbow. "Where's Travis?"

"Eating ice cream."

"How wholesome of him."

"He plans to follow the hot fudge sundae with his usual quota of beer."

Ida wrinkled her nose. "That's disgusting. Did you tell him that's disgusting?"

"More or less. But he's a big boy."

"You don't have to tell me. All three of you are pure eye candy."

Mac's face heated. "Cut it out, Ida."

"Not on your life. Age has its privileges. Anyway, I'm done if you want to go over and chat with Anastasia."

"Can I see your picture, first?"

"I was hoping you'd ask." Ida opened the professional-looking folder that Anastasia now used to protect a finished portrait.

Six months ago she'd sketched Mac and had simply handed him the sheet of paper. These days the presentation was far more elegant. He'd had her sketch of him framed, but he still didn't know what to do with it. Hanging it up in his house seemed conceited.

He looked at Anastasia's vision of Ida, and it was perfect. Anastasia had caught the irreverence and the sparkle, plus an underlying wisdom that some people missed because Ida was so outrageous. She didn't appear young in the portrait, but not ancient, either. More like ageless, and certainly someone you'd want to know.

Mac glanced at Ida. "It's you."

"I *know*. That girl has some kind of magic. I've had her do my portrait six times, and this is the best. She just keeps getting better. When I croak, I want this in the paper with my obituary, not some studio shot when I was a kid of fifty."

"I hope you're not planning on croaking anytime soon."

"God, no. Too much going on. They want me to be in the documentary, and eventually Vince will marry Georgie, and I can't miss *that*."

Vince laughed. "You certainly can't. None of us can. I'd crawl through quicksand to see Vince Durant finally get hitched. He was so sure it wouldn't ever happen."

"He was at that, foolish boy." Ida smiled. "But I knew." Her thick glasses magnified the curiosity in her gaze. "When are you going to admit you have a thing for Anastasia?"